FitzDuncan's Navy

John J. Spearman

The Halberd Series

Gallantry in Action
In Harm's Way
True Allegiance
Surrender Demand

The Pike Series

Pike's Potential
Pike's Passage
Pike's Progress
Pike's Purpose

The FitzDuncan Series

FitzDuncan
FitzDuncan's Alchemy
FitzDuncan's Enlightenment
FitzDuncan's Fortune
FitzDuncan's Gambit
FitzDuncan's Hope
FitzDuncan's Inheritance

The Perseverance Andrews Series

The Defense of the Commonwealth
The Courage of the Commonwealth
The Resolve of the Commonwealth

The Cliff Rawlins Series

Rawlins' Redemption

ACKNOWLEDGMENTS

Many thanks to my editor, Martin Roy Hill, who has been of enormous help from the standpoints of both technical expertise and moral support.

Deepest gratitude for Thea Magerand, the marvelous artist whose artwork has brought Caz and Lucy (and now Fenwick!) alive. Every piece she has done for my books amazes me further.

Back in the day, the school I attended offered fencing as a sport. I was excited about it, until I learned that there was no banquet table loaded with food, nor was there a staircase, a chandelier, or curtain pulls from which to swing. I firmly believe the sport would be far more popular if they added these elements. The Olympic committee should consider it.

If you would like to stay abreast of my latest activity,
please visit my website: johnjspearmanauthor.com

1

"But I don't know a thing about sailing or ships!" I protested. "I get seasick!" The last hour had been overwhelming. I came to the castle for a meeting with the king. I thought it was to discuss crop estimates, though I had been entertaining suspicions that something else was happening of which I was unaware. My best guess was that my father would step aside as Earl of the Eastern March and I would take over and swear my oath of fealty to the king.

When I entered the room for the meeting, instead of only the king, an entire group of nobles was present, along with the queen, Fenwick, and my wife. After teasing me for a few minutes, His Majesty just informed me I was his choice as his successor. I then needed to formally renounce any claim to the Eastern March and any inheritance from my father. My father then adopted Fenwick as his son and heir. Immediately upon doing so, my father stepped aside as Earl of the Eastern March, and Fenwick swore an oath of fealty to the king.

The king's son, Prince Albert, had died on our return from visiting a group of nomads far to the east. In a pouring rain, the section of the narrow mountain trail on which he was riding gave way, dropping him at least two hundred feet down a sheer slope. Attached to a rope, I went to rescue him, only to find his neck broken and his body growing cold.

Albert's death left the king without an heir and also prompted our ages-old enemies, the Rhetian Empire, to launch an attack they had been preparing for over a year. I directed our outnumbered forces to a resounding victory.

In two days, at a ceremony following Fenwick's wedding to Julienne Traval, the king would formally adopt me and name me as his heir. For two days, I would have neither family nor title. Since I lived most of my life without either, that did not seem a hardship.

Immediately following the king's pronouncements and swearing of oaths, the discussion turned to the aftermath of our recent war with the Rhetian Empire. In the past, the Rhetians encouraged piracy following their defeat on the battlefield as a method of extracting some form of retribution. Nearly two hundred years earlier after the previous war, the kingdom of Aquileia resorted to issuing letters of marque and reprisal—essentially creating pirates to counter the Rhetian pirates. The council voted unanimously to follow a similar course of action without waiting.

The king, looking directly at me, had said, "Now, whoever shall we appoint to oversee this operation?"

All this was covered in my last batch of scribblings. I mention it only to refresh your memory, dear reader. My apologies if you find this recapitulation annoying.

My objections were both legitimate. I knew next to nothing about ships or sailing. On my few sea voyages thus far, I suffered horrible seasickness, ameliorated only after my wife provided me with ginger oil to spread on my upper lip and licorice to calm my stomach until I adjusted to the rise and fall of the ship's deck.

Besides the nautical challenge, my brain was swimming with other issues that were raised by the dramatic changes that just took place, for which I was not at all prepared. I wanted to address them before tackling any sort of new task—especially one like becoming the commander of a pirate navy. Lucy and I would need to move. Would we move into the castle or be allowed to continue to reside in our house in the city? We would need to collect our belongings from Easton Manor and transport them to whichever place would be our home.

It meant walking away from the Eastern March and all the good things we accomplished there, and many that were still in progress. That saddened me more than just a little. My father, with whom I had been building a relationship for the last three years, was no longer legally my father. The king would become my father in a few days. Our relationship had become friendly and respectful after a tenuous beginning, but I would not say we were close.

Lucy would become a princess and eventually the queen, but I knew there were things she wanted to accomplish that might need to be sacrificed in order to fill those roles. Earlier in the meeting she indicated her support of these changes, but I worried about her goals and dreams. We needed to talk. Her happiness was essential to me.

Lucy and the queen had a terrific relationship, and I, too, felt close to Queen Liliana—closer than I did the king—so that was an asset rather than a worry. But how would our friends respond to our new status? In the last few years, I observed the king and his late son, Albert, and saw the difficulties they faced since the office and the person inhabited the same flesh.

A few weeks earlier, I was contemplating how my life would change, now that we seemed to have solved the biggest problems facing the March. Now, I would have an entire kingdom about which to worry. My life, and Lucy's, would be one of constant duties and obligations.

"Dear, I think it would be best if we postpone this particular discussion for a few days," Queen Liliana suggested. "Look at Caz. He was flummoxed a few minutes ago. Now he is positively drowning, if you'll pardon the expression."

"As you will all still be in the city," the king said, looking at the rest of the group, "are there any objections to resuming this discussion in three days?"

Shaking of heads and murmurs of "No, Your Majesty" followed.

"Let us reconvene then."

The king stood, indicating the end of the meeting. Everyone rose. As they exited, all of them offered their hands and their congratulations. My father and Fenwick stayed.

"Caz, I'm sure you have many questions," Liliana offered. "With whom would you like to speak first?"

"Your Majesties," I replied. "Later, I would like to talk with Duncan and Fenwick. That conversation can take place at our house if we will be allowed to return there today."

"There is no reason why you should not be able to return to your house," the king said. "At the moment, you have no official status."

"Then, Duncan, Fenwick, I would appreciate if you would return to our house and remain until Lucy and I are finished here," I requested. I used my father's first name because he was no longer legally my father. It was awkward, and it bothered me to use it.

Both men nodded and left the room.

"Come. Sit. And not so far away," the king invited.

Lucy and I moved to their end of the massive table. I took the seat closest to the king. Lucy sat beside the queen.

"I have so many questions already, Your Majesty, that I hardly know where to begin," I said.

"Let's start with that," he said. "Your Majesty is still appropriate in public settings. We are not in public. I would prefer Mark. If that is too difficult for you now, I will accept 'Sir' for a short time."

"You already know to call me Lily," the queen added.

"Where should we plan to live?" I asked.

"Wherever you choose," the king replied. "Though I suspect you will find it vastly more convenient to live here, in the castle. There will hardly be a day when your presence will not be required here unless you are away fulfilling some other duties."

"We understand that your lives are being uprooted," the queen added. "If it helps to keep your house in the city for a time, please do."

"But eventually, you want us here," I said.

"We want you to be happy," Lily said. "Mark is correct. You will find it much easier to be here rather than riding back and forth all the time. There are also security concerns."

I looked at Lucy. She smiled, then shrugged. I raised my eyebrows, and she shook her head slightly.

"Lucy and I will need to discuss this," I said to the king and queen. "For now—at least for a short time, I think we will stay at the house."

"That's fine, dear," Lily answered.

"May I ask how long it has been since you decided this?" I asked the king.

"I knew before we reached Reedsford on our return," he replied. "Actually, that's not true. I knew shortly after you brought us the news of Albert's death, but I would not admit it to myself. Then I sent you away to Rhetia with Fenwick and kicked myself every day until you returned for putting you at such risk. Then we went to war, where your leadership and guidance produced an overwhelming victory in less than a month. I had expected we would be fighting for at least a year and probably longer. After sending the Rhetians back home, by the time we reached Reedsford, all the others were convinced, with Shames and Pilaro agreeing to my choice but still harboring misgivings, as they mentioned. Earl Montgomery and the Dukes of Manton, Gulick, and Caurus were supportive from the first time I mentioned it. Chaldic and Lords Hepworth and Manafort expressed their support after the Battle of Hamil Creek."

"How long did my father know?" I asked.

"I shared my thinking with him when he arrived at Reedsford before we met the enemy. He was strongly in favor, though it saddens him greatly," the king stated.

"It grieves me as well," I said. "We were estranged for most of my life."

"I don't think you are aware of how much you restored your father," the king said. "He knows, and the rest of us have surely seen it. He carries an enormous debt of gratitude. I promised him I would encourage both of you to maintain your relationship."

"Thank you, sir. I hope to. How long has Fenwick known?"

"He claims he knew before I sent you two to Rhetia," the king said. "He can be rather cheeky, you know."

Lucy and I both laughed out loud, having lived with Fenwick's impertinence the last few years.

"Upon your return, he chastised me at some length for sending you on that errand—for risking your life when you were clearly the best choice to succeed me," the king said.

"Thank you for sharing this with me and for your steadfast belief in me," I said. "At the moment, I have no further questions for you. I am certain I will have more later. I would appreciate the opportunity to speak privately with my wife before we return to the house and see my father and Fenwick."

"The room is yours, Caz," the king said as he stood. "We will have a page waiting to escort you out when you are finished."

The king then crossed to me and embraced me, whispering, "Thank you" in my ear. Lily embraced Lucy, and then we switched partners for another hug. When they left the room, I held my arms open for Lucy. She stepped over to me, and we wrapped each other up. Both of us started to cry. Our bodies needed to release the huge emotions swirling within us. When we calmed down, I stepped back slightly so I could give her a small kiss.

"You've known for quite a long time, haven't you?" I asked.

She nodded—her cheeks still wet with tears. "If you lived," she whispered.

"And Fenwick and my father knew," I added. "Is that why you sent me out of the room when we had guests?"

"Yes and no," she replied. "Fenwick knows, so Julienne did too. Freddy knows from his father, so Greta knows. Quint also learned of it from his father therefore Siobhan was aware. Linc and Nellie, and Ratty and Inger still do not know, but we did warn them that Fenwick's wedding would be quite a memorable occasion."

"Lucy, what about your goals?" I asked after absorbing that information. "Your desire to share your knowledge and better the lives of the people?"

"I will still pursue them," she said, "but on a bigger stage."

"But you have said Lily has been prevented from doing anything like this," I commented.

"That's because there has been no one with ability who wore a crown in many generations," Lucy said. "The rumors of Lily's ability, from when she manifested Ceridwen Sospita in Eatonford and from what happened in Dunland, are just now beginning to gain an audience. Rumors about us are already more widespread. You have been concerned about the reaction to your bastardy—something that only a handful of disgruntled aristocrats find much fault with. You ought to be more curious about how people will respond to a future king and queen who have demonstrated their powerful magical abilities in front of hundreds of witnesses if not thousands."

"Should we not—"

"That is not what I am suggesting," Lucy interrupted, shaking her head vigorously. "Think of how the people of the March responded at the feast of Freyja."

I did as Lucy asked. It took a moment for me to center my thoughts on what she mentioned. Once I did, I understood her point.

"They were amazed and delighted," I said. "I think they also felt pride— that Lady Oritur and her ability belonged to them."

"I know you are embarrassed by the song the soldiers made up," Lucy said, "but it comes from the same feelings. Thousands of them saw you manifest Bellona when you defended the king. Your abilities are now well-known—and probably exaggerated with every retelling of the story."

I thought about what Lucy was saying. My embarrassment regarding the song was because I did not care for attention. During my formative years, when I was sent away to boarding school, attention was almost always negative. When I considered that the song may have come from their pride in being associated with me and in our tremendous accomplishments, it took on a different meaning. Thinking about it in this respect dazed me and filled me with humble gratitude.

"What about moving?" I asked after a lengthy pause.

"You won't be surprised to know that Lily has already shown me the section of the castle that would be ours," Lucy said.

"Of course she did," I replied. "I knew there was something going on behind the scenes, but I had no idea that it would be what just happened. At first, I thought you were pregnant."

"No, but now I can be," Lucy said, with a gleam in her eye.

"I don't understand."

"The laws of succession by adoption," she explained. "Any children we had before now would not be eligible to succeed you."

"You've known for that long?"

"I knew we would not have children right away," Lucy said. "A previous vision showed us raising them in our house here in the city. That sight was superseded by later events."

It struck me that this was an excellent example of why Lucy's grandmother instructed her never to reveal what she saw with her limited form of clairvoyance. Lucy later learned at the Temple of Njörun that her grandmother's strictures on this matter were the soundest advice—other warnings on different topics, not. Lucy was not perfect, though. Every so often, Lucy would let something slip through. I remembered now that when we bought the house in the city, she mentioned something about which child would be in what bedroom.

"So we should move?" I asked.

"Only if you wish," she said coyly. "Mark does make a good point about the convenience of being here, though."

"Would you enjoy being here?"

"No more and no less than being anywhere we will be together," she said. "I know you are fishing for information, but I can't help you. I'm sorry."

"Well, we will end up here eventually," I said. "And since we will already be disrupting our lives by moving everything from Easton back to the city, we might as well do everything all at once, I suppose. Otherwise, we need to go through the whole process twice."

"Mhm."

"Fine. But not until after this is all official," I said. "And the rooms Lily showed you?"

"Are marvelous," Lucy said with a giggle.

"Much as I would like to see them, I would rather go chat with my father—I can still call him that, can't I?"

Lucy nodded.

"And Fenwick."

"You sound as though you are angry with them," Lucy commented.

"I don't know what I feel right now," I confessed. "Perhaps I am—a bit. I'm sad to be leaving the March and all the things we set in motion. It won't mean the same to me when they come to fruition. Overall, I'm happy for my father, and I suppose I'm happy for Fenwick, too. I wonder how this will affect Julienne and her plans to take the reins of Traval & Company. It will be difficult for her to pursue that and be Lady Easton at the same time."

"I suspect Ariana will be willing to assist in those responsibilities," Lucy said. "Your father is stepping aside, not stepping away."

"Have you already discussed this with her?" I asked.

"Yes," Lucy said with a sly smile. "She was closely involved in organizing the Harvest Fair while you were elsewhere. That was one of the things I was most concerned about, but she has promised me it will continue."

"Still, Ari will not be Lady Easton. Of course, you never held the title either, but you certainly fulfilled the duties!"

We left the room, and a page was waiting. He escorted us across the bridge. The guards on the other side whistled up a hackney for us quickly.

When we arrived at the house, we found my father and Fenwick in the parlor, waiting for us. Both wore the guilty expressions of boys caught with their hands in the cookie jar. They were dismayed to have been discovered and felt slightly guilty because I was upset, but they were not necessarily sorry for their actions. Ariana was seated next to my father, holding his hand.

"Well, it has been quite a morning, hasn't it?" I remarked as I took a seat facing them.

Neither of them replied. Both kept their eyes down slightly and would not look at me. Seeing them this way banished whatever small bit of ire I might have felt at their deception. I realized there was no way they could have warned me what was to come.

"C'mon, you two," I said. "I'm not angry. What happened is wonderful for all of us, and I understand His Majesty probably swore you to secrecy."

2

Hearing that, they both relaxed. Fenwick looked up with a cheeky smile. My father's expression was a mixture of emotions.

"His Majesty told me, Fenwick—excuse me, *Lord Easton*—that you were upset with him for sending me with you to Rhetia," I said.

"Well, I did think it was reckless," he said. "In my mind, you were the only logical choice to succeed Albert. I'm glad you came along with me, though, or I might still be stuck on that island."

"And you, father—and you are still my father—I have enjoyed building our relationship. I am unwilling to set it aside. I am concerned about the projects we started. Lucy suggested that you were stepping aside, not stepping away. Is that correct?"

"I will never abandon the March," he said. "So Lucy's assessment is accurate. Besides, Fenwick knows absolutely nothing and would bollix everything up. I will also remain a member of the king's council. You need only ask, and I will do everything in my power to help you."

"I hoped so," I said. "Will Julienne continue with the family firm?"

"For the time being," Fenwick replied. "For the next few years, your father will continue to play a large role in the governance of the March, as will Ariana. I believe His Majesty intends to grant them titles as Lord and Lady Charles."

"We will assist Fenwick with the social obligations for the next few years," Ariana said. "I'm looking forward to it."

"In the meantime, Julienne will search for a qualified candidate or candidates to whom she can entrust the business," Fenwick explained. "She will still retain oversight of the firm but will turn over the operations to someone else. We hope that she will be able to fulfill her responsibilities as Lady Easton and keep an eye on the business. It will be a juggling act, but I am confident she will succeed."

"And you?" Lucy asked Fenwick. "Are you pleased by all this?"

"How could I not be pleased?" Fenwick answered. "It's amazing when I think about it. Granted, I was not nearly as surprised as you were—"

"You were not surprised to be named Lord Easton?" I asked incredulously.

"I did not say that," Fenwick protested. "I said that you were more unaware than I was. Admit it. You had not even the faintest idea of what would happen today."

"Fine—I admit it," I said grudgingly.

"Where I have felt nearly since Albert's death that you were the best possible choice to replace him," Fenwick said. "As a result, I speculated what the king would do about the March, given your father's wish to step aside. His Majesty had just completed redistributing the former Braintree and Morningstar holdings to the more capable men of our generation. He picked the best he could find who were landless, and there were not any others of the same caliber left. In thinking of who His Majesty might choose, I allowed myself to dream a little. The more I considered it, the more sense it made."

"Then Fenwick mentioned his idea to me," my father said. "I thought it was damned cheeky of him at first. As time passed, it made more and more sense to me. When we were out west, I brought it to His Majesty's attention. He liked Fenwick better than any alternative candidates."

"Will he still expect you to fulfill your other duties?" I asked.

"He has not said anything," Fenwick admitted, "but he was never shy about sending you all over to resolve problems that arose, was he?"

"No," I said with a small chuckle, thinking of the more than half-dozen assignments the king had given me in the last few years.

'I would imagine he will continue to make use of the two of us as he has before," Fenwick said. "As he did with Albert."

"You will help me with this pirate thing," I said firmly, making it a statement and not a question.

"I would imagine so," Fenwick replied with a sly smile.

"Good. Because I don't have any idea of where to begin," I confessed.

"Where will you live?" Ariana asked.

Lucy looked at me before answering, "The castle."

I nodded in agreement.

"What will you do with this place?" my father asked.

"I haven't had the chance to consider that yet," I admitted.

"I'll buy it if you wish to sell," Fenwick offered.

"Only if you keep Roberta on," Lucy stipulated.

"Of course I would," Fenwick said. "Just as I hope the staff at Easton Manor remains. Unless you want Theo …"

"No, thank you," I stated quickly.

Lucy started to laugh. I gave her a questioning look. It took her a moment to recover herself.

"Can you imagine Theo in the castle? Treating guests of state the way he used to act toward you?" she said, beginning to cackle again.

"Fenwick, we will need to visit the towns of the March after your wedding," my father said. "Rumors will arrive immediately, and we need to quash them as quickly as possible."

"Should I join you?" I asked.

"It would be helpful," my father said, "and probably pleasant for you. People will be happy for you. But we must clear your absence with Mark."

"When we finish that, I will need Fenwick's guidance regarding my next assignment," I said. "My lack of nautical knowledge is profound."

"Fenwick, my son," my father said, half in jest since Fenwick was legally his son now, "I'm afraid that any prolonged period of conjugation in connubial bliss will be postponed—at least until we have toured the March."

"Father," Fenwick replied, matching my father's tone, "Lord Easton must always be prepared to sacrifice personal pleasure for the good of the March."

"Oh, well said!" I remarked with a snicker.

"Lucy, is there furniture in the rooms the queen showed you?" I asked.

"Yes. They are fully and splendidly furnished," she said with a smile.

"I was thinking," I said, "that if that were the case, how many things do we really need to move from Easton and from here?"

"Our personal belongings, of course," she said. "The contents of my workshop at the manor, a few small pieces that came from home, and that's about all."

"We had quite a few pieces made when we moved here. Not to mention all the furniture we needed to replace in the manor. You don't want any of it?"

She shook her head with a sly smile. I read that to indicate she had already thought this through. Lucy was always one or two steps ahead of me.

"So, one or two wagon loads from the manor and not even a full load from here," I summed up. "That certainly makes things easier. I would like to see these rooms, though."

Fenwick agreed to the price I set on the house, which took into account all the repairs we needed to make when we bought it, as well as the furnishings. He and I went to my solicitor, Graham Throckmorton, to arrange the sale and transfer of the deed. I could tell Graham wanted to ask why I was selling, but he was tactful enough not to inquire.

My father insisted on repaying us for the renovations we made to the manor and for the furniture we bought. Lucy and I both tried to refuse, but he was insistent. I asked him why.

"You paid to set things to rights because my accounts, and the accounts for the March, contained nothing but cobwebs at the time," he said with a hint of anger. "We have discussed this before, and you know how I feel about it."

"Father—er, Duncan, you must stop berating yourself for what Veronica did. It's in the past and cannot be changed. Lucy and I were happy to step in. We never thought twice about it," I said.

"A testament to your character," he stated. "The fact remains that you should not have needed to do anything. At that time, though, the March was bankrupt. Now, thanks to you, and the reopening of the river and Port Charles, we enjoy healthy balances that will only grow larger, especially when the jute farmstead begins to produce. It will make this tired old man happy if you will let me repay you."

"Tired old man, my ass!" I countered. "You forget that neither Lucy nor I are deaf. We hear what you and Ari get up to at night."

"Well, perhaps not so tired as I was a couple of years ago," my father admitted with an embarrassed grin.

"Besides," I said, "as a part of the royal family, what should I do with my investments? Do I add them to the crown's vast holdings?"

"I can tell you that the princes had their own accounts, separate from the crown's," he said. "Upon Wim's death, his assets were transferred to Albert."

"Why would the prince have accounts separate from the crown?" I asked.

"A variety of reasons," my father said. "It is important for the prince to have the wherewithal to display generosity and support the causes he favors as an individual. Also, if you have more than one child, you will need to provide for those who are not your successor. The crown accounts are for crown affairs—not for the maintenance of the extended family. This is something you need to discuss with Mark, but your assets would be added to those left behind by Albert."

It was not all work and worry during those two days. Fenwick and Julienne came for dinner the night of the meeting. Julienne had shared with her mother (one of the worst social climbers I will ever encounter) that Fenwick was now Lord Easton. Her mother was rapturous at the news. Her father was concerned about how it would affect the plan to turn the company over to Julienne.

The following day, Lucy and I went to the castle. Lily was waiting for us and showed us where our quarters would be. What I saw far exceeded my expectations.

Castles are built for military purposes—defense. As such, they have thick stone walls. Windows are a liability since they provide potential access to an enemy outside. As a result, castles tend to be dark and dank. Most of the parts of the castle I had seen before fit this mold (and yes, that's a pun—mold and mildew are a constant nuisance).

The rooms Lily showed us were obviously constructed much later than the original part of the castle. Defense was no longer the imperative. They were several flights of stairs up from ground level. Though the walls were made of stone, they were whitewashed. Every room had huge windows, with views overlooking the city and a beautiful garden just below. The ceilings were at least sixteen feet high, and the overall impression was one of light and space.

As Lucy told me, the furnishings were splendid. The rugs were so thick I felt my feet would sink to the ankles. The furniture was beautiful and seemed perfectly placed. Most of the furnishings elsewhere in the castle were darker hues of blues and maroons, but here they were pastels, except for the rugs.

The rooms were on two floors. Above were three bedchambers, a sitting room, and a study. Below were a small parlor, a study, a large reception room, a large dining room, a pantry, and a full kitchen. Each of the bedrooms had its own lavatory attached. The largest bedroom also had an enormous closet, accessed through a smaller room.

"My boudoir," Lucy said with a giggle.

"Your what?" I asked.

"My dressing room," she explained. "Where I shall prepare myself to appear beautiful for you and the people."

"Oh. A waste of space then," I quipped. "Your beauty needs no such enhancement."

"Flatterer."

"Just being honest."

"You will have a maid and a cook," Lily said. "If you would like one, you might consider a batman."

"A what?" I asked, not certain I heard her correctly.

"A batman," she repeated. "A personal servant. Think of the position as a secretary who also helps you dress and maintains your clothing and appearance."

"Majors and Minors, no!" I laughed. "If we need a secretary, I am sure we will bring one on. As far as my appearance, I follow Lucy's orders."

"As Mark does mine," Lily said with a smile.

"Will we hire the maid and the cook?" I asked.

"They are already part of the staff," Lily said. "We kept them on after … Anyway, Lucy will meet them and decide whether to keep them on or find someone else. There is one last thing I need to show you."

Lily took us back to the entrance to the apartment. Next to the door, there was a bell pull. She tugged on it.

"To save you time, pull on this to summon a page," Lily said.

Sure enough, less than five minutes later, a breathless page appeared at the door. We dismissed the lad quickly, apologizing for summoning him needlessly. This was a feature I knew would prove useful.

When we returned to the house, Lucy started making lists of what should be taken to the castle. She would go over them with Roberta. While we were away, Roberta would have everything packed and transported.

That evening Freddy and Greta, and Quint and Siobhan joined us. They teased me about how surprised I was by the king's pronouncement. Freddy and Quint learned from their fathers that it was likely to happen while they were returning home from Reedsford. It was as light-hearted a gathering as ever, which pleased me and reassured me that my new position might not be an obstacle to our continued friendship.

It occurred to me that I already had the beginnings of an advisory council similar to the king's. Freddy and Quint would be members, and Fenwick, too, of course. Ratty Hawkins would be a valued member, especially since his star was on the rise in his family's company. Tom Gibson might be another.

Though Ratty and Tom were not members of the nobility, they were representative of the rising middle class. I began to think of others. Perhaps young Lord Houlsin and Lord Chafter.

"You are miles away, aren't you, Caz?" Greta commented.

"Majors and Minors!" I muttered as I snapped out of my reverie. "I was, Greta. My apologies, everyone."

"What was on your mind that seized your attention?" Quint asked.

"Nothing I should be thinking about in such pleasant company," I said. "Spirits have been high and the mood, light. I would rather keep it that way."

"It still astounds me that you were caught by surprise," Freddy said. "Even Lord Compote would have figured it out."

"How is Lord Compote?" Lucy asked.

"He shows up unexpectedly every so often," Greta said. "Thankfully, not in public."

"Come now, poppet," Freddy said, using his Lord Compote voice, leaning to his left with his head almost on Greta's chest as he ogled her décolletage. "You always enjoy a bit of the old slap and tickle with Lord Compote. Admit it."

As he ended his statement, Greta shrieked and nearly jumped out of her seat. She swatted his right arm, which had made its way under her dress. After she succeeded in removing it, she began to giggle.

"I've heard stories about Lord Compote but didn't know whether to believe them," Siobhan said. "They are all true, aren't they?"

The night before Fenwick's wedding, my father and Ariana were invited to have dinner with Freddy's parents, so Lucy and I dined alone. On the eve of my becoming the crown prince, I wanted only Lucy's company. I thought about how my life had changed so profoundly since meeting her. Lucy was the catalyst of everything that had happened since.

We were quiet through the meal. Afterward, we retired to the parlor. When I sat down, Lucy planted herself on my lap.

"It has been an incredible journey so far, my love," I commented as I held her close.

"It has," she agreed. "And it's not close to being finished."

"I am reluctant to ask for fear of making you uncomfortable, but how long have you known? You knew before Fenwick and I went to Rhetia that it would happen if I survived. Was it so recently or further back?" I asked.

Lucy was quiet while she considered what she could tell me. That indicated to me there were other things she had seen that were related, which she could not mention. It made me regret asking.

"I'm sorry, my love," I said. "I didn't mean for—"

"It's alright," she said. "The answer is easy. It's coming up with the right words to describe it that is difficult."

I looked at her quizzically.

"You must understand. I had a strong sense of premonition when we first met—when you and Freddy came asking about the Dark Arts."

"You knew then?" I asked incredulously.

"No," she shook her head. "The feeling was only that we were destined to be together, and it thrilled me more than I know how to describe. I saw nothing of the future. What I felt was a captivating sense of rightness and completion. My first fleeting glimpse of a possible royal future was a little later, but you must understand and accept that I was already in love with you from our first meeting.

What I saw did not influence my feelings for you. It was only the briefest moment anyway and unlike my usual forethoughts."

"Now I'm even more intrigued," I said. "When?"

"In Eatonford," Lucy said. "When I was fighting to break Esme's hold on you."

"I'll always remember that," I said. "You made my heart ache with your love. You've made me feel that way since, just as deep and powerful, but that was the first time."

"Really? When was the last time?"

"When you allowed Freyja to share your body on her feast day, I was dumbstruck."

"Interesting," she commented. "Back to your question, in Eatonford, when I was in the midst of that struggle, there were flickering images of you and of us. Some have already happened. Some I can't tell you about yet. As far as being certain, just before Albert, Fenwick, and you departed to visit the horse nomads, I saw the meeting and the king asking you to be his successor."

"When we left, you seemed melancholy," I said. "I figured out why after Albert's death. You knew."

"I did. And I couldn't say anything. Sometimes, the ability is as much a curse as it is a boon."

3

Fenwick's wedding took place in the biggest Temple of the Three Major Gods in the kingdom the next morning—the summer solstice. It was scheduled for half past eleven, when both hands of the clock would be moving upward, a sign of good luck according to one of our many superstitions in Aquileia. The actual moment of the solstice would not occur until later that evening. Thus, the length of the day was still increasing at the time of the marriage—another sign of good fortune.

I stood with Fenwick as his bridesman. Julienne had chosen her childhood friend, a woman named Bitsy Shepherd, as her bridesmaid. There were over two hundred people in attendance, including the king and queen. The head priest conducted the simple ceremony uniting Fenwick and Julienne in the presence of both human and divine witnesses.

When the ritual was completed, we all moved outside. We stopped in front of the altar atop the massive steps outside the Temple. Beginning three days before, announcements were posted throughout the city and in nearby towns, alerting the public to a major address from the king. The announcements also mentioned that the king was sponsoring sacrifices to the Gods in celebration of the solstice, with free food and drink for all. People had shown up in the thousands.

The summer solstice was one of our most festive holidays. The crowd was colorfully dressed and in a cheerful mood. Our speedy victory over the Rhetians just a few weeks before added to the good spirits. The promise of free food and drink on this holiday contributed in addition. The crowd began to cheer as they saw us emerge from the Temple.

The smell of roasting meat from the sacrifices filled the air as I advanced in front of the altar. The king came to face me. Surrounding us in a semicircle that wrapped around the altar were the members of his council, with Lucy and the queen placed on either end, closest to us. As we assembled, the crowd quieted.

"Hroth," the king began, addressing the high priest using his formal title but pitching his voice to carry well into the square, "since Albert's untimely passing, the kingdom has lacked a successor. This is a dangerous condition and one we wish to remedy today. We have chosen a man who has proved himself worthy in every way of being our heir. His service to us on many occasions has been invaluable. His leadership in the recent war resulted in our overwhelming victory, saved countless lives, and preserved the realm. We wish, in the presence of the Gods and all those here assembled, to adopt him as our son and heir."

"Is this the man?" the priest asked in a voice equally loud, indicating me.

"It is."

I withdrew my sword and handed it, hilt first, to the priest. At his nod, I knelt. The priest then laid the flat of my sword on the top of my head. The crowd was so quiet it felt like they were all holding their breath.

"Do you swear to honor the Gods above all things and the Three Major Gods above all others, and renounce all the works of the Lord of the Seven Hells?" he asked in a voice that filled the square.

"I do," I replied firmly.

"Do you promise to defend this realm against all enemies, foreign and domestic, to the limit of your ability until death shall claim you?"

"I do."

"Will love the king, your sovereign and father, and the queen, your sovereign lady and mother, and defend them and their rights to the utmost as long as they both shall live?"

"I will."

The priest handed my sword to the king.

"In the presence of the Gods and men, you have sworn oaths. These oaths bind you to the king, your sovereign and father, and to the queen, your sovereign lady and mother." Turning to the king, he asked, "Is this your son?"

"This is our son, our heir, and the successor to the throne," the king responded, speaking clearly, reaching even the far corners of the square. "This we declare in the presence of the Three Major Gods, all lesser Gods and other divine beings, and the people of Aquileia."

The crowd broke its silence and roared its approval. The sudden volume of noise stunned me. While the crowd was cheering, Queen Liliana gestured for Lucy to kneel next to me. When Lucy joined me, the priest came forward with a circlet. He gestured for me to bow my head so he could put it on. Someone handed the queen a brilliantly bejeweled tiara, which she placed on Lucy.

"To these symbols of their new position, I add one more," the king announced. Taking my left hand, he slid a heavy gold ring on my middle finger. As he did, he said, "This ring, bearing Prince Casimir's unique royal seal, is the final symbol of his authority."

The king bid us stand. Lucy entwined her arm with mine as Queen Liliana did the same with the king. The king held up a hand, and the noise died away gradually.

"His Royal Highness, Prince Casimir FitzDuncan Barry Gau, and Her Royal Highness Princess Lucille!" he pronounced.

The crowd roared yet again, even more loudly—if it was possible. The noise lasted a few minutes before it started to fade. A new sound rose from the assembled people. They began singing the song the soldiers had made up about me. Someone remembered to change my name since I was no longer Lord Oritur. Not only did Casimir rhyme, it also matched the meter. The chorus was as follows:

> Under Casimir's firm command,
> They died by thousands at our hand,
> With halberd, pike, and horseman's lance,
> They saw us come and shit their pants.
> The king fell, Casimir stood fast
> None of our foes beyond him passed.
> Rhetians lay in mounds of dead,
> The grass underfoot soaked blood red.

For the first time, hearing the song did not embarrass me. Because of Lucy's wise counsel, I heard the pride of the people coming through the words. I felt them claiming me as theirs. It moved me and humbled me.

When the song finished, the crowd grew quiet. The king stepped forward. As he did, he put his hand in the middle of my back and had me join him.

"Welcome, one and all, to the Feast of Midsommar," he called out, using the ancient term for the holiday. "We have decreed a day of feasting, celebration, and thanksgiving throughout the realm. The kingdom of Aquileia has much in which to rejoice. It is proper for us to take time to thank all the Gods, Major and Minor, and all the divine beings, for the blessings which they have shared with us."

The king paused and bowed his head. I did the same. There was so much for which I was grateful. I sent silent prayers to the Gods.

The crowd was entirely silent during this pause. I imagined all of them were doing as I just did. As a people, we were indeed fortunate.

"The Gods saw fit to grant us a tremendous victory over our age-old foes, who attacked us without provocation," the king continued. "The Gods sent us this man, now our worthy successor, whose praises you just now were singing."

The crowd laughed.

"His leadership is responsible for our swift and absolute success. But as we celebrate today, let us also remember the fallen—the heroes who died defending our realm and their loved ones. No war is won without cost. Though Prince Casimir kept our losses to a minimum, many still paid with their lives. Remember them, and treat their loved ones with compassion and charity, as the Gods would wish."

The crowd murmured its assent.

"The sacrifices have been made," the king continued, "in the names of Prince Casimir, Princess Lucille, Lord and Lady Easton, who were united in marriage only minutes ago, and in honor of those who gave their lives to defend us all. The priests tell us all is ready. Enjoy the Feast of Midsommar, and celebrate our many blessings!"

Cheering at a deafening level greeted this statement. Lucy came and took my arm, as the queen did with the king's. Together, we climbed down the steps of the Temple to the bottom.

On any other occasion, the Castle Shield would stand between the king and the public. Not today. The four of us stood exposed. A few brave souls shook my hand or the king's. Many knuckled their forelocks as they passed or bowed or curtsied.

After an hour, when the crowd was largely dispersed, engaged in eating and drinking, an ornately decorated carriage arrived at the foot of the steps. The four of us entered. When the door shut, we pulled away.

"Welcome to the family," Liliana said.

"Indeed, welcome," Mark added. "Now, we must get to work."

"Mark! Can't you let him get used to everything first?" Liliana chided.

"I'm sorry, but we have pressing issues," Mark said. "Caz, tomorrow we meet again with the council. There are some things we need to review beforehand."

"In regard to making me a pirate admiral?" I asked.

"Yes. Work has already begun," Mark said. "Fenwick has some, ahem, interesting, ahem, connections from his past. He gathered several of them and had them meet with naval architects to design a ship ideally suited for what we had in mind. We will review the designs after lunch. Then you and I will discuss the logistics."

"Regarding?"

"After the meeting tomorrow, you will deliver a set of the plans to the three largest shipwrights in Aquileia. Another set will be sent by the Royal Post to Newcastle's largest shipwright, and a set to his counterpart in Aurora. They will be asked to respond with their bids in three weeks. That will give you the time to make your tour of the Eastern March with Duncan and Fenwick. When you return, we will review the bids and issue contracts."

"Thank you for allowing me to return to the March," I said.

"You will need to accompany him, Lucy," Liliana said. "You need to wrap things up with your students and receive the accolades you are due from the residents of the March."

"I will also need to pack up the few things we will bring from the manor," Lucy said. "Most having to do with the project you and I discussed."

"Once contracts are let, you will have several months before any of the vessels are ready for action," Mark said.

After lunch, the king led me to a study. Waiting for us were two men. The seneschal introduced them as naval architects Giuseppe Mellone and Thomas Baldini. There were plans spread out on the table in front of them.

"After discussing the, ahem, requirements, we found ourselves in complete agreement regarding the type of ship you need," Mellone said. "It is called a caravel. They are not much used today. As a cargo ship, they do not have enough capacity. As a warship, they are too big to make effective use of oars. For a coastal raider, however, they are nearly perfect. These are the ships Sir Samuel utilized the last time the kingdom undertook a venture of this type."

"You are familiar with Sir Samuel Krum, Your Highness?" Baldini asked.

I must admit I did not recognize that he was speaking to me at first. It took a second for me to figure it out. I almost physically started when I understood.

"Quite familiar," I replied. "In the past, I spent a great deal of time in the administrative wing of the Palace of Justice. Portraits of the previous Principals of the City Watch hang on the walls. Of all of them, the only one I ever wished to meet was Sir Samuel. The rest of them look fat and comfortable. Sir Samuel was clearly a man of action. I am aware of his success as a privateer."

"The caravel is capable of running down any ship on the ocean as long as there is a breeze. They are remarkably fast before the wind and able to sail into the wind better than other ships of any size. A crew of a dozen men is sufficient to sail them effectively, but they can carry as many as three dozen soldiers in addition to the crew," Baldini explained.

"Are these plans complete?" the king asked.

"Yes. Six copies, as you requested, Your Majesty," Mellone replied.

"Very well. Gentlemen, please review the plans in exhaustive detail with Prince Casimir. He freely admits to having little sailing knowledge, so he needs a complete education," the king instructed. "The prince needs to be able to speak intelligently by tomorrow."

"To what level, Your Majesty?" Mellone asked.

"He needs to understand the ship's capabilities, its weaponry, and all the major working parts," the king said. "If you have a reference book that can educate him regarding the finer points, we would appreciate it if you would lend it to him for a time."

With that, Mark departed, leaving me with Mellone and Baldini. I examined the plans on the table. The ship drawn on the paper was marked as being fifty feet long but only fifteen feet wide. From the top looking down, the ship was roughly elliptical in shape, though the bow was pointed and the stern was squared off.

Each ship carried two tall masts, and one of the drawings indicated they used sails that were triangular in shape. The bottom had only a shallow keel. One of the very few things I had learned about sailing (from Fenwick, of course) was that a keel was necessary in order to sail into the wind. I decided I would lead with that.

"Gentlemen, one of the few things I thought I knew about ships was that a keel was necessary to sail upwind," I said. "The keel you show is small, yet Mr. Baldini said that this type of ship sails into the wind better than other large ships. Would you please explain this?"

"You are not wrong about keels, Your Highness," he replied, "but perhaps the explanation provided to you was lacking some information. On lighter vessels, a deeper keel helps keep the ship upright and prevents her from skimming across the surface from the force of the wind. Often, the keel contains additional weight, in the form of lead, to ensure the vessel maintains an upright posture. Does that make sense?"

I nodded.

"Our caravels," he said, "will be sheathed with lead—"

"Excuse me?" I blurted.

"The wooden hull of the ship," Mellone explained, "will be covered with overlapping thin sheets of lead, attached with copper tacks. I understand that lead, which is so heavy, and a ship meant to float seems antithetical. In this design, the weight of the lead will not be any threat to the buoyancy of the vessel."

"But it will provide the upright stability that a deeper keel does. Even though shallow, you see the keel of the ship runs the full length. It is enough to prevent the ship from yielding to the wind," Mellone added. "There are other significant benefits to the lead sheathing we must explain."

"The greatest threat to a ship is underwater," Baldini said, "in the form of the shipworm. Shipworms attack wood. It is why you see the wharves here in the port all rest on stone pilings. Wood pilings are eaten through by these pests, sometimes in less than a year."

"And the lead prevents them from reaching the wood," I surmised.

"Your Highness, it does more than prevent them. It positively repels them," Mellone said. "It also repels barnacles and weeds, both of which damage the wood of a ship's hull, but not as badly as the worms. The biggest advantage of keeping barnacles and weeds from growing on your hull is speed. A clean hull travels through the water more easily and, therefore, more swiftly."

"The shallow keel also allows ships of this type to sail in shallower waters than many," Baldini said.

"Let us move on," Mellone suggested, "and begin discussing the decks, or levels, of the ship."

I shrugged my agreement. Over the course of the next few hours, Baldini and Mellone went over the drawings with me, explaining everything. I quickly realized I needed to take notes, and I had a page get me paper, quill, and ink. We needed to backtrack to cover some items I had not written down.

The two men explained the difference between a halyard, a sheet, and a line. Before this, I would have called them all ropes. They taught me the names of the different parts of the ship. The one I found most interesting was the forecastle, which the sailors called the fo'c'sle, pronounced folk-suhl, or the raised section in the bow of the ship.

Before we finished, I begged them to draw a quick sketch of the ship with the names of the different sections so I could study while I was away. Mellone, who was of burly build with thickly muscled arms and meaty hands, did the honors. It was astounding to see the smooth grace with which he wielded the quill. It was completely at odds with his beefy appearance. His strokes were sure and delicate, and his lettering was precise.

In a matter of only a few minutes, he produced an accurate rendering. From time to time, Baldini made suggestions. When he finished, many of the terms I had written down were included. They both offered to guide me around a ship in the harbor when I returned from the March.

"There is no substitute for seeing it yourself and laying hands on things," Mellone said.

When he finished the sketch, I took the three leather tubes that contained the drawings. I would deliver them to the shipwrights. Baldini wrote down their names and told me where I would find their offices.

A page was waiting outside the door. I turned Mellone and Baldini over to him to escort out. Then I went in search of the king. Though I was learning my way around inside the castle, I ended up lost. As I was standing there, trying to figure out where to go, the queen came into the corridor.

"Lily, I'm lost," I admitted. "I'm supposed to see Mark now."

"I'll be happy to take you to him," she said as she linked her arm with mine. "You'll figure it out eventually. What makes it difficult is that after the original castle was built, there were expansions. Each expansion has its own arrangement and doesn't match up with the previous building because the outer walls were constructed for defense. In some cases, there are three expansions in the same general direction from the center, and there is no direct route from one to the next. That is actually by design."

We reached the king's office, and she left me there. I knocked and heard the king bid me to enter. He was seated at the same desk where I met him for the first time. It struck me how much things changed in the last few years.

"So, Caz, are you drowning in nautical knowledge?" he joked.

"I think I'm keeping my nose above the water, but only just," I said. "Mellone and Baldini were kind enough to give me some information to study."

"Tomorrow, after the meeting, take the plans to the three shipwrights here in Aquileia," Mark said. "Instruct them to return their bids to the castle for your attention in three weeks. My secretary is writing up the formal bid requests as we speak. He will give them to you before you leave. Once you have delivered the materials to the shipwrights, you are free to return to the March, provided you are present the day the bids are due."

"I understand."

"Good. Now, we need to speak about logistics," Mark said. "We will build an initial fleet of six of these ships. You need to find captains and crews. Each ship can hold three dozen soldiers. I doubt you will need that many—two dozen should suffice. That comes to six captains, sixty-six sailors, and one hundred and forty-four men at arms. You are certainly qualified to select the men at arms.

Fenwick will assist you in hiring captains. Captains generally find their own crews."

We discussed a number of other items relating to the ships and manning them. When we finished, I realized my horse, Andy, was nowhere near. Lucy and I had walked from our house to the Temple, then ridden with the king and queen after the ceremony. I was able to find my way out to the front courtyard (with only a couple of wrong turns, which I caught and corrected). With the tubes containing the drawings and the letters under my arm, I crossed the bridge and approached the guard house. I asked the man to whistle up a hackney for me.

"Excuse me, Your Highness," he said deferentially, "but where are you going?"

"To my house," I explained.

"Your Highness," he said with a pained expression, "um, the crown prince does not travel by hackney. Neither does he go anywhere unescorted. I will have a carriage brought around and men of the Castle Shield to accompany you."

As you readers know, I pride myself on preventing my emotions from reaching my facial expressions. The guard's dictum was perfectly logical and made complete sense. It was also something I had not fully considered. I will admit I must have looked like a fish out of water, my mouth opening and closing with no sound coming out.

"Of course," I answered lamely when the power of speech returned.

4

It was at least twenty minutes while they prepared the carriage. When it arrived, I instructed the driver and the half-dozen men of the Castle Shield where I wished to go. Before I climbed into the carriage, the leader of the soldiers—a sergeant by the markings on his sleeve—cleared his throat.

"Your Highness, will you be going out again later?" he asked.

"I don't know, Sar'nt," I replied. "It will depend on what my wife wishes for me to do."

"Then we will stay."

Now I felt awful. Here it was the summer solstice, one of the major holidays of the year, and I would be forcing these men to remain at the house in case I went out. That did not sit well with me.

"Sar'nt, when we get there, I will ask Lucy if she needs me to go out," I said. "If she doesn't, I'll send you on your way. Someone will need to accompany me tomorrow morning, beginning at quarter past seven. We will collect my horse from the Foaming Boar, deliver these materials to three shipwrights, then return to collect Lucy and ride to Easton."

"Your Highness, begging your pardon," he said, "but one of the men can fetch your horse."

"Thank you, Sar'nt," I replied, "but I would like to do that myself. It should be amusing."

While we drove toward the house, I wondered how Jerry would react to my new status. Jerry was the stableboy at the inn, and a pleasantly cheeky lad. I hoped he would be a bit befuddled by my new position, but not overawed.

When I arrived at the house, I walked into a hive of activity. Roberta was in the kitchen with Roger, Freddy and Greta's man. They were preparing dinner for what looked like a large group of people. When I started up the stairs, Lucy heard me and called down. I followed her voice to our bedroom where she was laying out clothes for me—buff breeches and a sky-blue coat, with a paisley waistcoat She had changed out of the finery she wore for the ceremony into more usual garb.

"I saw quite a commotion in the kitchen," I commented.

"Indeed," Lucy replied with a smile. "There is a group coming for dinner. Are you finished with your business for today?"

"I am. Do you need me to go out between now and morning?" I asked. "The men of the Castle Shield came with me and want to know if they should wait."

"Just tell them no," she said. "I don't think I need you to go anywhere."

I ran downstairs and sent the men away. On my way up the stairs, I wondered how and when this dinner came about. Halfway up, Lucy's voice stopped me.

"Darling, I need a bath before I get dressed for the evening," she called. "Would you please tell Roger and Roberta?"

I did as requested, but helped Roger lift the large pot for heating water onto the stove, and pulled the first buckets of water from the well. The first two went into the pot for heating. The second two I put on the hoist. I would pull them up when I went upstairs.

After pouring the cold water into the tub, I sent the empty buckets back down on the hoist. Two buckets of cold water, with four of hot, produced the optimal temperature. It was not long before Roger hollered to tell me the last buckets were ready. I poured them in and went to return them to the hoist.

Lucy, as naked as the day she was born, passed me and trailed her hand seductively across my chest as she passed. My eyes riveted to her, I walked into the door jamb, clanking the buckets and making a fool of myself. Lucy laughed and disappeared into the lavatory but stuck her hand out and beckoned me with a crooked finger.

I scurried back to the bedroom after throwing the buckets onto the hoist. As fast as I could, I began to remove my formal clothes. Hopping on one foot, I managed to tear one of my fine white stockings in my haste. I was almost out of my underclothes, when my brain finally registered the clothing she set out for me to wear later.

It was the suit I wore when we married. Today was the second anniversary of our wedding. I—a complete dunce and horrible husband—had no gift to give my wife in honor of the day.

I trudged into the lavatory with my head hanging. Lucy had added something to the bathwater that made it smell marvelous, but I barely noticed at the moment. She looked up at me.

"What's wrong?" she asked.

"What's wrong is I am the worst husband in Aquileia," I said. "It is our anniversary, and I completely neglected to get you a present."

"Nonsense!" she said, and her laugh was brilliant like the ringing of a silver bell. "You made me a princess! There can be no greater gift."

She beckoned me closer. I knelt down next to the tub. She reached her wet hand around my neck and drew me close, giving me a passionate kiss.

"I didn't get you anything either," she confessed with a giggle. "Now get in here and do my back."

"I knew the day was coming," she said as I slid in behind her, "but every time I thought of it, I was busy with other things. When I wasn't busy and could have done something about it, I didn't remember, with everything else going on around us. I knew your mind was elsewhere—who would not have been distracted!—so I did not fret. Instead, I found our wedding clothes, and we will wear them tonight. Greta and Freddy are doing the same.

"Who is coming to this dinner?" I asked.

"Everyone," she replied with a laugh.

"Who is everyone?"

"Well, actually, there are two dinners," she explained. "The dinner here will be your father and Ari, the Travals, my parents, Freddy's parents, and Greta's parents. The other party is at Freddy's because his dining table is big enough to seat everyone. We will greet the older generation here, then walk across to Freddy's."

"I wonder if Madam Traval will remember how thoroughly she slandered me when I was just Casimir FitzDuncan," I mused.

"Don't fuss, darling," Lucy advised. "I imagine she has a selective memory and couldn't possibly recall."

I laughed.

"And who will be at our dinner?"

"Linc and Nellie, Quint and Siobhan, Ratty and Inger, Tom Gibson and Sophie Cohill, RJ Sweetland and Camilla Winsor, Fenwick and Julienne, and Freddy and Greta, of course," she listed. "We invited Julienne's friend Bitsy and her beau, but they had family obligations they could not escape."

"I'm glad Tom Gibson is invited," I said. "I wasn't aware that anyone knew him."

"Since he and Sophie started seeing one another—his mother and her parents just agreed to the match, by the way—Sophie has been getting him out in public more. Nellie and Inger have seen them on a number of occasions and decided he is perfectly charming. They have known Sophie forever. Though Tom is on the quiet side, he seems very sweet and absolutely adores Sophie."

"I'm happy for him," I said.

I started to share with Lucy my idea of creating my own council of advisors, including Tom and Ratty, but she turned around, put her finger on my lips, and said, "I didn't invite you into my bath to discuss the problems of the world, Prince Casimir. Start scrubbing. The water is cooling down."

When we dried off, we began dressing. I put on the clothes Lucy laid out and a cravat to match. I found Lucy had replaced the suede boots that I wore for the wedding, which were later ruined. These were perfect copies and matched the buff color of my breeches perfectly.

Lucy was wearing the same colors as I was, but where I was blue, she was in buff, and the other way around. As soon as she finished dressing, she gave me a peck on the cheek and headed down the stairs. When she turned on the landing, she saw my look of puzzlement.

"Greta and I are helping with one another's hair," she explained. "I'll be back soon."

No sooner did Lucy leave than Freddy walked in. He hollered, and I responded. I quickly trotted downstairs. As I was dressed in my wedding clothes, Freddy was likewise clad in his.

"They banished me from my own house," he complained, using his 'Lord Compote' voice.

"Why on earth would they do that, Lord Compote?" I asked.

"Well, poppet became upset when I stuck my tongue in her ear," he protested innocently, "even though I do it all the time, and it makes her giggle and squirm so cutely. Then she tossed me out when I pinched muffin's bum."

"What did muffin say?"

"Well, she didn't actually *say* anything," he replied. "She squeaked very adorably, I must say. Her cheeks flushed a becoming shade of pink, and she jumped a little."

"Well, I'm sorry, Lord Compote, Women are such a mystery to me," I said, shaking my head. "I always coveted your deep understanding."

"A mystery," he said. "That must be it. Poppet is giving me a puzzle to solve. Tilt the sherry decanter, dear friend, whilst I ponder."

I went to the sideboard and poured each of us a glass. Freddy had taken his usual sprawled posture on the sofa. I handed him his glass and sat in the chair facing him.

"Freddy, if Roger is over here with Roberta, fixing dinner for our parents, who is in the kitchen at your house?" I asked.

"Theo," he responded dryly.

"Nice try," I said. "Theo is in Easton."

"Esther and Wanda, from Lucy's and my parents' houses respectively," he said.

"I hope you are not as much of an idiot as I am," I said. "I forgot to get an anniversary present for Lucy."

A look of horror appeared on Freddy's face. I immediately felt sorry for him. As I was about to comfort him, he began to laugh.

"Of course I did. Why? You didn't?"

I shook my head sadly. "At least Lucy also forgot to get a present."

"Well, you've had a tumultuous time of it lately," Freddy said. "So has Lucy."

"Still, I feel bad," I said.

"Well, you're the prince now. Don't you get to use a whipping boy for when you make mistakes?" he asked.

"What a wonderful idea, Freddy! Now, whomever shall I choose?" I asked, leaning close to him and looking at him intently.

He laughed, knowing I was not serious. Our conversation turned to other topics. I mentioned my plan of creating my own advisory group, like the king's. Freddy liked the concept, and we bounced ideas back and forth.

Lucy came in, looking mindbogglingly lovely. As at our wedding, her golden hair was arranged in a thick braid over her left shoulder. She wore a crown of flowers and herbs.

"Lord Compote," she called, "Poppet says you are allowed to return if you promise to behave."

"Thank you, muffin," he said as he uncoiled himself from the sofa and approached her, "but where's the fun in that?'

Lucy squeaked and jumped. Her face flushed. Her hands flew to her backside.

"See you soon, muffin," Freddy called over his shoulder as he departed.

"He pinched you again?" I asked.

"Yes," she said with a chagrined look. "I can't believe I let him get away with it a second time!"

"Well, Lord Compote does have a certain way about him," I teased. "Now—this dinner—I imagine you and Greta came up with this idea in the last few days?"

"I wish we could claim credit for it," Lucy said, "but it was Siobhan and Julienne. They asked if they could host a party to celebrate. Unfortunately, Fenwick's and Quint's places ended up being too small for everyone we all felt should be included, so Greta volunteered."

My father and Ariana arrived just then. They scurried upstairs, telling us they needed to change. Their guests were arriving within the half hour.

"Come sit," Lucy said, patting the sofa. "I'd hop in your lap, but it's a bit too warm for that, plus my bum's been pinched—twice!"

"I had my first inkling today of what Mark said about it being vastly more convenient to live in the castle," I said, sharing the guards' insistence on my using a carriage and having an escort.

"Well then, we shouldn't tell them you are going across the street to Freddy's house," Lucy teased, making her eye twinkle as she did.

Her parents arrived first, followed by Freddy's. Ariana and my father came downstairs at this time. The Travals and the Hawkinses arrived together, with Herbert Traval and Benjamin Hawkins in a lively discussion. Christina Hawkins and Louise Traval brought up the rear.

The older generation all congratulated Lucy and me on the adoption and our elevation that morning. As Lucy predicted, Madam Traval chose not to remember that I was the same person from several years before. Before Lucy and I departed, we saw that Herbert Traval and Benjamin Hawkins had already cornered my father about some issue. I imagined it concerned Port Charles. That was no longer of the same concern to me as a few months before, and it made me sad. Lucy saw where I was looking and took my arm.

"Come, Prince Casimir, we must go mingle with our adoring subjects," she said.

Once we were out the door, she added, "Caz, as the crown prince, there will be many other opportunities for you to change things for the better, as you did with the Pheas River and Port Charles. That one is far enough along that you are no longer needed. You will find other projects."

Lucy often knew the right thing to say to snap me out of melancholy. This was exactly what I needed to hear. I squeezed her hand in gratitude.

When we knocked on Freddy's door, Freddy answered. He allowed Lucy in, then slammed the door in my face. I immediately guessed Freddy was mimicking Theo.

I knocked again. Freddy opened the door. He looked around, pretending not to see me. He slammed it shut again.

Again, I knocked. The door opened. Freddy stood motionless.

"Hello, Theo. Is Lord Rawlinsford in?" I asked.

"I'll see," Freddy replied, in an uncanny rendering of Theo's deep voice, then he slammed the door again.

I knocked for the fourth time. By now, I could hear everyone laughing. Most of the guests knew about Theo. They quickly educated those who didn't. The door opened.

"Greta!" I called. "Theo won't let me in!"

"Theo!" she hollered. "Let Caz in and treat him nicely, or I'll spank your bare bottom again."

"Won't you please come in," Freddy mumbled in Theo's monotone while displaying a devastatingly accurate version of Theo's most insincere smile.

"Why, thank you, Theo," I said.

I shrugged off my jacket and unbuckled my sword belt. I gave them to "Theo" to hang up. As Theo did countless times, Freddy waited until I advanced two paces past him, then dropped them to the floor, my sword clanging on the slate.

The others were watching from down the hall. I did not see what Freddy did, though I heard it. Greta and Fenwick both doubled over in laughter. While they were laughing, Freddy took my arm and escorted me inside.

"Thought you might miss Theo," he said. "I suspect he too longs for the days when he could abuse you so freely. In Easton, he can only be grumpy. Where you're concerned, I believe he much prefers being rude."

"Lucy was wondering whether we should bring him to the castle with us," I said.

There was a brief moment of silence while everyone processed what I said. Then, those who knew Theo the most began to guffaw. Once again, I saw Greta and Fenwick with their hands on their knees.

"Thank you, Freddy," I said quietly. "That got us off to a wonderful start."

For the next half hour, we shared some of the most outrageous Theo stories. There was one I dearly wanted to tell that showed another side of Theo, but I could not. After my first encounter with Fenwick, when I lay in the street more dead than alive, Theo carried my unconscious body to my rooms. Though I would be forever grateful to Theo for that, I would not embarrass Fenwick. Indeed, Fenwick's transformation since then was even more dramatic than mine. I had no wish to rub his nose in the past.

In the previous three years, I had enjoyed many merry evenings. This was the best yet. It seemed everyone came prepared with a hilarious story that most of the others had not heard. Fenwick managed to make the story of our Rhetian adventure comically entertaining. When he reached the part where we were imprisoned in the Rhetian fort, I broke in and described the food they gave us.

"Many different people have demanded that I eat it over the years," I said dryly. "Now I know what it tastes like."

Fenwick picked up the narrative after everyone finished laughing. He told of our escape from the fort and finding the boat. Though I remembered our voyage in the little boat as awful and frightening, Fenwick found the humor in our predicament. When he told of our time on the island, he maintained the fib that our fire was spotted by a passing Traval ship.

Lucy and I walked back to our house just after midnight. Her parents and Freddy's, and my father and Ariana, were still chatting and laughing. We said good night, which seemed to make them realize the hour.

5

At a quarter past seven the next morning, I was dressed, fed, and ready. Six members of the Castle Shield arrived precisely on time. They brought an extra mount for me to ride. We headed to the Foaming Boar and pulled around to the rear where the stable was. Every stall was occupied, and there were three horses tied up outside. Clearly, the inn was busy for the holiday.

Despite the early hour, Jerry was busy grooming a horse when we rode in. He noticed the men of the Castle Shield first. He froze in mid-brushstroke when I appeared from behind them.

The poor lad did not know what to do as I slid from the saddle. He knew me best as Mr. Caz, the man who rumpled his hair. Then I became Lord Oritur, which Jerry never quite grasped. Now that I was the crown prince, I figured he would be completely bamboozled. It didn't seem as though I was wrong. The brush dropped from his hand as he raised it to knuckle his forelock. Then, realizing that wasn't necessarily the proper way to greet a prince, he started to bow but immediately thought maybe he should go to one knee. I stopped him.

"Jerry! Stop!" I said firmly but kindly. "I'm still me—the same person who is going to try to rumple your hair, even though you're getting too big for that. And by princely decree, I shall not only allow you to continue to be cheeky with me, but I shall positively encourage it."

It took Jerry a moment to process what I told him. I could see when he understood by the naughty gleam in his eye. He took a couple of steps.

"I was there yesterday," he said, "and I was thinkin' 'Cor! I knew him when he weren't nobody special.' Though I am happy for you, Prince Caz."

"Thank you, Jerry."

"Mostly because Andy is now a prince's horse, and I've known all along he was too good for the likes of nobody special, like you was," Jerry teased. "So now Andy gets to be with all the other royal horses, and get his feed served to him on a purple pillow, which is what he deserves."

I laughed and darted my hand forward to rumple his hair. Jerry was taller now and not able to duck under the way he used to. I got a few hard rubs in before he twisted away. He glared at me with mock anger, but his smile gave him away.

"It looks like you're busy," I said, "and I'm in a hurry. I'll saddle Andy my—"

"No, Your Highness," he responded with an exaggerated bow, "it will be my greatest pleasure to prepare Andy for your royal bum to perch upon. Won't take but a minute."

The soldiers were listening. I could tell from the smiles they were trying to control. I decided to joke with Jerry some more.

"Just think, Jerry," I said as he put a blanket on Andy. "Touching that saddle, you can say to yourself, 'This saddle held the Prince's ass.' You probably won't want to wash your hands after."

"Nah," he replied as he hoisted the saddle onto Andy's back. "I'll scald 'em in boiling water, I will."

When Jerry finished, I held out my hand for him to shake. Sensing a trick, Jerry moved cautiously to accept it. We clasped only briefly before he stepped quickly away.

"Tomorrow, Princess Lucy and I will be leaving. After that, we might not see you again for a long time, Jerry. You might want to prepare your farewells for her. Just to warn you, she will probably want a hug," I said.

"And I will gladly give her one," Jerry said. "Not you, though. Uck!"

With my escort, I returned to the castle for the resumption of the meeting. The queen and Lucy did not join us, but everyone else from the meeting when I learned I was to be the king's successor was. Instead of sitting opposite the king, I was placed at his right hand.

Around the table were the Dukes of Chaldic, Caurus, Manton, and Gulick, Earl Montgomery, my father, Lord Hepworth, Lord Pilaro, and Lord Shames. They were standing by their chairs. When the king sat, we all followed suit.

"Prince Casimir has volunteered to oversee our nautical endeavors," the king said. "We have plans from the naval architects, which he will deliver to the shipwrights here in Aquileia. Plans are also being sent to a shipwright in Aurora and one in Newcastle. We have asked for them to return their bids in three weeks. In the meantime, His Highness will be returning to the Eastern March to make his farewells."

Following his opening statement, we showed the architects' drawings and explained the advantages of the type of ship. We discussed the method by which the crown would be repaid for the cost of construction. Freddy's father, David, the Duke of Manton, then brought up an interesting point.

"In looking back through the accounts from Sir Samuel's day," he said, "Sir Samuel did not limit himself to preying only on Rhetian vessels."

'How did we not end up at war with the whole world?" I asked.

"By warning the countries on the Surrounded Sea, and other countries on the southern continent, not to do business with the Rhetian Empire," he said. "According to a convention that has been followed since the fall of the Old Empire, countries at war are permitted to impose blockades against their opponents. We must inform the other countries of our intention and give them time to comply, but after a certain period of time, their cargos are fair game."

"Cargos?" Earl Montgomery asked.

"Only the cargo is subject to seizure," David said. "This is why the concept of a prize court is necessary. Any Rhetian ship we capture is ours. There is no adjudication required. For other vessels, a magistrate must rule. Typically, the cargo is forfeit, but the ship is allowed to return to its owner."

"Even so, isn't that a bit—provocative?" Lord Hepworth asked.

"In Sir Samuel's day, the formal declaration of the blockade was delivered by the crown prince," David said, aiming a smug look at me.

The meeting lasted another hour. I now knew what I would be doing while we were waiting for the ships to be completed. Fenwick and I would be taking a diplomatic tour of the southern continent.

After the meeting, I made the rounds of the three shipwrights. I delivered the tubes with the drawings and the instructions. All three were familiar with Mellone and Baldini and promised to seek them out with any questions.

We returned to the house. The soldiers took Andy with them. They would bring him back the next morning.

That evening, in contrast to the revelry of the night before, Lucy and I enjoyed a quiet dinner with Ariana and my father. We shared some of the highlights of the previous evening with each other. Later, as Lucy and I were climbing the stairs, I realized this was the last night that this would be our house. Lucy seemed to read my mind and held me close until I felt better.

The next morning a dozen men of the Castle Shield were waiting for us. They would accompany Lucy, my father, Ariana, Fenwick, Julienne, and me to Easton. When they saw me carrying Lucy's and my saddlebags, they jumped to grab them from me.

My father had already brought his and Ariana's horses from the Foaming Boar. Lucy and I rode double, accompanied by six soldiers, and went to retrieve Bella. Lucy wanted to say farewell to Jerry. In contrast to how he behaved with me, Jerry gave Lucy a hug. Tears filled both their eyes as we departed.

Julienne and Fenwick were waiting at the house when we returned, and we all set off. The Castle Shield stayed a discreet distance ahead of and behind us—out of earshot. Even though we would probably not touch on any sensitive topics, I appreciated their tact.

The first day's ride was fairly quiet. I think both groups were talked out from the dinners the night before. We arrived at the inn where we would spend the night.

The innkeeper told us we were fortunate. The day before, he was full with holiday travelers, including many who were returning home from going to see the adoption of the new crown prince and the Feast of Midsommar. When I asked about lodgings for the men of the Castle Shield, he made the connection. At that point, he began to fall all over himself to try to help us. He apologized profusely that he did not have enough beds for the soldiers but would offer them a chance to sleep in the stable loft. I took it to the sergeant.

"Sar'nt, the innkeeper doesn't have enough rooms," I said. "Stable loft, or set up camp outside of town?"

"Stable loft will be a might warm, Your Highness," he replied. "We'll find a spot—don't worry."

"Fine, but allow me to pay for your dinner and breakfast," I said.

"Not necessary, Your Highness," he replied, patting his coin pouch. "I drew traveling funds."

"I don't know how these things work, Sar'nt," I apologized. "This is all new to me."

"Your Highness, you don't need to apologize to me for nothing," he replied with a grin. "If part of my job means I sleep on the ground, it don't bother me none at all. And riding with you, Your Highness, is an honor for us. I was there when we filled the ditch with Rhetians, then at Lake Mago, at Hamil Creek, and at Farsall. Everyone in the Shield was part of the last three, but only a few of us were part of the first battle. Later, we all saw you save the king. Cor, I'll not soon forget that sight! The whole time, you slept on the ground like us and ate the same grub. Before that, I was there when we ambushed the nomads and later when we went over the mountains to see 'em. I watched you go down that cliff to try to save Prince Albert. Makes me kinda proud to be in charge of this detachment, Your Highness."

That evening, over dinner, my father mentioned something from the evening before.

"Julienne, your father and Ben Hawkins tried to sound me out regarding whether they should make an offer to buy Coombs out," he said. "They say the business is slipping away from him."

"They will be too late," Julienne said. "I told my father this already, but he ignored me. Remember the gentleman who bought the five harborfront properties adjacent to the ones I purchased? His name is Martin Albrecht. His negotiations to buy a controlling interest of Coombs are nearly complete."

"What?" I exclaimed.

"Do you also recall when I told you about the speculators who lost money, betting that prices last fall would be much higher?" Julienne asked.

My father and I nodded.

"For every person who thought prices would rise, there has to be another who thinks they will decrease or stay the same," Julienne explained. "Albrecht is a smaller trader based in Newcastle who learned of the Port Charles project. He bet every ducat he had and every ducat he could borrow that prices would be no higher. Depending on how things worked out, he would either be a ruined man or make a killing. He made a killing. At the auction, he bought the land with the idea of erecting his own warehouse. The decline of Coombs has presented another opportunity. I tried to tell my father this, and I'm pretty sure Ratty did the same with his father and older brother, but—"

I laughed.

"They didn't listen to Ratty when he told them about the potential of Port Charles," Fenwick said. "And they didn't listen to him about this. If they don't wise up and put Ratty in charge over Ben Junior, he might hop over to Albrecht, and then Hawkins will fade away like Coombs is now."

"Would Ratty do that?" Lucy asked. "Something like that could tear a family apart."

Fenwick's response was to lay his finger beside his nose, indicating he knew something but wasn't telling. Lucy gasped. My father laughed.

"If Ratty is as smart as we all think he is," he said, "then he will leave something incriminating where his father can spot it. Ben Senior will be horrified, but I think he already knows that Ben Junior is best suited to be nothing more than the head clerk. He won't let Ratty get away."

"You sound confident," Lucy remarked.

"Ben Hawkins and Julienne's father just need to remember how they made it to where they are," my father said. "Years ago, they were both young and hungry like this Albrecht. They would get a piece of information and dig until they knew enough to have an edge. The more established trading companies are always averse to risk. In their younger days, both Ben Hawkins and your father, Julienne, would know from the investigation they did whether the risk was manageable. It's how he and Ben bankrupted my father-in-law."

"What?" Julienne exclaimed.

"It's a long story," my father said, "and one that doesn't matter now. Caz knows the whole of it. I bear neither your father nor Ben Hawkins any ill will at all over it. They were smart, hard-working, and aggressive. My father-in-law was none of those things. Similar to Coombs right now, in many respects."

Lucy adroitly changed the subject by asking if anyone knew when Ratty and Inger Fairchild might announce their betrothal. The discussion then moved to Tom Gibson and Sophie Cohill. When we finished dissecting their relationship, we moved to RJ Sweetland and Camilla Winsor.

We arrived at Easton Manor two days later. It struck me as Lucy and I climbed the stairs to our bedroom that, like the house in the city, it would not be "ours" by the time I returned from touring the March with my father and Fenwick. While we men were away, Lucy would be arranging to pack and ship to the castle the things we wished to keep. In my case, that was clothing. She also had her workshop.

In the morning, my father drafted letters to the mayors and heads of the villages and towns, alerting them to our visits. He gave them to armsmen to deliver. When he finished, he rode with me to Bannister Brothers, the bank that held my accounts. My father insisted on repaying me for the repairs to the manor and the furniture we replaced. We arranged the transfer, and then I informed Richard Bannister that I would be transferring my account to the capital. He looked puzzled.

"Lord Oritur, I'm afraid I do not understand," he said. "How can you be leaving the March?"

My father's laughter prevented me from answering.

"Richard, you really should get out more," my father said. "He is no longer Lord Oritur. The preferred form of address is 'Your Highness.' You might be the only one in the building who has not heard the news."

"Oh!" Bannister gasped. "Majors and Minors! I apologize, Your Highness. I meant no disrespect. As your father suggests, I tend to be somewhat oblivious to things outside the bank. What on earth has taken place?"

"Well," I chuckled, "perhaps you ought to ask your staff to keep you abreast. Duncan is no longer legally my father—"

"Majors and Minors!" Bannister gasped.

My father and I told him about all the changes. He asked us to pause so he could write them down. When we finished, he seemed stunned. It took us a few minutes to pull him back to the task for which we came.

6

The next day, my father, Ariana, Julienne, Fenwick, and I, accompanied by half of the men of the Castle Shield who had ridden east with us, set off to visit every town and village in the March. At every stop, the reaction of the people was mixed. They were happy for Lucy and me, but sad we were leaving the March. Learning that Fenwick was from Northrup and that the king ennobled him because of his ability and service to the realm helped them begin with a more or less favorable attitude toward him.

Our visit to Northrup was interesting. There were still people who remembered Fenwick from his youth. After he ran away from his foster parents, the Banfields, the mayor at the time took it upon herself to find out why. Apparently, the Banfields had been honest about how poorly they treated Fenwick, claiming it was their right since they agreed to take him in after his mother died.

The people of Northrup did not agree with them and shunned the Banfields from that point onward. The couple moved away two years later. No one knew or cared where they went. The mayor from those days was still alive and came to embrace Fenwick at the end of our meeting.

"My poor child," she said as tears rolled down her cheeks. "If we had known, we would never have put you with them. We sent inquiries, trying to find you after you left, but had no success."

"Thank you, Mayor Boyd," Fenwick replied. "It was not the easiest road for me, but it led me to my current position in life. How could I not be pleased to have become Lord Easton and to claim Duncan as my father and Prince Casimir as a friend?"

During our tour, we also met with the armsmen. A small number of them had left to join the Rangers who patrol our border with the Rhetian Empire. The remainder were beginning to serve as roving constables. My father and Fenwick already approved of what I said next.

"Should any of you find your new duties less exciting than you hoped, I have an alternative that you may find attractive. If you ever dreamed of becoming a pirate and seeing the world beyond Aquileia, in a few months I will be in command of a naval force that will begin preying on Rhetian ships. I am not looking for answers today since our ships will not be built for several months yet. If you are interested, please write to me. When we are ready to take to the seas, I will inform you."

Lucy joined us halfway through our tour, along with the other members of the Castle Shield. Everyone was especially sad she was leaving. One question that was asked at every stop concerned the future of the Harvest Fair. When Ariana and Julienne assured them that it would continue and that they would do everything they could to make it even better, the people were pleased.

When we reached Hillstead, I mentioned I would be returning to Easton. Fenwick and my father tried to convince me to come with them to Port Charles. I tried to explain.

"To see the progress and all the building activity," I said, shaking my head, "should make me happy that things are turning out so well. But I'm afraid it will have the opposite effect. It's no longer my project—it belongs to you. Lucy is leaving with Julienne, and she will need my help in Easton."

"Lucy does not need your assistance," Fenwick said. "You will only get in her way. Come with us. Take pride in making this happen. Yes, you will not see it to completion. I hope that it is because you have identified other opportunities in the kingdom and are working to make those become reality."

"Things are well in hand, dear," Lucy confirmed. "Go see Port Charles."

As I suspected, Port Charles was a hive of activity. We could hear it before we could see it. The rhythmic beating of hammers driving nails into wood reached our ears before we exited the woods.

The town center was beginning to take shape. The biggest building in that section was the inn. Looking past to the harborfront, Traval & Company was adding to their warehouse. Hawkins Trading Company's huge facility on the opposite side of the harbor was well underway. Between the mouth of the river and Traval's operation, another huge warehouse was being built.

"Albrecht's?" I asked Fenwick.

He nodded.

We rode across the river to the jute farm. The large house where my father and Ariana would live was framed and under roof. The manufactory building was further along, and the cottages for the tenants appeared to be completed.

The fields were full of tall green plants. The jute was at least two feet taller than a man at this point. Mr. Balboa, the supervisor of the farmstead and an expert on the growing of jute whom we brought over from Mooresa, saw us and scurried over.

"Hallo, Hallo!" he called in his thick accent, his face beaming. "See? I told good crop, is good, good, good crop. Still one munt to grow."

"How much taller do these plants get?" I wondered.

Fenwick asked Balboa in Mooren. The two carried on a lengthy conversation. When it finished, Balboa trotted away.

"Bye!" he called over his shoulder.

"Mr. Balboa is quite happy, which I am sure you guessed," Fenwick said. "The harvest will exceed his expectations. He credits the quality of the soil. From the size of this year's yield, he thinks we should implement a two-crop rotation— half the land in jute, the other half in legumes, switching every year. He says the growing season will not permit two plantings a year."

"That's right," my father said. "I remember he mentioned that the water the plants soak in is good fertilizer for legumes afterward, and the legumes enrich the soil."

"Yes," Fenwick confirmed. "As a result, he wants a pump and a wagon with a large tank to spread the water. He will prepare drawings."

When we returned to Easton, Lucy was prepared for us to return to the capital. Julienne had already departed. With the help of the men of the Castle Shield who stayed behind with her earlier, all the belongings we were taking were packed in crates. Theo would deliver them to Commerford, where they would travel downriver to the port and the Traval warehouse. A Traval ship would collect them and deliver them to the capital.

Fenwick would return with us, while my father and Ariana would remain in Easton for a day or two before setting off to Mooresa. Fenwick would be assisting me in the diplomatic mission to the southern continent. We would return to the capital before the bids from the shipwrights were due.

Leaving the manor the next morning was quite emotional for me. I spent the first two-thirds of my youth there before I was sent away. I had never thought I would return, let alone as my father's heir. When I did, Lucy and I had poured ourselves freely into our new roles.

The success I enjoyed against the nomads was something of which I was proud. The Harvest Fairs and the feast days we held for Andvar and Freyja also filled me with a deep sense of satisfaction, and Lucy may have played a greater part in those than I did. Lucy also left behind her students. Through her efforts, every town and village now had a qualified healer. It was an amazing legacy.

We said farewell to the staff. Theo was probably delighted I was leaving, but saying goodbye to Lucy brought tears to his eyes. As we rode out the gate, Fenwick assured me he would care for the manor and the people at least as well as we did. I noticed tears in his eyes. I would not have said anything, but Lucy did.

"Fenwick, dear, what's wrong?"

"As much as your lives have changed in recent years, Lucy—and Caz," he said through a tightened throat, "mine has nearly kept pace. And to think, it came about as a result of me trying to kill you. The Gods have an odd sense of humor. Now I, an orphan from Northrup of no special family, am Lord Easton. Not only am I responsible for this household, but I am also accountable for the welfare of all the people we met in the last two and a half weeks. I owe it to you to see Port Charles grow and prosper. It's daunting."

We rode in silence for a time until I quipped, "At least Theo tolerates you."

"Only because Toby does," Fenwick noted. "If the dog didn't care for me, Theo would treat me worse than you, and that's saying something!"

That brought laughter that lightened our hearts. Our conversation picked up. The soldiers accompanying us had noticed our earlier mood and kept quiet. Now, they started to chatter among themselves.

When we arrived in the capital, we went in different directions. Fenwick was heading to the house that, until recently, was ours. Lucy and I, along with our escort, returned to the castle. Roberta would already have sent the things over from the house that Lucy had designated.

The short ride after bidding Fenwick goodbye was another emotional time. Tonight, we would sleep in the castle—not as guests, but as residents. Lucy sensed my disquiet and leaned over and clasped my hand as we rode. As always, Lucy's touch brought a feeling of calm comfort and quiet confidence. When she released my hand a minute or two later, my attitude had transformed completely.

When we reached the guardhouse, Lucy and I dismounted. When I went to shoulder my saddlebags, Sergeant Hewko looked at me disapprovingly. I retracted my hands quickly as though I had been stung. It went against my grain to have others wait on me, but the sergeant explained things to me while we were on the road.

"Your Highness, I have been allowing you to groom your horse and the princess's, but you really should get out of the habit," he said. "I understand you enjoy it and have no desire to seem privileged, but it just isn't proper. It's one thing if we're in the field, living rough. At the castle, well, it just won't do, Your Highness."

Lucy and I thanked the men for accompanying us. They took Andy and Bella with them, and Lucy and I walked across the bridge. The seneschal met us on the other side.

"The king and queen request your presence for dinner in just over an hour," he informed us.

We headed to our apartment. Lucy asked our maid Wilma to prepare a bath for us. After three days of travel in the summer heat, we needed to freshen up before dining with the king and queen.

My father now, I thought. The idea was still odd. It would take more time for me to accept it.

After Lucy asked Wilma to draw us a bath, I went to one of the armoires, looking for a change of clothing. While we were away, Roberta had sent the things Lucy designated from the house. The armoire I opened was full of men's clothing, but I recognized only a fraction of it.

"Lucy?" I hollered.

"Yes?"

"Whose clothing is in the armoire?"

I began to paw through the items. The fabrics were sumptuous, with rich colors. I drew one jacket out and held it up. It looked to be the right size to fit me. I noticed everything in the armoire was lighter in weight, suitable for summer. Looking at the bottom, there were also different pairs of shoes and boots.

Some of the clothing Roberta would have sent over was heavier for winter temperatures. I checked the armoire to the left of the first. This held more men's clothing but of heavier cloth.

Lucy walked up and was looking in the first armoire. She was fingering the fabrics. She turned to me with a broad smile.

"Is there another tailor other than Hamed who has your measurements?" she asked.

My first reaction was to shake my head, but in the middle of doing that, I remembered. Before Fenwick and I went on our first assignment together, he took me to the king's tailor. He outfitted me for our trip to Scaramouche.

"Yes," I admitted after I recalled it. "The king's own tailor. And the cobbler who is associated with him."

"That explains where they came from," Lucy said with a grin. "Someone bought you some clothes. The big question is whether it was Mark or Lily. The clothes are fabulous."

"Not very practical," I mumbled.

"For what?" Lucy asked.

"For—"

"For riding against nomads?" Lucy asked. "For breaking into people's houses? For all the other activities in which you used to engage?"

"Yes," I mumbled, realizing the point Lucy was making.

"Other than the clothing I made you buy, what else in your wardrobe was suitable for the crown prince?" she asked.

I could not answer. Lucy knew the answer as well as I did. I was not a slob, but my clothes tended to be practical and sturdy.

After our bath, I dressed in some of the new clothing. I allowed Lucy to pick an outfit for me. Everything fit perfectly, and I will admit I looked good.

Lucy snuck up behind me as I glanced in the mirror. Standing on tiptoes, she draped her arms over my chest and put her chin on my shoulder.

"Hm?" she prodded.

"I look *regal*," I said.

She cuffed me on the side of the head as she pulled away.

When we met the king and queen, I thanked them for the clothes. Lily looked confused. Mark merely waved his hand dismissively.

Over dinner, Mark wanted to know about our trip—specifically how the people of the March reacted to Fenwick's elevation in status. While he and I were chatting, Lucy and Lily had their own conversation. When dinner was served, our separate conversations paused.

After the plates were cleared away, Mark cleared his throat gently and said, "Tomorrow, we open the bids from the shipwrights. You, Fenwick, and I will review them, then let the contracts. As long as their bids are reasonable, I would like to give the shipwright in Aurora and the one in Newcastle each a ship to build. Both have good reputations, and I feel sending work their way helps maintain their business. I feel it is a good thing to have viable shipwrights in the three major ports. Eventually, I hope we have one in Port Charles also. Regardless, that leaves four ships for the three shipwrights here in Aquileia. Fenwick will have more to report on them."

With that, he excused himself. The queen stayed a bit longer. I suspected this was by design.

"I have someone I would like you to meet, Lucy," she said. "She is a farmer's daughter, and I noticed her last Freyday."

"What is her name?"

"I don't know," Lily replied. "I *saw* her, so to speak, at a distance."

From the queen's inflection, I took it to mean that she perceived the girl's aura. This was an ability that manifested for some of those with affinity to the Goddess Freyja. Lucy's dominant supernatural connection was to Freyja, while for the queen, it was one of her lesser two. Both could see the auras of supernatural affinity. As I have described in earlier writings, affinity does not automatically translate into ability. The affinity must be woken first.

"What did you see?" Lucy asked.

"Her dominant is Freyja," the queen explained. "Her lessers are Sadu and Mielvanir. I do not believe she is aware of her affinities."

As I have described elsewhere in my journals, Freyja is the Goddess of love, with an emphasis on romance and sexual pleasure. Mielvanir is the God of travel and commerce. Sadu is the Goddess of art, literature, and music.

"Why do you want me to meet her?" Lucy asked.

"I want you to recruit her—offer her employment," Lily said. "My hope is that by proximity to the two of us, her affinities awaken."

"And?" Lucy inquired.

"Lucy, dear, we need a scout," Lily explained. "I was planning on using you in this role, before …"

Her voice trailed off. I knew that Lily was thinking of Albert's death and our subsequent elevation. The queen had lost both her sons. One had turned out to be far more evil than anyone would ever have suspected. The other spent most of his early years as an arrogant, entitled snob before a crisis forced him to examine himself. From that point, Albert set himself on the right path and became a man of whom any parent would be proud.

"With your elevation, you cannot travel as freely," the queen resumed after a moment. "But this girl, if we can help her rouse her affinities and if she can perceive auras, might be able to travel the kingdom for us."

"To seek?" I asked.

"To find someone with an affinity for Ceridwen Sospita," the queen replied, "And if the Gods bless us, someone for whom Ceridwen Sospita is his or her dominant. I want to pass along the knowledge I have gained. There was no one to teach me. I have been diligent in searching for any information I could find. We have already seen two instances where Ceridwen Sospita was needed—in Eatonford and Dunland."

"How did people deal with the Dark Arts in the absence of someone with your abilities, Lily?" I asked.

"With great difficulty," she responded with a sigh. "It would take the combined efforts of a number of priests of the Three Majors, all protected by wards. Even then, there would be casualties. One reason we were successful is we intervened fairly early. For priests of the Three Major Gods to become involved, usually things need to reach a crisis state. It has been hard work to learn what I know. I want to pass it along."

"Lily, you are not that old," Lucy commented.

"I'm old enough to be your mother," Lily replied. "In fact, I am now your mother-in-law. It may take time for her to find anyone. The first person she finds may not be suitable."

"In what way?" I asked.

"They might be dumb as a box of rocks," Lily replied. "Having supernatural affinity is no guarantee of intelligence. Just because every person you know with ability is clever, Caz, doesn't mean they all are. As a matter of fact, even being clever does not mean you have all the answers. You mentioned that you are afflicted with seasickness. Have you ever tried connecting with Eir to solve that problem?"

Lucy and I both looked at one another sheepishly, then began to laugh. Eir is the Goddess of health and was a lesser affinity Lucy and I both possessed. Lucy had taught me to connect with Eir to increase the speed of my recovery after being wounded. Eir would almost certainly provide me with the ability to counteract my seasickness.

"You know, I could have used that advice a long time ago, *mother*," I said, teasing her.

"I'm sure that's true," she replied with a smile. "The thought only came to me after you mentioned your problem in the meeting. It woke me in the middle of the night, I'll have you know—from a sound sleep. My point is that even the brightest of us will not think of everything. Having a student to teach may cause me to consider things in a different light."

"Well, tomorrow is Freyday," Lucy remarked. "Let's go find this young lady—"

"Good. It will give us something to do while Caz and Mark are fussing about with boats," Lily said.

"Ships," I corrected.

They both gave me a look.

7

In the morning, I woke with my nose buried in Lucy's hair. It was my favorite smell in all the world. Lucy was tucked up in front of me, clasping my hand tightly to her bosom. She must have sensed I was awake, even though I did not think I moved at all. She twisted around and kissed the tip of my nose, then rolled away with a giggle.

I waited while Lucy used the lavatory, then went to perform my morning ablutions. While I was busy, Lucy picked another new set of clothes for me to wear. She was already dressed and went to see about breakfast. When I finished dressing, I sauntered to our dining room.

I should not have been surprised to see Fenwick already seated, looking cool and calm, but it did give me a start. He was dressed in the clothes he wore for his wedding. He was sipping a cup of something. I sniffed.

"Qava?" I asked.

"Yes."

"From my kitchen?"

"Yes."

"Lucy!" I hollered.

"I must say, Your Highness, you look rather smart this morning," he said, "for a jumped-up bastard."

"And to look at you, Lord Easton, in those handsome clothes, no one would ever be able to see the runaway farm boy," I replied.

"You forgot the 'orphaned' part, Your Highness," Fenwick remarked.

"I did, didn't I?" I said. "I shall have to do better next time."

The cook came out, bearing a carafe on a silver tray. Lucy followed her. The cook set the tray on the table.

"Caz," Lucy said, "please meet Jenny, our cook. Fenwick has already had the pleasure."

"Hello, Jenny," I said.

She blushed and curtsied, saying, "Your Highness."

Jenny was a bit plump but had an open, friendly expression. She scurried back into the kitchen. I looked at Lucy with my eyebrows raised.

"She is worried half to death about making a good impression," Lucy explained. "She feared she would lose her position when Albert died."

"I hope you explained that Caz is used to finding rat droppings, dead mice, and insects in his breakfast," Fenwick quipped.

Lucy swatted him on the back of the head as she passed. In the meantime, I poured myself a cup of qava. My solicitor, Graham Throckmorton, had introduced me to the stuff, and I acquired the taste for it quickly. It was not common in Aquileia, so I was used to going without.

I took a sip. It was perfect—not too strong, not too weak. I sighed with satisfaction.

"If she cooks as well as she brews qava, Jenny has no need to worry," I said.

Almost as if she heard me, Jenny came bustling back in, bearing a bowl of fruit and another bowl with muffins. After depositing them, she whisked away. She returned a moment later with plates of food. She stood waiting for Lucy and me to sit so she could serve us.

Lucy and I plopped down across from Fenwick. Jenny served Lucy first, then me, leaving Fenwick for last. An omelet with cheese, some bacon, and a bit of fried potato.

"To what do we owe the unexpected honor of your company, Fenwick?" I asked.

"Well, I wanted to see your new abode," he replied. "Now that I'm living in both your old ones. Besides, you enjoy my little impromptu visits."

"Maybe Lucy does," I said.

Lucy smacked me on the shoulder.

"Ow!"

"After we go through the bids," Fenwick said, "you and I are heading to the harbor. I will introduce you to the first three candidates for commanding our new ships."

In addition to the king, Mellone and Baldini were also waiting in the small room where we would open the bids. Once Fenwick and I arrived, the king slid the documents over to me, indicating I should open them. I slid my finger through and broke the seals one by one, then withdrew the enclosed papers. As I unfolded them, I scanned them quickly.

The letters all wasted quite a bit of ink and paper thanking us for the opportunity, blah-blah-blah. I wanted to see the numbers. Flipping through the pages, most of them finally reached the point of stating their bid on the third page.

"Go ahead and read them aloud, Prince Casimir," the king said. "Feel free to skip ahead to the part where it gets interesting."

The first was from one of the local shipwrights. He quoted a price of ten thousand five hundred ducats to build one ship, twenty thousand ducats to build two, and twenty-eight thousand for three. He stated he would be able to have two finished within a hundred days of being given a contract for the work. He then proposed alternatives to the material specified by Mellone and Baldini.

"Skip that," the king said.

I moved on. The next was from the shipwright in Aurora. His bid was twelve thousand ducats for one ship, with completion in one hundred and twenty days. He did not suggest alternatives to the specifications.

The next two were from the other shipwrights here in Aquileia. Both quoted eleven thousand ducats for one ship. One of them offered a price of ten thousand, five hundred for a second ship. Both promised the ships would be finished within a hundred and ten days.

The last was from Newcastle. His bid was eleven thousand five hundred, with completion in a hundred and twenty days. He offered no alternatives to the architects' design. Instead, he praised their work, stating they had listed the best materials for ships of this type. When I finished, I set the last one down.

"What do you think, Prince Casimir?" the king asked.

"The one who proposed alternatives to what Mr. Baldini and Mr. Mellone requested troubles me," I said. "His suggestion makes me wonder if he will be looking to make other substitutions without our knowledge. If I were to eliminate one of them based only on these documents, I would rule him out."

"Lord Easton?" the king asked.

"From what my contacts have related to me, I would agree with His Highness' suggestion," Fenwick stated. "Two years ago, Andexler was the finest shipwright in Aquileia. Unfortunately, Reg Andexler died, leaving the business to his son. The son is interested only in profits and spends little time at the shipyard."

"We agree," Baldini confirmed. "Andexler is not what it used to be."

"Of the remaining two shipwrights in Aquileia, would you commission both to build two ships, Prince Casimir?" the king asked.

"Here, my lack of knowledge thwarts me, Your Majesty," I replied. "I do not know enough about shipbuilding to know whether there would be any efficiencies for the shipwright in building two identical ships at the same time. Common sense tells me there should be some savings, but I lack confidence in my answer."

"Mr. Mellone? Mr. Baldini?" the king inquired.

The two looked at one another. Baldini shrugged. Mellone nodded.

"There is a small savings, Your Majesty," Mellone explained. "Most of the savings in creating a second ship comes from not needing to create the forms used to shape the wood a second time. Was this bid was from Charles Finley?"

"It was, and please explain how the savings are generated, Mr. Mellone?" I asked.

"Certainly, Your Highness," he said. "In crafting the hull of the ship, the wooden planks need to be curved. This is done by soaking the planks and then clamping them to wooden forms to make them bend to fit precisely with one another and in the specified shape of the hull. No one in the realm has built a caravel in recent years, so the forms will need to be created. The same forms can be used for a second ship. The five hundred ducat reduction for a second ship sounds about right."

"Do you think the other shipwright will accept five hundred ducats less to build a second ship?" the king asked.

Mellone and Baldini looked at one another, and then Mellone asked, "Is Hooper & Company the one who did not address building a second ship?"

"It is," I replied.

"Arlen Hooper is by nature a pessimist," Mellone said. "From what I know of him, he probably talked himself out of naming a figure for a second ship, convinced he would not be given the opportunity. He will accept the same terms as Finley."

"Prince Casimir, are there any changes to the financial terms that they request?" the king asked.

In the bid document we sent, we described a thirty percent payment to begin work, another thirty percent at the construction midpoint, and thirty percent when the ship launched. The remaining ten percent would be withheld until the ship completed sailing trials. According to Baldini and Mellone, these were fairly standard terms.

In reading through the bids, the shipwrights in Aurora and Newcastle stated they would be willing to accept the terms but humbly pleaded for more money at the beginning of the contract. Both suggested payments of forty-thirty-twenty-ten. I summarized this information for the king.

"And are you inclined to grant their humble plea?" the king asked me.

"I am," I said. "For these two shipwrights, a ship like ours will probably be larger than their usual projects and will be different in construction. I imagine their costs in the beginning will be higher, as I suspect they have no great stores of the lumber we have specified. That will mean their costs to begin the project will be higher. The two shipwrights here in Aquileia probably have enough to get started. Their initial costs will be less."

"Mr. Baldini? Mr. Mellone?" the king asked.

"His Highness is probably correct in his assumptions, Your Majesty," Baldini responded. "The shipwrights in Newcastle and Aurora build mostly fishing boats. Our ships will be larger, more sophisticated, and use different materials. They have stated that they will abide by the terms you set, but I suspect it will put a strain on their business."

The king looked to me, with his eyebrow cocked.

"Your Majesty, I would prefer if they gave their full attention to building our ships, and not worrying about paying their bills," I said.

"Well put," the king agreed. He turned around. "Thomas," he said, addressing his secretary sitting at a small table in the corner, "did you get all that?"

"Yes, Your Majesty."

"Good. Send the contracts out, with the payment terms amended for Aurora and Newcastle and adding a second ship for Hooper," the king said, then turned to Baldini and Mellone. "Thank you for your assistance, gentlemen. We expect you to be a familiar presence in the shipyards until all six are complete."

The two naval architects departed, as did the secretary.

"What do you have planned for Prince Casimir, Lord Easton?" the king asked.

"I have scheduled a lunch meeting with three men who I believe will make excellent captains once the ships are built," Fenwick replied. "Then I need to confirm the transportation arrangements to the southern continent for His Highness and me. Julienne set things in motion when she returned and should have an answer regarding when we can leave later today."

"We have already sent letters to the various governments alerting them to an upcoming visit," the king said.

"Your Majesty, I have two things I would like to discuss with you," I said.

"Should Lord Easton stay?"

"For the first, yes. The other does not concern him, but he can stay if he wishes." I replied with a shrug.

"What is the first issue?" Mark asked.

"In our previous travels," I explained, "one or the other of us has played the role of servant to the other and to Albert. That will be impossible on our upcoming diplomatic mission. Neither of us has a servant of this type."

"Ah. Yes," Mark responded. "You will each need a man to accompany you. I will pass this on to Mr. Williston. He will take care of it. A pity you can't take Lord Compote and his saucy maids with you."

I looked at the king incredulously.

"Albert and Fenwick have regaled me with the tales," he said with a grin. "And the other issue?"

"I would like to discuss what to do with my financial accounts."

"Lord Easton, you are free to go," the king said.

"If it is acceptable, I shall wait in your apartment, Your Highness?" Fenwick suggested.

I nodded. Fenwick stood and bowed, then left the room. The king leaned forward. He smiled broadly once the door shut.

"So, what to do about your not inconsiderable holdings, eh, Caz?" he said with a grin.

"A good portion of which is due to your generosity in the Spadewell matter," I said.

"Albert's generosity," the king responded. "He wanted you to have that money. All I did was not fight him too vigorously."

"Mark," I said, "I did not know that. He gave you the credit. It does not surprise me, though. Once Albert turned himself around, he did so in every way possible. He earned my friendship and my respect and showed himself to be the type of man any father would be proud to claim."

"Thank you, Caz," Mark said. "It gladdens me to hear that, while at the same time, it makes my heart heavy with loss. I have told you that you redeemed your father when he was lost. You saved Albert before that."

"I beg your pardon, Mark," I stated firmly but quietly. "I did not save Albert. Albert saved himself."

"Without you, he would not have had the opportunity," Mark replied.

"But it was Albert who recognized that it *was* an opportunity," I said. "And it was Albert who threw himself into his own redemption. It had to be extremely painful for him, but he addressed it squarely."

"I know that. But without you, Albert would not have seen the need to change his behavior," Mark said. "I give due credit to my son, but you were the catalyst—just as you were for your father."

"My father was more difficult," I commented.

"Of course he was," Mark replied. "He was mired in misery for decades. He thought it was inescapable. You helped him find his way back. There is something you should keep in mind, Caz. Not everything that happens to you is entirely about you. When I named you Lord Oritur, the hope that you would help your father was an important part of my decision. The other part was my wish to stabilize the border. Of course, you did that and so much more. But enough. Finances. Your accounts are with Pierre Luin and Bannister Brothers, are they not?"

"They are," I answered, surprised that Mark knew.

"What sort of return does Mr. Luin produce for you?" he asked smugly.

"Between twelve and fifteen percent per annum," I replied.

"Majors and Minors!" Mark hissed. "Are you sure of those figures?"

"Yes. I can get my ledgers—"

"No need. How long has Mr. Luin been achieving these results for you?"

"Since the beginning," I replied. "Seven years or so, now."

"Caz, the crown accounts—much larger than yours, I assure you—earn between six and eight percent per annum," he said. "And I was happy that we were doing so well. How is your money invested?"

"Pierre buys partial ownership of a number of small business concerns throughout the city," I said, "as well as smaller commercial buildings. Fenwick moved his accounts to Pierre as well once I told him what my results were."

"Clearly, we will need to meet Mr. Luin," Mark said while shaking his head. "Caz, Albert's estate—which is now yours—is just under eight hundred and fifty thousand ducats."

"Majors and Minors!" I gasped.

"Keep in mind that the money is for your children," Mark said. "And Lily and I hope you and Lucy have as many as you desire. Some you will set aside for your successor. You will divide the remainder between the others to provide them with a comfortable living. The crown will not pay their expenses. That is something you must instill in them all along. Now, if we are finished, I believe Fenwick is waiting for you. When you finish with him, you need to meet with Major Grunevald to discuss your upcoming trip."

"There you are," Fenwick said as I entered our apartment. "Your lovely wife just departed with the queen to cause a commotion in the market."

"Cause a commotion?"

"Two lovely women, surrounded by the Castle Shield—everyone will know within seconds it is Queen Liliana and Princess Lucy," Fenwick said. "I don't think you have quite grasped that your days of being able to wander freely are over," Fenwick said.

"I have been reminded of that several times recently," I admitted. "And it is irritating, I must admit. I hope the three men we will be meeting will not be distressed by the presence of a half-dozen of the Castle Shield."

"Oh, it will make them uncomfortable," Fenwick said, "but it should not scare them away."

"Good."

"Do you still have the drawing that the architects made for you?" Fenwick asked.

I nodded.

"Bring it," he said. "I want to show these gentlemen what sort of ships they'll be sailing. None of them have ever seen a caravel, I'd wager. They've heard of them, of course."

"While I have you here, I want to float an idea past you," I said.

"*Float?*" Fenwick asked. "Was that on purpose?"

"Of course, it was," I replied smoothly. "Just making sure you're awake. I was thinking the Persimmon Islands might be an ideal location for us to establish a forward base of operations."

"The little I have been told about them says they do not provide a good anchorage," Fenwick said.

"I'm not talking about a port in a storm," I said, "but in terms of a place for resupply. It would enable us to keep our ships closer to Rhetia for longer periods. We have months before the ships will be finished. In that time, we can construct a fortified position on one of the islands."

"It's not a bad idea," Fenwick admitted, "but let's *float* it by the gentlemen at lunch."

"I have one other troublesome question," I said. "What do we do about prisoners?"

"What did Sir Samuel Krum do with them?" Fenwick asked.

"I don't know and am almost afraid to learn," I said. "My suspicion is that he sold them into slavery on the southern continent."

"That would be my guess, too. It also depends on the type of ship we capture. A cargo vessel would be manned by Rhetians. Taking Rhetian pirates … Well, you saw those people."

"How many of the pirates were actually from Rhetia?" I asked.

"I'm pretty sure none were," Fenwick replied. "Their only connection to Rhetia is the port. None of the countries on the southern continent tolerate piracy. Only Rhetia allows it."

"The pirates are unbelievers, then," I said.

"I think the Rhetians think the pirates are almost sub-human, so their nonbelief doesn't matter. They also do not allow them out of a small area of the port," Fenwick explained.

"We could return the crews from the cargo ships to Rhetia," I said.

"Returning them to Rhetia exposes our ship to additional danger, so that's not a good choice," Fenwick mused.

"The ships will all return here to Aquileia for prize court. Perhaps we can ransom the true Rhetians. As far as the pirates, prison," I concluded.

8

Accompanied by half a dozen soldiers, Fenwick and I rode to a section of the waterfront. We tied our horses in front of a tavern. Two members of the Castle Shield entered first. As they did, the noise level in the tavern dropped precipitously. A pair of men in breastplates and helmets clearly made the tavern's patrons nervous.

Fenwick went in right behind them and found the three men with whom we were to meet. In appearance, they were not quite as disreputable as Fenwick's friend Bebo—the Scaramangan "opportunist"—but they all seemed to have a harder edge to them than the captains and sailing masters I'd encountered otherwise. Fenwick introduced me. He gave their names as Moser, Hardy, and Hughley. They did not stand up and bobbed their heads instead of bowing. Fenwick gestured for me to begin the discussion.

"The crown has just let contracts for six ships of this type," I said, pulling out the drawing. "We expect completion in four months."

"These are—caravels?" Hardy said uncertainly.

"Yes," I responded.

"Why caravels?" Moser asked.

"Supposed to be fast," Hardy said. "Good sailors, especially into the wind. Shallow draft—can get close to shore."

"Why have I never seen one?" Moser inquired.

"They don't have large enough holds to make them profitable for carrying cargo," Hardy explained, "and they are much more expensive than the Liburnians other people use."

"Other people?" I asked.

"Rhetian pirates and others like them," Fenwick responded.

"I see they are armed with ballistae and catapults," Hughley remarked. "From where it is positioned, the catapult would be useless under sail. The ballista looks handy, though."

"Crew size?" Moser asked.

"A dozen," Fenwick responded. "With room to carry another two or three dozen fighters."

"That's an awful lot of people on a ship that size," Hughley commented.

"His Highness suggested we consider establishing a supply outpost on one of the Persimmon Islands," Fenwick said. "That might make it more practical to sail with such a large number."

"Have you ever been to the Persimmon Islands?" Moser asked belligerently.

"Twice," I answered. "I understand that the shoals make it an unsafe anchorage, but that is not what I had in mind. My idea was to construct a fortified position where we could store supplies. It would enable you to spend more time hunting and eliminate the need to return to Aquileia every few weeks."

"Is there enough water?" Hardy inquired.

"On the island where Lord Easton and I spent the most time—a few weeks—there was a spring that seemed more than adequate," I said. "If that proves to be too cumbersome for refilling water casks, we can arrange for regular deliveries from Aquileia."

'It's worth considering," Hughley said to the other two.

They both shrugged and nodded slightly.

"You're just going to give us these ships?" Moser asked.

"Yes and no," I replied. "You will bring any ships you capture to Aquileia. A magistrate will judge whether they are legitimate prizes of war—"

"What do you mean, 'judge?' If we capture a Rhetian ship, it's ours," Moser protested.

"We are declaring a formal blockade of the Rhetian Empire," I said. "That means you can stop *any* ship sailing to or from there. You would capture the ship and take it to Aquileia. The judge would then make a ruling—usually for a foreign vessel the cargo is forfeit, but the ship may go free. For a ship flying the

Rhetian flag—or no flag for that matter—the ship is ours as well. After this, the cargo, or the ship and the cargo, are sold at public auction. The crown keeps a quarter of the proceeds. That pays for the ship."

"What about after the ship is paid for?" Hardy asked.

"We still keep a fourth," I replied. "We deserve to make some money out of this, too."

"And the three-quarters?" Hughley inquired.

"Yours to split as you see fit," Fenwick said. "Keep in mind, you'll have your crews, plus the men-at-arms we will supply to you. They won't work for free, I imagine."

"How many men-at-arms?" Moser asked.

"We thought two dozen per ship would be enough to deal with any adversaries," I said.

"Too many," Moser said. "A dozen and a half, tops. That will also allow us to stay out longer."

"What if you capture a Rhetian ship?" I asked. "You want to get it to Aquileia but don't want to leave the area. You detach some of your crew to sail it and some of the men-at-arms to keep the Rhetians under control. How short-handed do you want to be?"

"That's a good point, Moser," Hughley said. "How would you return our crews to us? Or would we need to travel to Aquileia to retrieve them?"

"If we establish a supply base in the Persimmon Islands, I would imagine we would send them there," I said.

"That's sounding more and more like a good idea," Hardy said. "Who pays for supplies?"

I looked to Fenwick for the answer.

"The crown," he said.

"That's more than fair," Hughley admitted. "Count me in."

"You'll supply your own crew," Fenwick said. "We will provide the men-at-arms. You'll get the ship in four months."

Moser and Hardy looked at one another. Hardy shrugged. Moser nodded to himself.

"We're on board," he said. "How do we do this? With a contract?"

"It's called a letter of marque and reprisal," I said. "It spells out the terms of what we discussed, but it also declares that you are an agent of the Aquileian government acting on our behalf. It gives you the authority to enforce the blockade."

"Who are your other three captains?" Hughley asked.

"That's actually an area where we could use your advice," Fenwick said. "I knew of the three of you. The other names I had are no longer interested. Can you think of three others like yourselves who would see this as the strong opportunity it is?"

"Well, that's another set of questions we had for you, Fenwick," Moser said.

"Would it help if I told you that a couple of the families of the captains who sailed under Sir Samuel two hundred years ago are still enjoying the benefits?" Fenwick asked. "It has been six or seven generations, and as you might expect, some of the families squandered their inheritances in that time. Two, however, are still quite wealthy—all due to the money they reaped under Sir Samuel's command."

"And who will be in command?" Moser asked.

"I will," I said.

"No offense, prince, but what do you know about sailing?" Hughley asked.

"Not much," I admitted, "but I won't be commanding a ship."

"You won't be sailing with us?" Hardy asked.

"I will if you invite me to join you," I said. "Right now, my sailing knowledge is limited. My fighting has always been on land. I would be an asset when you close with an enemy, even though I would not be much help in steering the ship to the right spot."

"Well, they do sing songs about your ability to fight," Hughley cracked.

"Lord Easton and I are about to embark on a long voyage to communicate the news of the blockade to the countries on the southern continent. I will be an eager student, and I promise by the time I return, I will know the difference between a halyard and a sheet, as well as much more. I can also promise I will never try to tell you how to sail your ships."

"We will hold you to that," Moser said.

"Returning to my question," Fenwick interjected. "Can you think of three others who would appreciate this opportunity?"

Hardy, Moser, and Hughley looked at one another. Hughley shrugged. Moser nodded.

"We can get you three more," Hardy said. "Let us talk between ourselves to figure out who deserves it the most."

"We need the names later today, if possible," Fenwick said.

"Five minutes is all we need," Hardy said.

"We will wait outside," Fenwick said.

"I thought you said we were having lunch," I jibed Fenwick as we left the tavern. "Where's the food?"

"You don't really want to eat here. Trust me," Fenwick replied. "There are food carts around the corner."

Fenwick knew of my weakness for such delicacies as meat and vegetables cooked on a stick, thinly sliced potatoes fried in oil, and dough fried in oil then drizzled with honey. These culinary delights were not served in any inn or tavern I knew. The only place to obtain them was from street vendors with food carts.

A minute later, Moser came out and said, "Barrett, Ward, and Turbot."

"Thank you," Fenwick said. "We will check into them. In the meantime, it will be four months before the ships are ready. His Highness and I will return before then. We will pull all the loose ends together at that time."

As Fenwick promised, there were food vendors nearby. We indulged ourselves, and I made sure the soldiers accompanying us were able to enjoy themselves just as much as I did. Fenwick then departed to see Julienne while the soldiers and I returned to the castle.

"His Majesty is looking for you," the seneschal told me when I walked across the bridge. "He is in his office."

I found my way, only needing to turn around twice. When I saw the guard down the corridor, standing outside the door, I breathed a sigh of relief. I knocked and was bade enter.

"Oh, good, you're here," the king said. "Have a seat."

"We met with three ship captains," I said. "They gave us the names of three others. Fenwick is checking up on them."

"Good. And you think these men are suitable?" Mark asked.

"I have no idea," I admitted. "We shall see, I suppose. Which reminds me—I think we should establish a presence on one of the Persimmon Islands. Though the Rhetians claim them, the only permanent residents are sheep. We should construct a fortification and use it as a supply point. It will enable the ships to stay on station without needing to return to Aquileia."

"What sort of fortification?"

"Wooden palisades—nothing more," I replied, "with a dozen soldiers. We will need a watchtower as well—located in a different spot. The fortification should be near the shore. We will place the tower on the high ground."

"Do you know on which of the islands you will place this supply base?" the king asked.

"Of the seven islands, I've only been on two. Both of them would be suitable. It might be that one of the other five is even better. One note of caution—there are not enough trees on the islands, so we will need to transport the necessary materials."

"You should meet with Colonel Yankton of the Shield," the king said. "He is the expert at constructing fortifications."

"We will need accurate topographical maps and nautical charts," I said. "Shoals surround the islands. An island that might be perfect land for our base might not be convenient for the ships."

"Contact the archivist for the maps and charts," Mark said. "Anything else?"

"I have one nagging question, sir," I said. "What will we do about prisoners?"

"Prisoners?"

"Yes. When we seize a vessel, there will be a crew and possibly passengers," I explained. "We will release those who can claim they are citizens of a country other than the Rhetian Empire. The others will be citizens of the empire or the mongrels that crew the pirate vessels they allow to operate from their ports. All of them will be delivered here to Aquileia when a captured ship is brought in for prize court. I would imagine we would ransom the Rhetian citizens and put the others in prison—is that correct, or would you prefer that we deal with them in some other manner?"

"That sounds reasonable," the king replied. "Except what do we do with the Rhetians if the empire does not pay the ransom?"

"That's why I am asking."

"What did Sir Samuel do?"

"Fenwick and I suspect he sold all of his captives into slavery," I said. "I have no love for the Rhetians, but …"

"Yes. Different times," the king mused. "Let's both think on this issue. We have time. There is one thing I need you to consider."

"Yes?"

"You will represent Aquileia on this trip," Mark said. "You need to set aside whatever doubts and uncertainty you have about your new position. On this mission, you will communicate our will—the will of the nation. We are at war with the Rhetian Empire, as we have been since they broke the treaty following Sir Samuel's death and as we were for hundreds of years before that. You are not traveling to negotiate or bargain with these governments. Instead, you are informing them of our planned action as a courtesy. If they take offense, ignore their protests. They have a choice of continuing to conduct trade with the Rhetians—in which case we will do our best to intercept their ships—or honor our blockade."

"Could this lead to war?" I asked.

"None of the countries on the southern continent are prepared for any sort of war with us," Mark said. "Their armies are small and poorly led. I believe that is by design since the rulers don't wish to fear a competent commander usurping their authority. Fenwick can tell you more. He is better acquainted with their politics than anyone."

There was a discreet knock on the door. After Mark called for the person to enter, the seneschal peered in. Mark nodded.

"Major Grunevald is waiting for you in your study," he said.

With that, our meeting was finished. I picked my way through the confusing corridors to find the entrance to Lucy's and my new residence. When I arrived, I found Fenwick and Major Grunevald in my study.

"Lord Easton and I have already covered most of what we needed to discuss," the major said. "He will confirm our departure, which is currently scheduled for the morning tide the day after tomorrow. It is late enough in the morning that we can load after daybreak."

"How many of the Castle Shield are accompanying us?" I asked.

"A full squadron," the major replied. "One hundred and twenty men and horses, plus your mounts. We will fill three carracks."

"Do we really need that many men?" I asked.

Both the major and Fenwick frowned at me.

"Yes," Fenwick replied. "Show of force, Your Highness."

"Understood," I said. "I just worry about the logistics."

"Not your problem, Your Highness," Grunevald stated. "I have already made all the arrangements."

That was something new for me. In all honesty, I had not considered the planning necessary for a trip like this. If it fell to me to organize, I would have been woefully behind schedule. I realized that the crown prince had more support than I considered. This was a good thing.

Grunevald departed. Fenwick and I moved to the parlor. He sprawled on the sofa.

"I was thinking I could bring Theo along on our trip," he cracked.

"If we are going to cause a diplomatic incident, I'd much prefer to have Lord Compote and all three of his saucy maids along," I replied.

"Three?"

"Lucy was one of the originals," I said.

"That's right," Fenwick said. "I forgot. Sadly, I don't think any of them can get away for as long as we will be gone."

"And we will be away for how long?" I asked.

"Well, we need to visit Scaramouche, Garo, Mooresa, Vanda, Hier, and Nagah," Fenwick replied. "At least two months, but it could be as many as three."

9

Lucy and Queen Liliana returned less than an hour after Fenwick departed. I heard them before I saw them. It sounded like they were conducting a tour of the castle.

I rose from where I was sitting in the study and went into the main hall of our apartment. With Lucy and the queen was a young woman. She was of moderate height, three or four inches shorter than Lucy. Her back was to me, so I could not guess her age at first. I reckoned she was the person the queen spotted in the market the week before.

"Caz, I'd like you to meet my new lady-in-waiting, Katie," Lucy said when she spied me over the stranger's shoulder. "Katie, Prince Casimir."

The woman turned to face me, and I saw she was young—in her middle teens, I guessed. With her head bowed, she executed a curtsy. When she lifted her face, I could see she was attractive. I would call her cute rather than pretty, but as she matured and her features lost the softness of youth, she promised to develop into a beautiful woman.

"I'm pleased to meet you, Katie," I said, bowing slightly.

Katie's mouth opened as though she would respond. She then closed it and blushed, looking down at her feet. I couldn't help but chuckle.

"Katie, if you are to be Lucy's lady-in-waiting, we will see a great deal of one another," I said. "I hope I'm not *that* frightening."

"It's just … You're the prince," she mumbled. "They sing songs about you. I'm just nobody special."

"Katie, I'm afraid I must disagree. The fact that the princess and the queen chose to add you to our household means you are someone special," I said. "I urge you to take advantage of the opportunity they have given you."

"Oh, I will, Your Highness," Katie said. "It's just a bit overwhelming. I had no idea what was in store for me when I woke up this morning."

"That happens to us a lot," I joked. "It was very nice to meet you, Katie. I'm sure I'm interrupting whatever my wife and Her Majesty were planning to do with you right now, so I'll take my leave and let them continue."

I retreated to the study and let them resume integrating Katie into whatever her duties would be. Before I sat down, I remembered I needed to find the archivist to find maps and charts of the Persimmon Islands. I went to the entrance of our apartment and tugged on the bell pull. A page appeared a few minutes later, and I had him take me to the archives.

It took some time for him to find the materials I sought. What he retrieved from the shelves was brittle with age. He unrolled them carefully, fearful of ripping them.

"Please, Your Highness," he begged, "let me have them copied before you take them."

"Allow me to examine them before you take them away," I asked.

While the archivist waited, I studied the maps and the charts. Manaway Island, where we rescued Julienne from Rhetian pirates, would be an acceptable location. To the eastern side, the water was deeper than most of the other islands, except for one.

As near as I could determine, the other island with a less shallow approach was the one where Fenwick and I were marooned. The map showed that it was called Hardscrabble Island. I would leave the choice of which island to Colonel Yankton.

This, of course, reminded me that I needed to meet him and discuss the project. I thanked the archivist and left, trying to find my way to the courtyard that served as the entrance to the castle. When I found it, after only one false start down a blind corridor, I was proud of myself.

After crossing the bridge, I went to the gatehouse and asked where I could find the colonel. The guard stepped aside and whistled loudly across the yard. One of the other soldiers came trotting over.

"Take His Highness to see Colonel Yankton," the guard instructed.

I had met the colonel before, during the battles with the Rhetians. He had been in command of constructing our fortifications. When I met him, he called himself a "military engineer." I did not understand until later when I saw the earthworks beginning to take shape.

We met briefly in his small office. I shared my idea of establishing a fortified supply base on one of the Persimmon Islands. He understood immediately.

"The archivist is preparing fresh copies of the maps," I said. "The existing ones are quite old—faded and brittle. When he finishes them, Manaway and Hardscrabble Islands are the two most attractive locations. I will be away for at least the next two months—possibly three—and hope you can investigate the two locations further and begin work on building a stronghold of some type."

"This sounds like an interesting challenge, Your Highness," he said. "I look forward to it."

When I returned to our apartment, Lucy was not there. I set off in search of the library. Since Fenwick and I were traveling to the southern continent, I wanted to look at an atlas to see where we would go.

Once again, I got horribly lost. I found myself in the corridor where the king's office was. I asked the guard to point me in the proper direction.

In the library, an atlas was already spread open on a reading table. It took me no time to find the maps I sought. I started with Scaramouche, the easternmost destination. Nagah, to the west and south, would be our last stop. It would require us to pass through the Rhetian Straits twice—once going, then returning.

The Rhetian Straits separate the Surrounded Sea from the Occasum Ocean. Much further west lay three landmasses. I don't know whether they were considered large islands or small continents. The atlas did not include them. Bold adventurers had traveled to them and from them. They were too far away for trade to be economically feasible. It took at least a month to sail to the nearest of the three, and that was with favorable winds. It took longer to return.

The Rhetian Straits would be fertile grounds for our privateers, I reckoned. Rhetian freebooters hung around that area, hoping to prey on commercial traffic to and from Nagah and Hier. Most ships that sailed that route took precautions to be well-defended before leaving port, but there were some that took chances.

I'd visited Scaramouche and Mooresa. Garo, Vanda, Hier, and Nagah were unknown territory. Fenwick was familiar with all of them and fluent in their tongues.

Not long after I returned to our residence, there was a knock at our door. It took me a minute to realize what the sound was. I jumped up, but Wilma reached the door well before I did. Mr. Williston was standing there with another man only a couple of years younger than he. His apple-cheeked face looked familiar. I realized he accompanied Prince Albert on our trip to Scaramouche.

Mr. Williston was the deputy master of the Royal Household. When Lucy and I moved to Easton Manor and were trying to set things to rights, the queen lent us his assistance. It would have taken us far longer to get things organized without his help. We learned a tremendous amount from him.

"Your Highness," Williston said with a slight bow, "may I present James Gilbert. It is my understanding that you will need a servant to accompany you on your upcoming diplomatic mission. Mr. Gilbert is eminently qualified to assist you."

"Mr. Williston, Mr. Gilbert," I said, gesturing for them to enter. "I've never had a servant before. In the past, I've pretended to be one, but I can't say I knew what I was doing."

"Well, if anyone paid any attention to you at all, you were not performing correctly," Gilbert said. "My goal on this journey will be to anticipate your needs so well that you never notice me. Now, if I may, Your Highness, I would like to examine your wardrobe. We shall be traveling for two months in a sultry climate. We need to make sure we bring enough of the proper clothing to meet your needs."

I led the two men to the armoires that contained my clothing—new and old. Gilbert leaned in and started to flip through the lighter-weight clothes. When he opened the drawer on the bottom where my shirts, underclothes, and stockings were, he tsk-ed.

"Your Highness, you will need three times the number of what I see here,' Gilbert said. "The heat of the climate and the lack of laundry facilities, you see. His Majesty's tailor has your measurements?"

"Yes."

"Very well," Gilbert said. "It's short notice, but you are the crown prince. They will be ready in time. Where are your chests? You will need two for a journey of this length."

I had two trunks, but they were full of other things—my "Reg Ashe" clothes, for instance. Now that I considered it, I would never need those things again. Even worse, the battered appearance of the cheap chests I owned was in no way suitable for my new station. Thankfully, Mr. Williston decerned from my uncomfortable expression what the problem was.

"His Highness does not have anything suitable, Mr. Gilbert," he said. "Another task for you."

"Mr. Williston," I said. "It occurs to me that Lord Easton, my traveling companion on this mission, would benefit from the same sort of assistance and oversight. We will be representing Aquileia in an official capacity, and it would not do for us to be seen as—"

"Quite right, Your Highness," he responded. "I will see to it presently."

"You're overdressed, Your High-and-Mighty-ness," Fenwick said the next morning when I entered the dining room. "We are joining Mr. Baldini and Mr. Mellone at the harbor to crawl around a ship and further your nautical education. I would suggest clothing you won't mind getting dirty."

"How dirty?" Lucy asked, entering right behind me.

"Filthy," Fenwick answered, "to the point of ruination."

"I know just the things," she said, turning on her heel and leaving the room.

"I don't know whether to thank you or curse you for setting Mr. Williston and Mr. Gilbert on me," Fenwick said. "There is no question that my wardrobe needs to be enhanced, given my recent elevation in status, but to do it on such short notice will be expensive."

"Mark stressed to me that the two of us will be the embodiment of Aquileia to these foreigners," I said. "I suppose I'm in a better state of preparedness since Mark just filled a couple of armoires with new clothing more suitable for my station, but even so, Mr. Gilbert is having a number of items made where he perceived a lack."

"I've laid some old clothes out for you," Lucy announced as she returned.

Hearing this, I left and returned to our bedroom. Lucy had found some of my "Reg Ashe" clothing. These were garments I bought to convey the image of a lower-class swindler trying to pass himself off as someone more successful. I could not imagine that I would ever need them again, so if they were ruined today, I would never miss them.

"Oi, Reg!" Fenwick exclaimed with a laugh when I returned to the dining room, recognizing the outfit.

"I remember when you asked Hamed to make these," Lucy said. "They were just enough out of fashion to be only slightly awkward then. Now? They're garish. I'm consigning the rest of them to the rag bin."

"Be my guest," I said, kissing the top of her head. "What have I missed?"

"I was just telling Fenwick about Katie," she said. "She was feeling a bit overwhelmed, as you can imagine—being plucked from the market by the queen and the new princess. She's bright, though. Lily and I didn't discuss the real reason we chose her, but I suspect she has figured it out. When she returns on Maniday to move in, I expect Lily and I will have a much more substantive discussion with her."

"She will live here?" I asked.

"Of course," Lucy replied with a laugh. "She will be my lady-in-waiting. She has to live here."

"Listen to you," I said. "A lady-in-waiting—what exactly does the job require?"

"Well, she won't be a servant," Lucy said. "Any more than I was Lily's servant when we went to Eatonford and then to Dunland. I was her lady-in-waiting on those adventures."

"You were, weren't you?" I recalled.

"At first, Katie will be a student, just like the people in the March were. Lily will help, too. Once her abilities blossom, Lily and I hope to train her, then send her throughout the kingdom."

"How did her father react?" Fenwick inquired.

"I think he's still stunned," Lucy laughed. "Katie is just old enough that he was probably beginning to think of marrying her off. If she comes to the castle, he won't need to worry about that."

"Plus, her prospects of finding an advantageous match will be much greater," Fenwick added.

"Let's hope that is still years away," Lucy said. "Lily and I hope to find others like her whom we can also enlist. One woman will not be enough to scour the entire realm."

Jenny came bustling in, bringing me some qava. As the day before, she prepared it perfectly. A moment later, she brought in breakfast for the three of us.

"What did you accomplish with the rest of yesterday?" Fenwick asked

"I found maps and charts for the Persimmon Islands," I said. "From what I could see, it turns out that the two islands we have visited will be the best for establishing a fortified supply point. The archivist needs to make new copies of the charts and provide them to Colonel Yankton. By the time we return from our journey, I hope construction is well underway. I also reviewed the atlas to see where we will be traveling. Then, Mr. Williston and Mr. Gilbert arrived."

"When they finished with him," Fenwick said to Lucy, "they paid me a visit. 'Your wardrobe is entirely unsuitable for a peer of the realm, Lord Easton. It simply will not do. As an exemplar of Aquileian nobility, you must present a better image.' Majors and Minors! The man intends to have all new clothing made for me before we depart. It's going to cost a fortune!"

Lucy gasped, then giggled. "When were you planning to leave?"

"Tomorrow," Fenwick said glumly.

"That *will* be expensive," Lucy laughed.

"Fenwick, what sort of trouble will we encounter in the countries we will be visiting?" I asked, changing the subject before he took the opportunity to complain some more.

"I don't anticipate any," he replied. "Other than unhappiness at our announcement of a blockade. Hier and Nagah are the only countries that trade enough with the Rhetians to cause any real hardship, but even they do more business with Aquileia. No one, however, especially the ruler of a country, enjoys being told by a foreigner what he can or cannot do. They will still observe the diplomatic niceties with us, but they may act a bit aggrieved."

"To be expected, I suppose," Lucy commented.

"The real commotion will come after we have seized one of their ships," Fenwick said. "He probably neglected to tell you this, but I suspect His Majesty will expect you to deal with their unhappy ambassadors."

"What if I am not here?" I asked. "It seems likely that I will be spending at least some of my time at sea or in the Persimmon Islands."

"Then they will await your return," Fenwick said loftily.

"Wonderful," I grumbled sarcastically. "Meanwhile, they will grow more angry by the day."

"Rank has its privileges," Fenwick quipped dryly.

Fenwick and I, accompanied by a half-dozen men of the Castle Shield, rode to the harbor. We found Mellone and Baldini waiting for us at the Traval wharf. They took us to a large ship tied up near the end of the quay.

"This is one of the three carracks on which we will be sailing tomorrow," Fenwick said.

"It's similar to the other ships we've taken before," I noted.

"Carracks are the standard cargo ship used in the Surrounded Sea," Baldini stated. "They have much greater capacity than a caravel. Carracks are sturdy and seaworthy—meaning that they can handle bad weather and rough seas. They are slow, though. A caravel could literally run circles around this ship in the open ocean."

"What are they doing down there?" I asked, pointing into the bowels of the ship.

"Reconfiguring the hold to accommodate your horses," Mellone said. "Two ships will need to carry forty horses. One will have forty-two."

Baldini and Mellone made me cover every inch of the ship. I went from the bilge to the crow's nest high up the mainmast. They made me crawl into the cable tiers and other tiny storage spaces forward, and the small nook where the rudder was attached to the ropes that controlled it. Once again, they reviewed the difference between the different lines ("Not ropes! Lines!" Mellone growled at me). I felt I now could tell the difference between stays, sheets, and halyards.

By the time we finished, I was beyond filthy. Splotches and smears of tar were all over my clothes. The skin of my hands seemed to have absorbed dirt, tar, and grime from every surface I touched. I hoped Lucy would know how to get rid of it.

When I returned to the castle, Lucy would not allow me into our residence until I undressed. I tried to protest, saying that the prince should not be required to strip naked in the hallway. Standing with her hands on her hips, she paid no attention to my complaint. Wilma stood behind her and giggled at my nakedness.

Before allowing me in, Lucy looked at my hands. With a sour expression, she pointed me to the lavatory. She headed in a different direction, telling me, "Don't you dare touch anything!"

She returned quite a few minutes later with soap, olive oil, a pan full of hot water, and a stiff brush. Lucy then stood and supervised me as I scrubbed and scrubbed, trying to clean my hands. Finally, she pronounced herself satisfied and allowed me to get dressed again.

10

We dined that evening with the king and queen. Fenwick and Julienne joined us as well. The conversation centered on the journey Fenwick and I would embark upon the next day.

While Fenwick and I both suspected our meetings with the rulers of the countries on the southern continent would be slightly prickly, neither of us was overly concerned. Mark agreed with us. Lily had one concern.

"Julienne, will this have any bearing on your trade with these countries?" she asked.

"If it does, it should be positive for the kingdom, if not for Traval & Company," Julienne replied. "The items the Rhetian Empire imports also have markets here. It may decrease prices for those goods, which will affect our profitability. Any negative impact, however, must be balanced by what our losses might be if the Rhetian-sponsored pirates were left unchecked. I would be more concerned that you will be able to conduct an effective blockade with only six ships. How many did Sir Samuel have under his command when we last mounted an effort of this type?"

"More than double that number," the king said, "eventually. He started with only three, then kept adding one or two ships every year until he had a fleet of sixteen. We haven't discussed the long-term plan, but we intend to use the money we generate from our initial efforts to pay for additional construction as we progress—just as Sir Samuel did."

"On a more aggressive schedule than Sir Samuel, it appears," I commented.

"Precisely," Mark agreed. "If the results of our first few months are encouraging, we will commission another half-dozen ships. We will evaluate their effectiveness before deciding how many more are needed."

When dinner ended, Lucy and I returned to our residence. The sun had just set and we could see the city in the twilight from our windows. I stood behind her and enfolded her in my arms. She put her hands over mine and leaned into me with a sigh.

"I'm not looking forward to being away from you for so long," I murmured. "It will be the longest we've been apart since we met."

"We will both be busy," she said. "Let's hope the time flies."

Our journey to Alygien, the main port in the country of Scaramouche, was uneventful. The weather was clear, and the winds were favorable. As the queen suggested, I used my connection with Eir to eliminate my seasickness. What a difference it made!

I took advantage of the trip to learn more about ship handling and navigation using an astrolabe. The sailing master enjoyed having an eager pupil and was happy to answer all my questions. He pointed out that the carrack was square-rigged, while our caravels would fly triangular lateen sails, which the carrack did not use. When Mellone and Baldini had said that a caravel could sail closer to the wind, it was very much an abstract concept to me. Aboard a ship, with practical demonstrations of what it meant to sail "into the wind" and a knowledgeable expert to explain, I grasped the idea firmly.

Scaramouche was as hot as ever, and the sun was relentless. Fenwick arranged to buy straw hats for all of us for the three-day ride to Sablanca, the capital. I sensed my horse, Andy, was happy to be back on land.

On the third day after landing, we approached Sablanca. Even from a distance, we could see the palace of the grand vizier. It was dazzlingly white in the bright midsummer sun, built on the highest ground in the city.

Just before reaching the gate to the structure, I asked Major Grunevald to have the men put on their helmets. The gates swung open just as we reached them, and we swept into the courtyard. Waiting for us on the steps to the entrance, in the shade, was the grand vizier himself.

Fenwick and I left the formation and rode to where he was standing. When we drew near, we stopped and dismounted. As Fenwick had coached me, I stepped forward and gave the slightest of bows—no more than a couple of inches from vertical. The grand vizier looked curiously. He began to speak.

"So this is the new prince," he remarked. "And you—the last time you visited, you were a servant. Now you are dressed like someone of rank?"

"This man is indeed now the prince, Your Excellency," Fenwick explained. "The man you met died in an unfortunate accident. Our king chose this man, Casimir, to be his successor. Prince Casimir is a mighty warrior, a man of courage and character. At the same time, our king ennobled me. On our last visit, it is true that I played the part of a humble servant. Now, I am Lord Easton."

"Aha!" the grand vizier exclaimed, then laughed. "Was that another deception? Like the lusty idiot who was ten times clever and just pretending to be a fool?"

"My ennobling is fairly recent, Your Excellency, but even then, I was not a mere servant," Fenwick explained.

"Marvelous!" the grand vizier said, clapping his hands.

He turned to a group of servants waiting and nodded his head at us. The servants sprang into action. They quickly unloaded our luggage from the wagon. Others took our horses.

Someone in what passed for a military uniform in Scaramouche came to speak with Major Grunevald. Grunevald couldn't understand, so Fenwick slipped over to translate. After a minute, Grunevald ordered his men to set up camp where the Scaramangan officer indicated.

When Fenwick finished with them, he returned and spoke briefly with the grand vizier. Then, two other servants—quite young—appeared. Fenwick gestured for me to follow the one. He took me to where I would spend the night.

The quarters were sumptuous. The carpets were the thickest I ever felt under my feet. The bed was enormous, covered in pillows. An entire wall was one long window, open to allow the late afternoon breeze to blow in. Despite the heat, the room was cool and comfortable.

Almost as soon as I entered, servants came in, filling a bath for me. After a week on the ship, then three days of riding in the heat, a bath was most welcome. I eased myself into the water with a sigh.

While I was cleaning up, Mr. Gilbert came and laid out clothes for me to wear to dinner. My dirty things vanished. I presumed he took them to wash them. This service and attention to my personal needs was something I was not accustomed to. I decided I could quickly become spoiled if I was not careful.

Fenwick came to the door shortly after I dressed. He, too, had enjoyed a bath and was clad in some of his new finery. Together, we went to where the grand vizier would host us for dinner.

In addition to the grand vizier, there were four other men present. Fenwick explained to me later that they were important people in Scaramouche. Fenwick handled the introductions. All I was required to do was nod at the appropriate time.

The dinner was superb. I enjoyed Scaramangan cuisine from the time I first tasted it. The dishes were typically much spicier than those of Aquileia. Another significant difference was eating with the right hand instead of using a fork.

"I find myself missing the vulgar fool who came on your last visit," the grand vizier said. "His antics were quite amusing, and his maid was pretty. When I learned later that he was merely playacting, I found it even more humorous. We Scaramangans enjoy these sorts of deceptions."

"His real name is Lord Rawlinsford," I explained. "He is a dear friend and a member of an important family in Aquileia. The maid is actually his wife. In addition, he introduced me to my wife, who is his cousin. I am relieved you perceived humor in our last visit. I was worried you would be angry."

"Ha!" he laughed and smiled broadly. "You came to trade electrum for tanzyan. We traded. Both sides received fair exchange. It's true some of my advisors were hoping to deceive you. They were embarrassed when their trick failed, and feared to tell me. I, on the other hand, was not unhappy. In fact, it gave me the best laugh I had enjoyed in years when I realized that it was your Lord Compote who foiled their plan. Given a choice, I would prefer my allies to be intelligent and perceptive."

"It pleases me to hear you use the word 'allies,' Your Excellency," I said. "Did you receive our letter regarding our intention to impose a blockade on the Rhetian Empire?"

"We did."

"And you understand and accept our need to do so?"

"We understand," he said. "As far as accepting, we prefer to do business with whomever we choose and do not enjoy being told we should not trade with someone. That said, we are not in a position to contest or enforce your wishes. We will inform our trading houses of your declaration. The trade we conduct with the Rhetians is minimal, but a couple of merchants may try to slip past you. If they do not succeed, they will know better than to seek relief from our government."

"Thank you, Your Excellency, for your wisdom and understanding," I said.

With that, the matter was closed. This, the visit that I felt held the most potential for being difficult, ended up being amiable. Our conversation turned to other things.

"Prince Casimir, are you aware they sing songs about you?" the grand vizier asked.

"I am," admitted with a blush.

"Are the things they sing about true? Are you a warrior-mage?" he inquired.

"Some have called me that, yes, Your Excellency," I admitted.

"Marvelous! So the tan-zyan was for you, then," he said. "Don't be nervous. We will not try to take it back. The two stones you obtained in the trade were better than some but not the finest quality tan-zyan we possess. We did not show you those. Just as I am certain your king retained the best examples of electrum that he owns."

"Yes, Your Excellency, one of the stones was for me," I admitted and held up my ring. I did not address the other part of his statement.

"Who was the other stone for?" the grand vizier asked. "We have not seen a warrior-mage among our people for generations. Could it be that Aquileia has two such men?"

"We do, Your Excellency," Fenwick said, holding up his own ring.

"Fantastic!" he exclaimed, clapping his hands. "Simply splendid!"

The grand vizier wanted to know more about the recent battles against the Rhetians. He was surprisingly well-informed about what happened, but only in general terms. I let Fenwick do most of the talking.

The four other men were silent the entire time. The grand vizier never introduced them, which I thought was odd. Still, they listened carefully as Fenwick told about the war.

The grand vizier then wanted to know more about Prince Albert's death. He was aware of how it happened but did not understand why we went across the mountains to meet the horse nomads. I took it upon myself to explain the history behind it. The grand vizier was fascinated.

"You know those nomads are probably distant kin to the rulers of Vanda at the end of the old empire," he said.

"How can that be?" I asked. "They are so far away."

"As I said, it goes back to the days of the old empire," the grand vizier explained. "In particular, the twilight of the empire. Do you know much about the old empire?"

"On my first visit to your country, Lord Easton took me to see ruins near Alygien," I said. "They were so interesting that when I returned to Aquileia, I read some books to learn more. I am interested in hearing how the rulers of Vanda might be related to the horse nomads. Please, continue."

"As you know, the old empire lasted for hundreds and hundreds of years. Their only rival for power was the Petomins to the east. At the height of its power, the old empire could have crushed the Petomins, but I think they decided it was not an economically sound idea to do so. It would cost more to keep the area pacified than they would glean in tax and tribute. Still, every other generation, the empire and the Petomins would clash.

"As time went on, the empire grew weaker, with different leaders of the army rebelling from time to time, attempting to gain the throne for themselves. The Petomins attacked, trying to take advantage of one of these civil wars. The factions in the empire put aside their differences to crush the Petomins. When that war ended, plague hit the cities of the empire and the Petomins, weakening both.

"Sensing an opportunity for plunder, a large group of horse nomads rode out of the north and swept through the Petomins and deep into the empire, finally stopping at what is now Vanda. The empire did not have the strength to dislodge the nomads, and the nomads did not have the strength to fight their way back to their homeland. An uneasy truce followed. Finally, a generation later, the emperor recognized the right of the nomads to occupy the land, provided they supplied him with annual levies of soldiers—a ridiculously small number, I might add.

"In effect, the emperor allowed them to establish their own separate kingdom within the empire's borders. They owed the emperor no tax or tribute other than the small number of men due every year. This weakened the empire still further. In less than a hundred years, the empire ceased to exist."

"And now, a thousand years later, the rulers of Vanda still trace themselves back to the horse nomads?" I asked.

"That is what they claim, though I believe the current ruling family has no more than a few drops of horse nomad blood in their veins if they have any at all," the grand vizier stated. "Vanda is no different from the rest of the countries on the north coast of the Surrounded Sea. Our ruling dynasties tend to be rather short-lived. I am the seventh generation of my family to rule Scaramouche, making us one of the more successful since the old empire faded away. Most don't survive past the third generation."

"Aquileia went through a similar period," Fenwick stated, "though our current ruling family has been in power for eleven generations, I believe."

"And with the addition of new blood, and of a warrior-mage at that, perhaps they will continue to hold power for another eleven or more," the grand vizier said.

"Do you worry about—?" I started to ask.

"These men," the grand vizier said, waving at the other four at the low table, "are the eldest sons of the most powerful families in Scaramouche. Two of them are replacements for older brothers who perished."

I realized then that these men were not officials of the court but hostages. Their purpose was to ensure the loyalty of their families. The casual remark by the grand vizier that two older brothers needed to be replaced indicated to me that they were killed due to the misbehavior of their families. While I was thinking about that, I missed a question the grand vizier directed to me.

"Excuse me," I said. "My mind went astray. Would you please ask me again?"

"From your reaction, I am guessing that your king does not follow the same practice?"

"We do not," Fenwick said. "We approach the problem in a different way. Aquileia employs a royal assassin. Our king inherited the man who worked for his father but did not replace him when he retired. That lasted for nearly twenty years and caused some difficulties. The king eventually brought someone on to perform those duties. Instead of keeping eldest sons as hostages, disloyal nobles in Aquileia who present a threat tend to have accidents."

"Fatal accidents," the grand vizier intimated.

Fenwick shrugged.

"Hm. That is an interesting concept," the grand vizier mused. "I will ponder it. Already I imagine it would be more effective and less expensive than our current practice. Do both of you know who this assassin is?"

"We do," Fenwick stated.

I was glad Fenwick answered because I might have laughed.

"The king has asked the current holder of the job to find his replacement," Fenwick continued. "The present employee has earned the king's trust and is being given other responsibilities."

"Interesting," the grand vizier commented. "So the assassin has been entirely loyal to the king? What safeguards did the king have in place to ensure that loyalty? That would be one of my biggest concerns."

"The assassin came from a very humble background. He had no relationships with any of the noble families. To seize power for himself, he would have needed to cultivate those people, and that would have been easily discovered."

"And then?"

"There is another man in the kingdom, equal or superior to the assassin in skill," Fenwick said. "If the assassin strayed …"

"What if that man decided to cause trouble?" the grand vizier asked.

"Then the assassin would have been ordered to kill him," Fenwick said with a wince and a shrug.

"So, I really need to find two assassins," the grand vizier said. "The one to keep the other honest."

11

We left Sablanca the next morning and returned to Alygien. When we arrived, we loaded ourselves back on the ships for the short sail to Garo. This country was immediately to the west of Scaramouche. Favorable winds delivered us to their main port and capital, Cyrene, in less than three days.

Having spotted our ships while still well off the coast, a royal delegation was waiting for us when we pulled up to the pier. Our visit would be brief—just overnight—so we did not disembark the horses. They took Fenwick and me in an open carriage up to the palace while the men of the Castle Shield marched alongside us.

Our meeting was civil enough, but the emir of Garo did not possess the sense of humor that the grand vizier displayed. Nor did he seem as friendly. He acknowledged receiving our official notice of the blockade, but I could tell he was slightly resentful. I tried to probe to see how deeply he was upset, but he revealed very little.

The emir had beady eyes set close together. From my first look, I was predisposed not to like the man. In the conversations that followed over dinner later, I became convinced we could not trust him either. Something else felt subtly wrong.

I accessed my link to Bellona and withdrew a tiny tendril of her power. With it, I tried to expand my senses beyond the room where we were, searching for the source of my disquiet. Whatever was bothering me was not in the near vicinity, but that did not reassure me.

"Fenwick," I whispered halfway through the meal, "we should return to the ships. I realize it is probably a breach of protocol or etiquette, but I do not feel safe staying under this roof tonight."

"It will be perceived as a snub, Your Highness, but I agree with you. Something is not quite right," Fenwick said. "I will make our excuses at the appropriate time."

When dinner was coming to an end, Fenwick said, "A thousand apologies, Your Excellency, but we must catch the tide in a short time. Please pardon us for not taking better advantage of your marvelous welcome, but we have fallen behind schedule on our journey and must depart."

Though the emir tried to hide it, I could tell he was unhappy at this news. My sense is that his displeasure centered on our returning to the ships this evening rather than our failing to accept his hospitality. That, of course, made me more eager to get away.

We left in the same carriage, surrounded by the Castle Shield on foot. We heard the commotion before we saw it. Arriving at the pier, there was a crowd of hundreds gathered by our ships, with about half waving torches and shouting. When they caught sight of us, the crowd turned our way.

"They are unhappy about our proposed blockade of Rhetia," Fenwick said, translating their shouts. "They are yelling, 'Free seas for free people,' and 'We are not Aquileian slaves,' along with more general curses."

It seemed to me as though a good portion of the crowd was composed of people who were ordered to be there. Their performance in the chants was lacking any sort of passion. Even of those who did join in, several in the crowd kept flicking their eyes back to glance at some men toward the rear. Still, something about being a part of a mob allows people to suspend their customary restraint. I feared that if the furor continued to build, some of those torches would begin flying toward our ships.

"Go talk to some of them," I told Fenwick, pointing to a couple of the ones who seemed to be in charge. "The emir is behind this. He's trying to make a point, but if these people don't disperse soon, something bad will happen that I think will be far worse than what the emir intended."

The Castle Shield formed a tight knot around me and bulled their way through the crowd. That certainly did not calm things down. From the corner of my eye, I noticed Fenwick slipping away.

Major Grunevald was waiting on my ship with nine of his men. Each of the other two ships had only ten members of the Shield before we returned. All thirty were cradling crossbows in their arms. When I climbed aboard, I went directly to him.

"We ended our evening early, major," I said. "Good thing, from the looks of it. Let's give them a chance to calm down on their own, but if they don't begin leaving in, say, ten minutes, have the men form up and clear the pier."

"I'm glad to see you, Your Highness," Grunevald said. "It's only become boisterous in the last half hour or so. Before that, they looked like a bunch of confused sheep."

"I sent Lord Easton to speak with some of the people we think are in charge," I said. "If he is successful, the crowd should begin to break up."

Whatever Fenwick said to the men we identified as the leaders was effective. The shouting started to lose some of its vigor. Before it stopped entirely, I could see people beginning to drift away from the pier. When there were only a couple of dozen people left, Fenwick climbed aboard.

"The emir wanted to make a point," Fenwick said. "He did not intend for them to cause any damage—"

"But mobs take on a life of their own," I interrupted.

"Exactly the point I made with the people who organized the whole thing," Fenwick said. "Even they could see things were building and might reach a boiling point. That's why they were willing to accept my suggestion to call a halt to the festivities."

I wondered how much of it was due to their common sense and reasonableness, and what sort of a part Fenwick's connection to Mielvanir played. Mielvanir is our minor God of travel and commerce. It was one of Fenwick's lesser abilities but explained the ease with which he learned foreign languages.

Though the tide would not turn for another couple of hours, there was an offshore breeze. We could at least pull away from the docks into the center of the harbor and remove any remaining temptation for someone to launch a torch on deck. I gave the order to the sailing master, and within minutes, we untied and began drifting away from the pier.

"Why do you think the emir staged this almost-riot?" I asked Fenwick.

"He just came to power a little more than a year ago," Fenwick replied. "I think he was trying to make a point to his people that he will not allow foreigners to push him around."

"Why? Has that been a problem here?" I inquired.

"Absolutely," Fenwick said. "Garo is small, lying in between Scaramouche and Mooresa. In the past, both countries have bullied Garo to a certain extent—not militarily, but economically. This emir is the first one in many years who does not owe his position to close ties with either the grand vizier of Scaramouche or the bashaw of Mooresa."

The winds changed direction, and it took us five days to reach Acrius, the chief port of Mooresa. We spent most of that time tacking (another term I learned) back and forth. I had been to Acrius before, playing the part of a servant to Lord Compote when he negotiated to buy jute sacks. My friend Freddy—Lord Rawlinsford—played the role of the dimwitted Compote to perfection. His unrelenting obtuseness ended up being an incredibly successful negotiating tactic. The Mooresans eventually grew so tired of his endless and repetitive questions that they gave him favorable pricing in order to end the meeting and save their sanity.

Acrius was the capital of Mooresa, so an official delegation was waiting for us when we arrived. We left the horses on the ships, and the Castle Shield accompanied our carriage on foot. The bashaw's palace was atop the highest point in Acrius, and the long climb in the heat of the day had to have been highly unpleasant for the soldiers.

My worry about this leg of the trip had to do with my father and Ariana's visit. They were to have come in place of Lord Compote to buy a slightly larger quantity than the previous year of the jute sacks used to ship grain and produce. Ariana was originally from Mooresa, something that should have ensured a decent welcome. By now, they should have concluded the negotiations and be on their way back to Aquileia. I hoped that was the case.

If my father and Ariana had not yet visited, then Fenwick and I were in a difficult spot. We were coming to make certain the bashaw knew we intended to enforce the blockade we announced. That might make my father's task more difficult. And, of course, if the bashaw knew we re-established our own jute growing operations, he would be furious, but I doubted any news of that would have reached him.

When we reached the bashaw's palace, servants took Fenwick and me to rather luxurious rooms. Almost immediately after we entered, other servants began preparing a bath for me. Given the heat and lack of opportunities to wash since visiting the grand vizier, I was quite grateful.

The ever-efficient Mr. Gilbert had laid out fresh clothing for me while I soaked. I had just finished dressing when Fenwick slipped into the room. He immediately sprawled on a low chair with over-stuffed cushions.

"Our father and Ariana have already come and gone," he announced with a slight smirk. "They departed the day before yesterday."

"That's a relief," I admitted. "Though, let me remind you, if he's your father, he cannot be mine anymore."

"You just took all the fun out of my attempt to tease you," Fenwick complained.

"Sorry, but that wasn't one of your better efforts," I said.

Our dinner with the bashaw was, for the most part, nearly as pleasant and light-hearted as the evening with the grand vizier. The bashaw was in an expansive mood. I suspected my father was not able to strike as good a bargain as Lord Compote. That would provide ample fodder for ribbing him in the future.

The bashaw did let something slip later in the evening that I thought odd. In discussing our journey so far and the visits we had yet to make, his face clouded when we mentioned Hier. Fenwick immediately caught the change in his expression and probed.

"Is something troubling happening in Hier?" he asked.

"We don't know," the bashaw admitted. "The last three ships that sailed for Iradiem, their chief port, have not returned. All of them are now overdue. It came to my attention only yesterday, so I apologize that I don't have more information to share. It is probably nothing more than adverse winds."

The winds were from the west, which would have made them entirely favorable to return to Mooresa. I let his comment pass, and the conversation turned to my father's recent visit. That segued into a discussion of the recent changes in Fenwick's and my status. The bashaw mentioned that he had heard the song about me. He wanted to hear about the war. The evening did not end until well after dark.

In the morning, we dined again with the bashaw. Afterward, he escorted us to the harbor and saw us board the ships. We pulled away from the pier, and when the tide started going out we flowed out of the harbor along with it.

There was a steady wind from the south now, and we made good progress toward Vanda. We arrived at the harbor of the city of Malan in the middle of the night and needed to wait for daylight before entering. By mid-morning, we rode the tide into the port.

The capital of Vanda, Nitis, was just over a two-day ride. We unloaded the horses. Fenwick and I would stay at an inn that night while most of the Castle Shield would encamp just outside the city.

Despite the blazing sun and oppressive heat, it was good to be on horseback. Andy appreciated it, too, after so long cooped up in the stall in the hold of the ship. I felt guilty about it and, when we reached the inn, wanted to groom him myself. Sergeant Hewko, however, would not permit it.

"No, Your Highness," he said sternly.

"Sar'nt, I'm not trying to prove anything about how modest I am or anything like that. I simply feel rotten that Andy has spent so much time on the ship. I'd like to try to make it up to him," I explained.

"Your Highness, I understand," Hewko said. "And that's why I take care of Andy myself—Davy, too. They're both real fine animals—intelligent, great temperaments, affectionate, and handsome, too."

As though he knew we were talking about him, Andy turned around. He took a couple of little steps toward me and nudged my head with his muzzle. Then he turned to Sergeant Hewko.

"Heavenly beings!" Hewko muttered. "It's like he knew exactly what we were saying."

"He might," I said, shaking my head in wonderment. "He's the best horse I've ever known, and I'm lucky to have him."

Andy huffed out a breath and let his lips flap. The sergeant and I looked at him, then at each other. We both burst into laughter. I patted Andy affectionately and then headed inside.

We arrived in Nitis late in the afternoon. The king and queen were waiting for us as we rode up. I dismounted and made my small bow while Fenwick translated. We were ushered inside to spacious quarters.

At dinner, Fenwick steered the conversation away from our recent war with the Rhetians to our visit across the desert and over the distant eastern mountains to the horse nomads. The king and queen were both keenly interested. It led us into a long discussion about Vanda and its history.

The queen claimed she was a descendant of the horse nomads. The king traced his lineage back to a different group of nomads who invaded Vanda from the south, hundreds of years after the horse nomads arrived. According to what they told us, the horse nomads were the first of three waves of hostile immigration into the territory. Each group of invaders ended up seizing control from the previous rulers. Even within each group, there were deadly rivalries, and clashes over succession were common.

"Before I was born, my father seized power from his second cousin," the king said.

"Do you worry that someone from that branch of the family might seek revenge?" Fenwick asked.

"Some have already tried," the king said with a shrug. "I keep a close eye on them. Their efforts were clumsy. None of them are terribly smart. It's why my father took the throne in the first place."

"The grand vizier of Scaramouche mentioned to us that power changed hands fairly often in the countries on the north coast," I said.

"His family has lasted longer than many, and I know why," the king said. "His focus is different. I am trying to imitate him—and your family, which has outlasted all of us."

"How so?" asked Fenwick.

"I believe the reason power changes hands so frequently is because people see that as the end goal. The first generation gains power. The second strengthens its grip. The third then indulges in it. At no time do they attempt to resolve the problems that affect the realm. That means there is always a ready source of discontent and unrest. The same problem brought about the end of the old empire. It was more important to the rulers to be seated on the throne, even though half the empire had turned to a pile of crap. Rather than clean up the crap, all their efforts were spent on maintaining themselves in power. At three different points I know of, underlings made great progress in addressing the underlying problems affecting the empire. In all three cases, the emperors ordered them to be assassinated because they represented a threat to his rule."

"So, what is the end goal?" Fenwick asked.

"Peace and prosperity for the realm," the king stated. "Power is a means to that end, not an end in itself."

"It is interesting to hear you put into words things I was taught by my grandfather as a boy—though he never phrased it so nakedly," I said. "He would just discuss examples of how different noble families managed their holdings. His strong belief was that anyone who did not manage a territory for the good of the residents was doing his king a disservice."

"I did not have such a good teacher," the king said. "It was up to me to figure it out on my own. Though you say your grandfather taught you? Not your father?"

"Future historians will have a difficult time depicting my family tree," I joked. "I was born out of wedlock."

"A bastard?" the queen gasped.

"I knew that and have been meaning to ask how you came to your current position," the king said. "I hoped a polite opportunity might present itself."

I told the story as succinctly as I could, but it still took some time as they interrupted my narrative with questions. How Fenwick and I met is something I glossed over, not wishing to make him feel uncomfortable. I also omitted to mention Lucy's and my supernatural abilities.

"There is something you left out, Your Highness," the king observed. "There is a song about you that some of the sailors from Aquileia sing in the dockside taverns. The tune is quite charming, and the chorus is easy to remember. One of the verses tells of you summoning the warrior goddess to save your king. Is it true? Are you a warrior-mage?"

"I am," I replied.

It made me slightly uncomfortable to discuss matters of this sort with someone who was nearly a stranger, though not nearly as much as it would have a year earlier. I remember how worried I was before I admitted it to my father. He already had a strong suspicion, which made it easier.

"Amazing," the queen murmured.

"I am not one of those who tries to deny the existence of magic in the world," the king said. "Many of my predecessors did. They feared it because they could not control it. Yet I have seen with my own eyes how villages in Vanda that have witches tend to prosper more than those who don't. After all, being able to gain the assistance of one of the Minor Gods would help any human endeavor, though the warrior goddess would be more useful to an entire realm than a single town."

"You may need to call upon your abilities if you are continuing to Hier," the queen remarked.

"Really? What is happening in Hier? The bashaw of Mooresa mentioned something might be wrong there," Fenwick said.

"We don't know that anything is wrong," the king said. "Some of our trading ships that called there are a few days late to return home. There is little traffic overland because of the mountains that lay in between us, but what little there is has also stopped. We heard rumors of unrest in Combrial, Hier's southern neighbor, and wonder if it spread northward."

"Do you think someone from Combrial has seized control of the government?" I asked.

"That would be my guess," the king admitted.

12

In the morning, we departed Nitis for Malan. Along the way, Fenwick and I debated whether to continue with our plan to visit Hier. We wondered if the unrest from Combrial had developed into war or even a change in regime.

"Well, Iradiem is also the capital," Fenwick said. "We can make a quick stop and assess the situation."

We reached Malan without incident and loaded back into the ships. When the tide turned, we sailed out of the harbor. The same steady southern wind was blowing, and we made good time to Iradiem, arriving in the early morning after four days at sea.

The tide was flowing in, so we entered the harbor. One thing I noticed that seemed different was the number of ships sitting idle at the wharves. I pointed it out to Fenwick.

"It's probably related to the unrest," he said.

As we drew closer, we saw that there was no activity at all on the docks. I'd never seen a waterfront deserted like this. Ordinarily, they were hives of activity.

With no dockworkers, it would make it more difficult to moor the ship. I made the decision to have only our ship tie up. We signaled to the other two to drop anchor in the harbor.

Our sailing master expertly guided the carrack up to the wharf, with almost all our forward progress eliminated by the time we reached it. A handful of our sailors nimbly jumped to the pier, and others threw them the mooring lines. Within minutes, we were snugged up to the dock.

I requested that Andy and Davy be lifted from the hold since I did not see any carriages or hackneys. Major Grunevald asked for his mount to be unloaded as well. The other men of the Castle Shield from our ship would proceed on foot. Within minutes, the three horses were smoothly hoisted to the pier, already saddled.

The thirty-nine men of the Castle Shield filed off the ship. When we reached the waterfront, they formed up around Major Grunevald, Fenwick, and me. Fenwick said he knew the way and pointed us to the south and west.

The eerie feeling I had from the lack of activity at the waterfront was compounded by the silence of the city. There was no one outside. We were leaving the warehouse district when I noticed the quiet chatter between the men of the Shield had stopped.

"Major Grunevald, I have a bad feeling about this," I said. "We should return to the ship."

He did not respond—not even the slightest twitch to indicate he heard me. Eyes straight ahead, he continued to ride. I pulled slightly ahead of him and repeated myself. He did not respond.

I saw a gleam of red deep in his eyes while the rest of his face seemed to lack expression completely. I'd seen that dull luster in the eyes and blank countenance before—in Dunland. When I turned to look at Fenwick, he was similarly affected.

The only logical conclusion was that they, and the foot soldiers surrounding us, were now in thrall to a practitioner of the Dark Arts. I was unaffected since I was wearing the ward the queen gave me a couple of years earlier. Untying my cravat and unbuttoning my collar, I reached into my shirt and pulled the necklace up and over my head.

Major Grunevald was closer, so I went to him first. I touched the ward to his hand. He immediately collapsed, unconscious, slumping forward, then sliding out of his saddle to the left.

I pulled Andy to the side to avoid stepping on him. The major's left foot was still in the stirrup and his mount stopped rather than drag him along. The men flowed around him on either side. I continued moving to the left, forcing Andy through the non-responsive men of the Castle Shield as they continued to march forward.

That caused enough of a disruption to the formation that it caught the attention of whoever was controlling them. Andy and I were now free of the group. I set him to a trot. In a short time, the men would not be able to catch us. They had yet to change course. Fenwick was a different matter. Looking over my shoulder, I saw him draw his blade and wheel his horse to pursue us.

I drew my own sword in order to defend myself but had no intention of trading blows with Fenwick. Instead, I hoped to touch my ward to him. It would knock him out, but I was unwilling to leave him behind, figuring I would need him at some point.

As Andy and I traveled down a side street, I kept us to the left side of the road. That would force Fenwick to try to fight us with his left hand. I felt that would be enough of an advantage to give me a chance to tag him with my ward. Andy and I did not increase our pace, staying at a trot. I wanted Fenwick to reach us.

Reaching within myself, I fully opened my link to Bellona. Andy and I both seemed to increase in size. It was only an illusion—we occupied no more physical space than before—but the strength that flowed through me was real. Looking over my shoulder, Fenwick and Davy were almost upon us, appearing just as large and menacing as Andy and I did.

When they came alongside, Fenwick jerked on Davy's reins to try to shove us against the wall of the building. At the same time, he slashed at me left-handed. Davy did nudge us, but not as hard as Fenwick intended. Perhaps Davy sensed the wrongness of what was taking place.

I caught Fenwick's slash with the hilt of my sword. With my own left hand, I touched the ward to the skin of Fenwick's hand. As with the major a few minutes before, Fenwick immediately slumped.

I reined Andy in. Davy stopped alongside us. I pulled Fenwick from his saddle. Removing his sword from his hand and retrieving the knife I knew he kept inside his boot, I thrust them through my own belt. With that done, I hoisted him back over his saddle, flopped over with his arms on one side and legs on the other. With that done, I closed my connection to Bellona and felt her power recede.

I mounted Andy, and we sidled over so I could take Davy's reins. We headed back to the wharf. I hoped the dark mage had not yet taken control of the ships. That wish did not come true, as I could see the sailors on foot at a distance, heading toward us. I wheeled us down a street to the right, traveled one block, then turned toward the harbor again.

There was no way I could sail the carrack by myself—I knew that. There should be rope in the harbor, though. I needed something I could use to bind Fenwick's hands and feet. He would regain consciousness at some point, and I wanted him restrained when that happened in case the mage regained control of him.

Exiting between two warehouse buildings, the waterfront was as deserted as when we arrived. I could see our other two ships easing their way inward to docks. By the time they tied up, I wanted to be gone.

Fortunately, there was a coil of rope at the end of the nearest wharf. I quickly cut two suitable lengths and trussed Fenwick up. Thinking that I might need rope to cobble the horses at some point, I cut two more lengths and coiled them around the front lip of my saddle.

I toyed with the idea of boarding the ship to retrieve other clothing and supplies, but a glance at the progress of the other two ships persuaded me against that. Mounting Andy and taking Davy's reins in hand, I decided to head east, back to Vanda. I had no food, no water, unsuitable clothing, and a captive who might still be under the control of the dark mage—who now controlled the city of Iradiem and, for all I knew, all of Hier.

"Majors and Minors, Fenwick," I sighed to his unconscious form, "you do drag me into the most challenging things!"

Though I decided to travel overland, I realized I did not know whether there was a coast road. For that matter, if there was, I needed to find it. I accessed Bellona again, tugging out the smallest tendril of our connection. It is difficult to put into words what I did then—my vocabulary fails me when I try to explain the supernatural. The easiest way to describe it is how I thought of it—I stretched out my senses while thinking of a major road to the east.

Almost as soon as I did this, I knew which way to head. Yet even though I was using only the smallest amount of power, I felt it pull on my reserves. When I threw open my link to the Goddess earlier, I must have used almost all the asomatous energy in my body. I touched the tan-zyan stone on my ring to the diamond in the pommel of my sword. That brought me access to the energy I had stored in the diamond. The stored energy then flowed through the ring and into me. When I felt full, I stopped. Again, I am using physical terms to describe something that did not take place in the realm of our normal senses, but I do not know how to describe it otherwise.

I found the main road—a grand boulevard through the middle of the silent city. The only sounds were of the breeze, the occasional bird, and the clacking of the horseshoes on the cobbles. We saw no one.

I wondered where all the people were. How did they feed themselves? Did they even feel hunger? Were they frozen in place, in their homes, waiting for the mage to make use of them? I was tempted to explore in order to learn more, but the necessity of keeping watch on Fenwick prevented me.

We reached the gate in the tall and thick walls surrounding the city. Shortly after riding through, Fenwick began to stir. I quickly dismounted and lifted his head, grabbing his hair. The same dull red gleam was present behind his eyes. I pulled my ward up over my head again and touched it to Fenwick's neck. He collapsed.

I reckoned that Fenwick remained unconscious for roughly the same amount of time the mage in Dunland had when we touched him with one of our wards. Checking his bonds, I could see his hands were slightly blue. I decided to untie him for now to allow his circulation to flow, but I would need to truss him up again before he next woke.

Back in the saddle, we continued on the road. By ship, it took us four days with favorable wind to reach Iradiem from Malan. I wondered how much longer it would take to ride there. My first guess was that it would require at least twice as many days. Then I remembered the mountains we passed that lay in between Vanda and Hier. That would add even more time.

I had some money. Though it was in Aquileian coin, silver and gold have universal value. We would need cloaks for the night when it grew cold, something to carry water, food for us and the horses, and a better idea of where we were going and what to expect along the way. Obtaining these things was dependent on how far the dark mage's sway extended.

I did not know enough about the Dark Arts to venture a guess as to his reach. It seemed logical that there would be limits to the control a mage could exercise. I remembered in Eatonford, where the girl, Esme, was possessed by a grimoire, her direct control was limited to the household. The town, several miles away, was largely free from her influence, except for a spell she cast that alerted her when her name was used.

Similarly, in Dunland, the entire town was under the mage's control, but Count Dunland's manor was not. The count, however, was still affected by spells the mage cast upon him. From this, I reckoned there must be geographical limitations regarding holding people in thrall. I hoped that this sort of constraint would prevent the mage from sending anyone in pursuit of us.

From those experiences, I knew spells could be extended further. There probably was a cost in terms of the mage's use of asomatous energy, I guessed. If you cast a spell too widely, could it drain you? Then, there was a question of re-establishing control of a thrall. I imagined there was some linkage that would make it possible for the mage to "find" Fenwick when he regained consciousness. Whether that was subject to geographic limitations was another unknown.

When the mage in Dunland seized Fenwick's will, I broke the connection by touching him with my ward. The mage did not re-establish control afterward. Here, though, the mage's influence reappeared as soon as Fenwick regained consciousness. How far would that power extend?

As we rode away from the city, we entered an area of lush farms. The fields seemed to be tended, but I did not see any people. When I judged we were approaching the time when Fenwick might regain consciousness, I stopped and bound his hands and feet again.

Not long after, I noticed him squirming, trying to slide off Davy's back. I dismounted quickly. Grabbing him by the hair again, I lifted his head. His eyes still showed the red luster deep within. I touched him with my ward, and he collapsed again. After loosening his bonds, we continued.

I wondered whether I made a mistake by trying to bring Fenwick with me. If I could not trust him to remain free of the mage's control, his presence could be a burden that would make the overland trip to Vanda impossible. I would be afraid to sleep or leave him for any length of time.

The last time I felt this helpless was when Fenwick and I were marooned on one of the Persimmon Islands. That thought reminded me of a way I could contact Lucy to inform her of what happened. I searched within myself for the reddish-brown mote that was my connection to Shasha, the sparrowhawk who had attached her mind to mine.

From the view I accessed through her eyes, it seemed as though she was near Bannock Hill in the Eastern March. She was perched in a treetop. I sensed she was pleased I contacted her. That pleasure quickly faded as she sensed my troubled mind.

You are ill-at-ease, Caz.

"I am, Shasha," I thought in reply, though instead of her name, I remembered the sound of her wing beats that it represented. "Can you still contact the owl?"

It has been days upon days since I last sensed the owl's presence here.

"The owl is near Lucy, in the city," I thought, and pictured a map of Aquileia in my mind, trying to show how to traverse the distance between the Eastern March and the capital. "We live there now."

Why?

"It's complicated. I promise to try to explain later. Would you be willing to go to the city to contact the owl?"

Is there hunting?

"Oh, yes," I thought, remembering for her a flock of pigeons in a market square.

I should get fat and lazy living there, she expressed with what I felt was a jocular tone. *I will go. When I contact the owl, I will reach out to you again.*

With that, she closed our link.

It was a three-day ride from Easton to Aquileia. How long it would take a sparrowhawk, I did not know. I also did not have any idea how Lucy could help me, but there was comfort in knowing that she would be aware of my predicament.

Continuing east, we neared the first town since leaving the city. At a minimum, the horses and I needed water. Given that it was the height of summer on the southern continent, it was quite hot. Food would be good as well, but if the mage's control extended this far, eating might need to wait until we were further along.

Entering, I saw no one outside. I did see a fountain in the center of town, though. When we reached it, I slid off Andy's back and allowed him and Davy both to drink. After looking around, I went to a different section of the fountain and cupped my hands to get some water. Fenwick wouldn't get any, but that was not my priority.

A voice came from the shadows. From the pitch of the voice, it was someone young—a boy or girl. It came from behind me, on the western side of the square. I looked up and tried to see who it was, but he or she was hidden in the shade.

"I'm Caz," I replied with a wave. "I'm from Aquileia."

The girl replied, but I could not understand her.

"Miela!" a voice screeched from within the building.

The girl scurried back inside. I climbed back into the saddle, took Davy's reins, and resumed our journey. For whatever reason, Miela was unaffected by the dark mage's command. I would like to have learned why. From the reluctance of anyone else to come outside, I reckoned they were frightened to go out. I wondered whether it was just a reaction to what some may have seen in the city or if the mage cast a spell to keep them inside.

Did it also mean the mage knew where I was? Would he ride out from the city to capture us? That was my biggest concern, though I doubted he would. Leaving would probably result in his losing control of the thousands who lived there. Of course, he could probably re-establish it once he returned, but in the meantime, how many would flee on the ships in the harbor? How far would they carry the news of what he was doing?

13

I stopped to tie Fenwick up again when I felt we were getting close to when he would wake up. Sure enough, less than a half-hour later, I saw him trying to slide from Davy's back. I stopped, dismounted, and yanked his head up. My frustration with the current situation showed as I was none too gentle. His eyes still had the red glow deep within. I touched my ward to his neck, and he slumped immediately.

We reached the next town near sunset. Praise all the heavenly beings, I saw people. True, it was only a handful, but they were outside and moving. They saw us coming and stopped, turning to face us. Others came outside and joined them. They looked at us curiously as we rode in. In their defense, I was rather finely dressed—not like the usual traveler—and I was bringing an unconscious body along. When I drew within fifty yards, one of them called out to me. I did not know the language and could not understand him. Translating was the reason Fenwick came on this trip, and he was unavailable.

"I apologize," I called back. "I'm from Aquileia, and I don't speak your language."

The man who called out to me held up his hand. I didn't know whether he wanted me to stop or to wait. I did both. A few minutes passed, then a woman arrived.

"You come city?" she asked, her accent heavy.

"Yes," I nodded.

"How?"

I guessed she wasn't asking about my mode of travel. That was obvious. She must have been asking how I was not captured in the thrall of the mage. I reached for my ward, fished it out of my shirt, and showed it to her.

"I have a ward," I said. "It protected me."

The topaz was small enough that she needed to approach more closely to see it. She moved hesitantly toward me. When she drew within five feet, she nodded and began retreating.

"Bulla," she said, addressing the townspeople.

The people watching then murmured understanding. They began talking among themselves. I hoped they were discussing whether to help me.

"Who him?" the woman asked, pointing at Fenwick's body.

"My friend," I said. "No bulla."

She explained to the others. Their conversation grew more heated. There was a clear line of disagreement. The man who stopped me originally stopped the disagreement and said something to the woman.

"Where go?" she inquired.

"Vanda, I hope, but I will need help—supplies. I have money."

The discussion after she relayed my request was less contentious. Several in the group were nodding. I hoped that was a positive sign for me.

"What you need?" she asked.

"Cloaks," I replied. "Blankets, water skins, food, food for horses—a feed bag would help."

For each item, I playacted its use. When I tried to demonstrate a feed bag, several of the group laughed. I shook my head and pointed to Andy's head. From the slight increase in their chuckling, they already figured that out.

"We help," the woman said, "but you no stay. You fine. Him, not."

"I understand," I replied, nodding. "May I water my horses?"

She passed my request on to the man. He waved us forward to the fountain. The group parted to allow us to pass through. He issued instructions, and some of the group trotted away.

I slid from Andy's back and allowed him to drink. Davy sidled up as well. The woman approached me.

"Who you?" she asked.

"The crown prince of Aquileia," I replied, figuring this might be the time to use my title.

"Crown prince?" she inquired.

"King," I said, putting one hand up in the air. "Crown prince," I added, with my left hand slightly lower. "Father, son," I continued, wiggling each hand in turn.

"Ah," she exclaimed.

She turned to the man and began explaining. His eyes grew wide. The two had a rapid back and forth.

"We respect, but still you go. Him," she said, pointing at Fenwick.

I nodded but added a smile to show that I was not angry. Some of the group who left minutes before started to return. In short order, they furnished me with everything I requested. They also provided saddle bags which I did not ask for, but needed. I rolled the blankets up and tied them behind the two saddles. Then, I filled the four water skins they provided.

Opening the bag of feed, I scooped out dinner for Andy and Davy into the feed bags, then drew them over their heads. When I felt I had everything secured, I turned to the man and reached for my coin pouch. He tried to wave me off, but I insisted. The material they gave me was worth at least a couple of ducats. I handed the man five of the gold coins.

"You no pay," the woman tried to explain. "You royal—no pay. Gift."

"Then this," I held out my hand with the coins, "is also a gift."

"Ah," she said, understanding my intent. "Gift for gift."

She explained to the man. He nodded his understanding and smiled. The woman turned to me.

"Thanks you for gift," she said with a grin.

"And I thank you for your gift to me," I answered.

I swung back up into the saddle. Andy and Davy came along, munching away. I waved goodbye as we left the town. They had given me some bread and roasted fowl. I ate while we rode, saving some for Fenwick.

When the horses finished their feed bags, I stopped and dismounted. I pulled the bags from their heads. While on the ground, I bound Fenwick's hands and feet again. He would be waking relatively soon.

Sure enough, just as the sun was setting behind us, I heard Fenwick groan. That was different from before. When he regained consciousness earlier, he made no sound.

"Fenwick?"

"Yes, Your Highness," he croaked.

"Thirsty?"

"Yes."

I reined Andy to a stop and dismounted. Crossing to Fenwick, I lifted his head—more gently this time—and looked into his eyes. There was no trace of the red glow. I went behind him and pulled the waist of his breeches so he could slide down. When his feet touched the ground, I steadied him, then put a water skin in his bound hands.

"I don't suppose there is any chance you will untie me?" he asked after he took a long drink.

"I'm considering it," I said. "Getting back to Vanda will be impossible if I need to keep watch over you the whole time. The problem is the extent of the mage's control. Every other time you've roused, he possessed you immediately. This is the first time he hasn't."

"You really don't trust me," he stated.

"If you saw what I did," I said, "you wouldn't even bother to ask."

He shrugged in acceptance.

"Are you hungry?" I asked.

"Starving."

I gave Fenwick his share of the bread and meat. He sat down and then tore into the roasted fowl. Only after he bit off, chewed, and swallowed three bites did he pause.

"I've lost a whole day," he commented. "What happened?"

I explained what took place. When I mentioned seeing the red gleam behind his eyes, Fenwick frowned. He was probably thinking back to the time in Dunland.

"At least I didn't try to kill you this time," he joked weakly.

"You did, only I was too quick and touched you with my ward on your first thrust," I said.

"Oh."

"Where is yours?" I asked.

"With my things on the ship," he replied glumly.

We sat in silence for a time. Twilight was fading to the dark of night, and I had no desire to continue further. I was drained, physically and emotionally. Crossing to the horses, I retrieved the cloaks and the blankets I rolled up. After I tossed them in Fenwick's direction, I took the extra rope I had and hobbled both horses to keep them from wandering too far in the night, then removed the saddles.

"I'm going to take a chance," I said when I finished. "Take this," I said as I pulled my ward off over my head. "Put it on, and I'll untie you."

"Are you sure that's a good idea?" Fenwick asked.

"No, but I can't think of any better choices," I replied. "You are the one the mage has some connection with. The ward should prevent him from re-establishing control over you. I'm gambling that I am too far away for him to put me in his thrall."

"What if you're wrong?" Fenwick asked.

"Then I'll probably kill you in your sleep," I said.

"There are worse ways to die," Fenwick joked weakly.

"I would like to avoid it. Lucy would be quite cross with me—probably for hours," I quipped in return as I loosened the ropes binding his wrists.

"You wouldn't miss me?" Fenwick asked with a hint of a whine.

"I suppose I would—sort of like when you have a stone in your boot. After you shake it out, there is that pleasant sensation of the irritation being absent," I teased.

"That was one of your better sets of cracks," Fenwick commented as he untied his feet.

"Perhaps dark circumstances bring out the best in me," I offered.

"When we reach Vanda, what then?" Fenwick asked, returning to a serious mood.

"I have no idea," I admitted. "When the sparrowhawk reaches the capital, I hope to let Lucy know what sort of trouble we are in."

"What can she do?"

"Not much," I grunted. "It's just that there is some peace of mind in knowing that she is aware of our troubles."

"Do you think she will come to Vanda?" Fenwick asked.

"No. She might send a ship to come collect us, though."

"What about the people we left behind in Iradiem?" Fenwick demanded.

"I've been pondering that much of the day," I said. "To retrieve them would require a significant military effort, and we would need the queen to play a leading role because of the presence of the Dark Arts. I doubt Mark will be willing to take on the risk. Though the situation in Hier is awful, it does not concern Aquileia much beyond our missing people. I would look for the other countries here on the southern continent to take the lead. In that case, we might offer assistance."

"And just abandon our men? The ships? Majors and Minors—the horses?" Fenwick queried.

I had not considered the plight of the horses on the ships. If the dark mage enthralled all the men and pulled them from the ships, there would be no one to take care of the animals. Stuck in the holds, with no food or water, they would not survive long, and they would meet a horrible end.

"Trust you to make me think of something more wretched than what I was already worrying about," I said, putting my head in my hands. "Gah! Even so, that does not change the overall situation. This is a local problem. I think the mage can exercise his control only so far, in terms of geography. That's what we saw in Dunland."

"True," Fenwick admitted, "but in Dunland, the mage also allowed his thralls to return to some semblance of normal life—at least as far as feeding themselves. Otherwise, no one would still have been alive by the time we showed up."

"Neither of us knows enough about the Dark Arts to know what this mage is capable of doing," I replied. "I would imagine he has the ability to make some of the people into his lieutenants, who then instruct and manage everyone else. He probably has some way of coercing people into following instructions. Beyond that, I'm at a loss."

"To deal with this properly, we need the queen's help," Fenwick said.

"Or someone like her," I countered. "Again, it's not truly our problem to solve—even with the men we left behind. Knowing the king as we do, there is simply no mathematics where the loss of a hundred and twenty men equals putting the queen in harm's way."

"Is there a way to neutralize the mage without the queen?" Fenwick asked.

"According to Lily, there is," I said, "but from her limited description, it will be difficult and dangerous."

"Difficult and dangerous is what we are known for, Caz," Fenwick remarked with a smile.

"Not without Mark's specific orders," I said, shaking my head. "Let the neighbors handle it. They have a pressing interest. We do not."

"You've changed," Fenwick stated.

"What are you talking about?" I demanded.

"Before, if I told you we needed to do something like this, you would have groused about it, but there was never any doubt that you would join me," he explained.

"If you'll recall, those assignments were given to you by the king," I pointed out. "When the king asks us to take this on, I'll complain about it—to you, not to him—and go along to make sure you don't mess things up. It's no different from before."

"I suppose you're right," he said after thinking quietly for several minutes. "It just irks me that I fell under the mage's control, and I want a measure of revenge."

"Believe me, I understand," I replied sympathetically, remembering the time in Dunland when the mage used me to attack Fenwick.

Fortunately, the queen was right there and broke the mage's hold on me before I did any harm. When I recovered my wits, it seemed like a horrible dream. I remember being mortified with embarrassment.

"So, what's next?" Fenwick inquired.

"Me going to sleep," I replied. "It has been rather an eventful day."

"For you, perhaps," Fenwick commented. "I missed most of it. By the way, will you give me back my sword?"

"I might as well," I said. "You'll just nab it from me when I fall asleep. No sense in putting you to the trouble. I'll even give you back your knife."

"Thank you. It might have been embarrassing groping you for it in the dark," Fenwick cracked.

I unrolled the blankets and stretched out on top of them. I covered myself with one of the cloaks. Fenwick just watched. He did not prepare to go to sleep. I suspected something was on his mind, so I tried to stay awake, waiting for him to air it out.

"It doesn't bother you?" he asked eventually. "Our people? The ships? You're willing to walk away and do nothing, except wait for someone else to take the lead in addressing this problem?"

"Predictable," I sighed.

"What?"

"I could tell you were still upset by our earlier discussion," I said. "You think that I don't care because I am not immediately intent on neutralizing this mage and freeing our people."

"I never said that," he protested.

"No, but you were thinking that—admit it," I countered.

"Fine," he sighed. "Yes, I was."

"Certainly I want to bring this mage down," I said. "It disturbs me greatly that so many of our people are under his control. I do not want to abandon them. And when I think about what will probably happen to the horses, I feel ill. The problem is that it's bigger than just me."

"What do you mean?" Fenwick asked.

"Before, in all my adventures, if I failed—and died—it was just me. Yes, Lucy would be affected, but she accepted the risks for the most part when she accepted me. Perhaps that is because of her clairvoyance and her knowledge that I *would* return. As a matter of fact, the only time she was truly upset was when you dragged me to Rhetia," I explained.

"She was not sure of your survival?" Fenwick asked.

"Later, she admitted she had a vision where I did not come back," I said, "but I could tell she was greatly troubled when you showed up that night. But, even if I fell, my father was still in place in the Eastern March. Things would not fall apart if I were gone."

"How is it different now? If you die, the king is still alive," Fenwick stated.

"The difference is that the king saw what I did in the Eastern March. Then he turned command of the army over to me against the Rhetians and it confirmed his earlier observations of my ability. He wants me to do for the kingdom what I did for the March," I said.

"Have you discussed this with him?" Fenwick asked.

"No, but why else would he have chosen me as his successor?" I argued. "If I were merely a man of good character and reasonably competent, there were others of noble blood he could have chosen who do not carry the same baggage as I do. I believe he selected me because he wants the crown prince to be transformative—someone to move the kingdom forward. That's one of the reasons I think Albert became more involved with me, and I suspect the king urged or encouraged it."

"Are you flattering yourself?" Fenwick teased.

"Having you around helps prevent that," I quipped. "In any event, resolving the situation we encountered here no longer involves just a risk for you and me. Much more is in potential jeopardy. And though I am probably overstepping my bounds, you should begin to think in the same way. The Eastern March is now yours. The health and prosperity of those people is on your shoulders."

"Huh," Fenwick grunted.

I let Fenwick chew on that thought while I drifted to sleep.

14

Morning arrived, and I was pleased to see that Fenwick and the horses were still there. Even better, all were still alive. That meant I had not been enthralled in the night and killed any of them unknowingly.

"Fenwick," I said, nudging him with my foot. "Let's get moving."

Fenwick rolled over slowly, opening one eye to look up at me. He sat up slowly, then twisted to his knees and started to straighten his blankets before rolling them up. When he finished, he stood, then stretched.

"Thank you for a sleepless night," he said, as he picked up his saddle and carried it over to Davy. "You gave me too much to think about, then were unavailable for further discussion."

"Reach any conclusions?" I asked.

"Nothing I care to discuss at the moment, other than to acknowledge you have a point," he said. "Things *are* different now. I have Julienne to consider, and the March."

We mounted up and started heading east. It was not long before we reached the next town. I was pleased to see a few people about. From a distance, they did not seem quite so pleased to see us. They stopped where they were and turned to watch us approach. Fenwick and I both raised a hand in what we hoped they viewed as a friendly greeting.

"Stop right there, please," Fenwick told me one of them said when we were fifty feet away from them. "Who are you? Where are you coming from?"

"We are from Aquileia," Fenwick replied to them. "We escaped Iradiem and are heading to Vanda."

"What is happening in Iradiem?" a woman asked. "No one has returned from there in more than two weeks. The people in the towns closer to the capital don't know either, but we are all frightened."

"From what we saw, a mage practicing the Dark Arts has taken control of the city," Fenwick explained. "Everyone there is in his power."

"Then how did you escape?" a man asked suspiciously.

"We were protected by a ward," Fenwick replied, sharing with me as he translated.

"Bulla," I corrected, interrupting him.

"What?" Fenwick said.

"They call it a bulla," I said.

"Fine," he said to me. "A bulla protected us," he told them.

"What sort of bulla?" a woman inquired.

Fenwick dismounted. He reached into his shirt and retrieved the topaz. Showing it to her, he approached slowly, trying to appear unthreatening. She took hesitant steps toward him. When she was close enough to identify it, she stopped.

"Topaz," she said (though she used their word, which I don't recall). "Is it the stone or a spell?"

"Both," Fenwick said.

The group talked among themselves. As we stood there, more people came outside and drifted over to the group. The discussion was not an argument, and all of them had something to say. Finally, the woman turned to us.

"What do you want?"

"Food would be welcome," Fenwick answered. "Information will help, on how far of a journey it is to Malan or Nitis in Vanda, and what towns lie ahead of us."

"Will you give us your bulla if we help you?"

"No," Fenwick said firmly.

He then explained how he was enthralled by the mage while I was not, and that he was wearing it now to prevent being recaptured. The ward would only protect one person regardless. The disappointment on their faces was clear. It did not cheer them when Fenwick told them we had money to pay for food.

"How do we protect ourselves from the mage?" the woman pleaded.

"If you know of a witch—a magic user—with skill against the Dark Arts, they might be able to make a bulla for you," Fenwick said.

That started another vigorous discussion among the group, which had grown to nearly twenty people by now. It seemed to me that they knew of at least one witch nearby and possibly another further away. Suddenly, they remembered we were there.

"We will give you some bread," the woman said, "but then we want you to leave. If someone comes for you, it would be best for us if you were gone."

"How far to the next village?" Fenwick asked.

"About four leagues," a man answered. "The further east you travel, the more distance between the villages. When you reach the mountains, you will have a two-day ride from the town on this side to the one on the Vanda side."

"How many days to the mountains?"

"On horseback? Five," he said.

A man brought us some bread. He refused to accept payment for it. The group waited for us to leave. Fenwick climbed back in the saddle, and we set off. The people stayed where they were, watching us go.

It was nearing midday when Fenwick commented, "Dust cloud behind us."

"Damn," I muttered. "Well, that answers one question."

"Which one?"

"Whether the mage converted some of the thralls into committed followers," I said. "I wonder what sort of hold the mage maintains over them at this distance?"

"The better question is whether we want to make it easier for them to catch us or more difficult," Fenwick suggested.

"If we were closer to the mountains, I would argue in favor of making it harder for them, with the hope we might lose them. Since the mountains are still days away, I would prefer to get this over with," I replied with a sardonic grin.

"I hope they're not our men," Fenwick commented.

"That's an awful thought," I agreed.

We waited as the group approached. When they drew closer, we could see there were six of them. Thankfully, they were wearing uniforms we did not recognize. They approached at a trot.

"That's close enough," Fenwick warned them in their language when they trotted to within forty yards of us. "What do you want?"

"You must come with us," one said.

"No."

They continued to approach, though at a walk. I looked to see if I could spot the red luster in the depth of their eyes. Though I could not be certain, it did not appear to be present. To me, that meant the mage was not exercising direct control over them. Still, the mage convinced them to serve him, either by threats of punishment or promises of rewards.

"You must come with us, or your men will suffer," he said.

"They are already suffering, I'm sure," Fenwick replied.

The group continued drawing closer and were now only fifteen yards away. Fenwick gave me a meaningful look. I nodded my agreement. We drew our swords. Reaching within myself, I summoned my connection to Bellona and threw it open.

As before, Andy and I instantly seemed to increase to a menacing size. Beside me, I saw Fenwick and Davy do the same. Bellona's power sang in my veins. With a gentle squeeze of my knees, Andy sprang toward the men. They had just freed their blades when we came upon them.

It is difficult for me to describe what it is like to be manifesting the Goddess of War. Time seemed to slow in almost every aspect except my movement and reactions. Those were quicker than I could ever achieve on my own. My blade moved as swiftly as thought and observation—like a reflex reaction but with no wasted motion and with uncanny accuracy.

In seconds, all six of them were dead or dying. I tamped down my link to the Goddess, then touched the tan-zyan stone in my ring to the diamond in the pommel of my sword to restore the asomatous energy I used. Before sheathing my sword, I leaned down and wiped the blood from both sides on the uniform of one of my fallen foes.

As I was closing my connection to Bellona, I felt a strange sense of satisfaction. That struck me as odd since I took no pleasure in killing these men. My mind gnawed on it for a few minutes.

"Fenwick, did you feel anything unusual just now?" I asked as we began to head east again.

"Unusual in what way?"

"A sense of approval for what we just did?"

"Well, yes, but it's not unusual," he replied.

Seeing the troubled look on my face, he quickly added, "I don't take my pleasure from killing people, Caz. That's not what I'm saying. It's the Goddess. She seems to like it when I use her power efficiently and rightly. Haven't you ever felt that before?"

"I have—a handful of times," I admitted after thinking back on other incidents.

"For instance," he continued, "your sword belt—I gave it to you, and it makes me happy to see you wear it. I think Bellona is just like us in that respect. She granted us this ability, and it probably pleases her when we use it appropriately."

"I wonder what we would feel if we ever used her power for the wrong reasons?"

"She has let me know when she is displeased," Fenwick said.

"When?" I inquired, thinking back to Fenwick's previous career as a paid assassin.

"The times I fought you," he said. "After our first two encounters, I felt she was displeased with me. I've told you before that I never felt any reluctance to dispose of any of my targets until you."

"Your reluctance didn't stop you from trying," I remarked.

"No, it didn't," he admitted, "but the Goddess did not approve. I sensed her disappointment."

"What about the time you attacked me when you were under the mage's control in Dunland?"

"All my senses were so jumbled when I recovered that I could not tell you what she may have tried to communicate to me," Fenwick explained. "I was not acting of my own will. I would like to think she understood that and forgave me."

We collected the horses. Using their reins and the rope I had, we arranged them in a string to follow us. It was not long after that when my vision was suddenly taken over. I saw the city of Aquileia from the air. It was later in the day there than it was where Fenwick and I were. Within myself, I found the mote that was Shasha and touched it with my mind.

Hello, Caz. I sense the owl now. What would you like me to share?

For those of you who do not remember, Shasha was able to communicate with Chauncey, the owl who is Lucy's familiar. They share thoughts, not words. From earlier experience, I learned that I could provide visual images to Shasha that could, through Chauncey, be revealed to Lucy.

First, I thought of the map of the southern continent, centered on Hier. Then, I remembered the sight of Major Grunevald and the red glow behind his eyes. I sent an image of the red in Fenwick's gaze that I saw before touching him with the ward. After that, I shared my current view from Andy's back—of Fenwick and I riding. Finally, I returned to the map, focusing on the location of Vanda.

"Please have the owl share those with Lucy."

The owl is unhappy with me. He was sleeping.

"This is more important to his mistress than his sleep. Then, the owl can show you where we live now. You should find plenty of hunting."

The people in the next town were just as distrustful as in the previous village. When Fenwick told them we left six bodies behind us on the road, their expressions grew fearful. We tried to reassure them but were not too successful. We gave them the horses and asked them to bury the bodies. They agreed on the condition that we leave immediately.

My vision changed suddenly, showing me a view from what I guessed was the top of the castle in Aquileia. Shasha was perched on one of the roof peaks. I touched her mote with my mind.

Your mate sends these.

Shasha shared an image of a ship under sail, and then of a map of Vanda. From this, I reckoned that Lucy would be sending a ship to Vanda to collect us. Whether she would be on the ship was not indicated. I would need to wait and see.

"Thank you."

I like this place. Hunting is absurdly easy. And there is a male nearby. That excites me.

"Really?" I thought back to her with a smile capturing my face. "Will you mate?"

I am not opposed.

"Well, good luck. And thank you for helping me."

How could I not? With that, she broke the connection.

In the villages we passed that day, the welcome was just as cool as before. As we traveled further from the capital, fearfulness began to give way to curiosity. Everyone kept his distance from us, though, and they were clearly relieved when we departed.

No other riders came after us in the following days. We were hit by occasional passing thunderstorms. As we drew closer to the mountains, the villages were smaller, and the distance between them longer.

The last village before we entered the mountains was almost friendly. They sold us some jerky, dried fruit, bread, and animal feed to last us until we reached the first settlement in Vanda. Though the prices they charged us were exorbitant, I did not complain. It did make Fenwick unhappy, though, and gave him something to grouse about for a day.

The road gave way to a trail after that last village. We started to climb. We reached the pass after a full day of riding. I will admit the cool air of the mountains was refreshing after the unrelenting heat we had been experiencing.

The first village we reached in Vanda was powerfully interested in us. We were the first visitors to cross from Hier in weeks, when normally there would be regular travel over the mountains during the summer. Our appearance also spurred questions. By now, the fine clothes we were wearing were much worse for the wear. They were never meant for the type of hard use to which we put them. Fenwick and I both were more than slightly bedraggled.

The warm welcome we received cooled rather sharply when we told them what was causing the trouble in Hier. I had been hoping to spend the night at the inn in the village. It was clear from the townspeople that they preferred for Fenwick and me to keep moving. They did allow us to eat a hot meal and buy some more supplies.

It took us five more days to reach Malan. We lost almost an entire day when Davy threw a shoe. Fortunately, there was a farrier in the nearest village. Rather than leave things to chance, I decided Andy should probably be reshod. The farrier was quite competent, but he did not work quickly.

When we reached the city in the afternoon, we went immediately to the harbor. Fenwick and I were both cheered to see a small, sleek ship flying the pennant of Traval & Company. I hoped it had brought Lucy, so we went to find out.

"Aye, the princess is here, Your Highness, along with a half-dozen of the Shield," the sailing master told us. "Miss Traval—er, Madam Fenwick—er, Lady Easton—came as well. We arrived on the morning tide. They are staying at an inn. I don't know which one, sorry to say."

"Since you gave us such good news, I'll forgive you for not knowing which inn," I said. "They should not be too difficult to find. Thank you."

"Indeed," Fenwick said to me as we departed, "there are only two establishments where I would want them to stay, and both are closer to the center of the city than the docks. None of the inns close by are—acceptable."

"I can only hope they allow us through the doors, looking the way we do," I cracked.

"Then I suppose we must rely on your regal bearing, Your Highness," Fenwick retorted.

"In that case, we might as well implore a passer-by to inquire for us," I said, laughing.

The ladies were in the second of the two inns to which Fenwick took us. As I predicted, after seeing our unshaven and disheveled appearance and our tattered clothing, the doorkeeper asked us to wait outside while he sent someone to call upon his guests. A few minutes later, Sergeant McClellan appeared.

"Majors and Minors!" he gasped, then quickly caught himself. "Begging your pardon, Your Highness, milord. It's just—you two are filthy."

"We know, sar'nt," I replied.

15

I nside the door, I could hear Lucy instructing the innkeeper to have baths prepared for the two of us. The doorman tried to apologize for making us wait outside, but Lucy forgave him before he could finish. She then appeared in the doorway.

"Hold right there," she said imperiously.

Though I longed to embrace her, I froze in my tracks. Her tone was deadly serious. She approached Fenwick, holding up her hand to indicate he should not move.

"You are wearing the ward?" she asked.

Fenwick showed her, holding the topaz with two fingers. He was preparing to take it off. Lucy shook her head.

She began reciting something using an archaic version of Aquileian. When she finished, she repeated it twice more. After the third recitation, I saw something change on Fenwick's face—as though he were more relaxed.

"You can take the ward off now," she said.

Lucy then addressed me and repeated the incantation three times. I felt nothing. When she finished, she sighed in relief.

"What just happened?" Fenwick asked.

"We will talk upstairs," Lucy cautioned. "Not here. Don't come any closer, Caz. You'll ruin my dress, and you smell like sour sweat and Andy."

"You know these men, Your Highness?" the innkeeper asked when we came through the front door.

"Indeed I do, Mr. Tomai," she responded with humor. "This is my husband, Prince Casimir, and the other gentleman is Lord Easton."

"I beg your pardon, Your Highness," Tomai said to me, bowing deeply. "I had no idea—"

"All is forgiven, Mr. Tomai—or will be once we have enjoyed the chance to clean up," I said. "We are aware we look like vagabonds."

We trooped upstairs, following Lucy, with the sergeant bringing up the rear. Another member of the Castle Shield was waiting at the landing of the top floor. A third man was stationed outside the room where Lucy took us.

Julienne was waiting inside the parlor of what seemed like a flat of rooms. She rose when the door opened and moved toward Fenwick, only to stop after two steps. Her nose wrinkled up as she caught the smell of us.

"I've ordered baths for them," Lucy explained.

"We need to open the windows," Julienne said as she crossed out of the room to do just that.

"What happened to me downstairs?" Fenwick asked. "You recited that phrase three times, and after the third time, I felt different."

"Lily taught me that incantation," Lucy explained. "She figured this mage would be more skilled than the one we encountered in Dunland. From what she has read, a mage skilled in the Dark Arts cannot only enthrall subjects but also establish a lasting connection that yokes you to him. The mage in Dunland did not know how to do that."

"That explains how you fell back under his power when you woke," I said.

"It doesn't explain why the mage did not claim me again after we traveled a certain distance from the city," Fenwick said. "Does distance play a part?"

"According to Lily, it does not," Lucy said, "but I need to know more about what happened."

I told the story of our misadventure so far. Lucy and Julienne listened attentively. Just as I was about to finish, there was a knock at the door. Maids were there with buckets of steaming water for baths. We allowed them in, and they filled a tub in an attached lavatory.

"The only explanation I can provide for why the mage did not regain control over you, Fenwick, is that he or she must have been focused on something else when you became lucid," Lucy explained. "And by the time he turned his mind back to you, you were wearing the ward, preventing contact."

"The ward broke the connection but did not dispel the bond?" I asked.

"Correct," Lucy stated. "If Fenwick took the ward off before I severed the mage's hold on him, he could have been recaptured—even here. Enough of this for now. We need to get you two cleaned up."

Lucy took me across the hall, explaining that this was her set of rooms. The one we were in first was Julienne's. Waiting for me was a bath. After riding for more than a week in the summer heat of the southern continent, I knew how awfully I smelled.

Lucy waited for me to finish outside. When she heard me stand up and step out of the bath, she entered. Stopping me in the midst of toweling myself dry, she enfolded me in a tight embrace.

"That's what I was hoping for," I sighed, my nose in her hair.

After a minute or two, Lucy stepped back. She pointed to the razor and shaving soap that were there for me. After I scraped the beard from my face, she directed me to the bedroom, where fresh clothes were laid out for me.

"I brought some of your clothes. When you and Fenwick are dressed, we need to talk some more," she said. "I simply couldn't bear to continue with both of you reeking so much."

"I knew it was bad," I admitted, "but one's nose grows accustomed."

Just as I was finished dressing, there was a rap on the door. Lucy opened it, and Julienne and Fenwick entered. They all sat down and I joined them.

"The king has sent messengers to Scaramouche, Garo, and Mooresa," Julienne said. "A member of our group is on the way to Nitis right now with a message for the king of Vanda."

"Mark has suggested that all of them come to Malan for a meeting to decide what to do about Hier," Lucy added. "He would like Aquileia's involvement in this crisis to be limited—extremely limited."

"So, the queen will not come," I said.

"She will not," Lucy confirmed, "and Mark would prefer it if you and Fenwick departed after sharing what you know."

"But we left a hundred and twenty men of the Castle Shield behind," I protested, "not to mention three of Traval's ships and their crews."

"I said Mark would prefer it if you returned home," Lucy reiterated. "He did not order it. The king realizes that it might be diplomatically impossible for you to extricate yourselves, but he urges you to make a strong attempt. This is not Aquileia's problem as much as it is Hier's neighbors."

"The king has offered to compensate us if the ships are irretrievable," Julienne added.

"What other resources can we expect?" Fenwick asked.

"None," Julienne stated. "As a matter of fact, Lucy is to return home with me tomorrow, now that you are here."

Fenwick and I shared a meaningful look.

"That reminds me," Lucy said.

She went into the bedroom. When she returned, she was holding a topaz ward in her hand. She gave it to Fenwick.

"Lily created this for you," Lucy said. "Where is your other one?"

"On the ship, in my trunk," he said.

Julienne shook her head and tsked him.

"Has Lily prepared anything else for us if we stay to fight this mage?" I asked.

"There's nothing more you or Fenwick could learn unless you spent years of study," Lucy said. "The wards are as good as anything. As far as neutralizing the mage, she wrote letters that are being delivered to the different rulers. They will need to kill him or her. That will leave all the thralls stupefied. They will need to assemble a group of priests of the Three Major Gods to break them free. The priests will know what to do."

"Will the soldiers be protected with wards like ours?" Fenwick asked.

"Not like the type we have," Lucy said. "There are non-physical wards the priests of the Three Major Gods can create to protect the soldiers, but they only last from sunup to sundown."

"After sundown?" I inquired.

"They need to reach the mage before sundown," Lucy said firmly in response.

"Why can't they create wards like ours?" Fenwick asked.

"They could if they have a person like Lily, whose dominant is Ceridwen Sospita, and he or she knows the proper spells. The amount of topaz available and the cost of it would be prohibitive, though," Lucy said. "I don't know how many soldiers it will take to reach the mage and kill him, but imagine it will be hundreds. Remember, they won't only be fighting Hier's soldiers. Every person in that city will be an enemy as long as the mage controls their thoughts and actions."

"And here I thought becoming a pirate admiral would be difficult," I commented.

"The king wrote letters for both of you that I have not given you yet," Lucy said. "I imagine he will urge you to return to Aquileia if what he wrote is similar to our discussions."

"Let us read them," Fenwick suggested.

Lucy went to the other room and brought them back. They looked identical—heavy cream paper, embossed in wax with the king's seal. She handed them to us.

> Caz—
>
> By now, Lucy will have told you my wish that you return to Aquileia as soon as is fitting. You know my unease concerning the supernatural. Where the Dark Arts are concerned, that anxiety increases almost to the point of physical discomfort. Once you have shared the nature of the problem in Hier with the rulers of the countries you have visited recently, I urge you to conclude your part in this sad business and depart.
>
> That said, I know you well enough by now to understand that you would leave reluctantly, if at all. Your competitive fire is part of your nature, as is your reluctance to leave a job unfinished. It also may happen also that the other rulers put you in a position where it will be difficult to refuse a call to arms.
>
> All I ask is that you make your decision after careful consideration. Should you decide to stay to see this through, I will support your choice. If that is the case, take the greatest care possible so you can return safely to Lucy, Lily, and me.
>
> —Mark

I finished reading my letter at the same time Fenwick finished reading his. We looked at one another. Fenwick then held his letter out for me to read. I gave mine to him.

Lord Easton—

In my letter to Caz, I urge him to return to Aquileia after you communicate the situation in Hier to the rulers upon whom you called recently. Provide him with good counsel. Help him make the decision that is best for Aquileia.

If, after careful and thoughtful reflection, the two of you decide to remain on the southern continent and assist the other rulers, I charge you with the duty to protect him to the utmost of your ability. In the event he decides to return, I expect you to accompany him. Under no circumstances should one of you remain without the other.

Should the two of you reach the conclusion that Aquileia's needs are best met by taking part in the clash to come, I will support your choice. Take the greatest care possible so you both return safely.

—Mark

When I finished reading, I handed Fenwick's letter to Julienne. Fenwick handed mine to Lucy. When they finished reading them, they traded.

"Your thoughts?" Lucy asked us.

"There are only a very few things in the world that frighten me," Fenwick said after I nodded for him to speak first. "The Dark Arts top the list. What happened to me in Dunland, and then again upon landing in Iradiem, proves to me I have good reason to fear. I lost control of my thoughts and actions without even knowing I was in danger. From a purely selfish point of view, I would join you on the ship for Aquileia when you sail tomorrow."

"But you won't, will you?" Julienne retorted.

"Blame Caz," Fenwick said. "He reminded me that I can no longer act with only my self-interest to guide my choices. I am no longer Fenwick the orphan, whose only duty was to himself. You are in my life, Julienne, and I need to consider your needs and desires. I am also Lord Easton now and responsible for the continued prosperity of the Eastern March. Finally, I am a trusted advisor to the crown prince and must weigh the needs of the realm when giving him advice. The king expects us to wait here to share what we learned with the leaders of the countries that have the most to fear from Hier. So, wait we must."

"And then?" Julienne asked.

"Well, I think His Majesty identified the possible obstacle that might prevent our swift return," Fenwick said. "There is a possibility that our leaving could damage Aquileia's standing with these countries. The reason is that Caz and I both admitted to possessing supernatural abilities. I know if I were the grand vizier of Scaramouche or the bashaw of Mooresa, I would employ every bit of leverage to make sure these 'warrior-mages' stayed."

"Caz?" Lucy inquired.

"Fenwick and I are of like mind," I said. "The Dark Arts scare me, and my experiences were with a young woman who was possessed by a spell book, and a mage with little training. It is possible, perhaps even probable, that the mage we will face in Iradiem is more skilled than the one in Dunland and more powerful than Esme was in Eatonford. But Mark has asked us to stay to meet with these rulers, so we must. They will want us to stay. My preference is to return home. That might not be the best solution for Aquileia, but I will endeavor to make it so. Besides, neither of us have our breastplates or helmets."

"We brought them," Lucy said quietly, "at the king's suggestion. He insisted on having the soldiers polish them before we packed them. At first, Mark was distressed that your armor was dinged and dented, even pierced and repaired in a couple of spots. His first thought, he told me, was that neither set of armor was grand enough for either of you. He changed his mind quickly, though, saying that the blemishes are signs of honorable use by real fighting men."

"I would hope so," Fenwick retorted, "since some of those dents came when we stood over him and protected him from the Rhetians."

"He did make mention of that," Lucy replied with a smile.

No sooner did Lucy say this when my stomach gurgled loudly.

"I believe His Highness is trying to tell us we should see about dinner," Julienne quipped.

Her comment drew a chuckle from all of us. We stood and headed downstairs. With Fenwick and I wearing fresh clothes and clean-shaven, the innkeeper fawned over us, bowing and scraping for us all the way to the dining room.

The meal was quite good. Fenwick and I directed the conversation away from our recent escape, speaking instead of our previous visits and sharing our impressions of the different rulers we met. I then asked what was happening at home.

"Martin Albrecht has bought the controlling interest in Coombs, as we suspected he would," Julienne said. "Ratty Hawkins is now the second-in-command at Hawkins."

"How did that happen?" I asked.

"Almost exactly as we predicted," Julienne laughed. "Ratty received a letter from Albrecht, offering him a job at a substantial increase in pay and the opportunity to earn a share of ownership. He left the letter on top of his desk when he left at the end of the day. His father happened to see it and was livid."

"Did Mr. Hawkins see the errors of his ways?" I asked.

"Not at first," Julienne said. "His immediate reaction was to screech at Ratty for communicating with Albrecht. Ratty, praise all the heavenly beings, stood up for himself. He pointed out that Albrecht contacted him, not the other way around. Ratty also scolded his father for ignoring him when he advised him about the potential of the Port Charles project and then about the opportunity to buy Coombs out. He then demanded that his father quit stalling the discussions with Inger's parents, threatening to elope with her. The next day, Ben Sr. announced some changes—Ben Jr. was now the head clerk, and Ratty was now second only to his father in the company. And Ratty and Inger just announced their betrothal."

"Good for you, Ratty," I laughed.

It was heavenly to spend the night in Lucy's arms. Being close to her always reaffirmed my confidence and restored my heart. Saying goodbye to her the next day was difficult. I planned to see her again soon. When I started to tell her that I decided I would be returning home as soon as Fenwick and I met with the rulers, she put her finger on my lips to stop me.

"Don't make promises, my love," she whispered. "You forget—I know your heart."

With that, she turned and headed up the gangway and onto the ship. Fenwick and I stood on the pier and watched as Lucy and Julienne sailed away. When the ship reached the harbor mouth, we turned and walked back to the inn.

16

Eight days after Lucy departed, the grand vizier of Scaramouche was the last to arrive. He disembarked from his ornately decorated ship with great pomp. The king and queen of Vanda met him at the waterfront. Their winter palace was nearby, and already they were providing lodging for the emir of Garo and the bashaw of Mooresa, along with their retinues. The grand vizier and his people would stay there as well.

Soldiers from all three countries were on the way, traveling overland. From what they told us, Garo and Mooresa each came with five hundred men, all mounted. Eight hundred horsemen were coming from Scaramouche. They were expected in a day or two. The king of Vanda committed seven hundred—the bulk of his army. That made sense since his realm neighbored Hier.

Fenwick and I retained our rooms at the inn. We were of like mind—to say our piece and depart. Julienne shared schedules with us before she left. A Traval ship was due to arrive in Malan sometime in the next two or three days, and we planned to sail back on her.

If we stayed in the palace with the other rulers, they would be able to badger us to try to get us to stay. I couldn't blame them. If situations were reversed, I would probably do the same. Fenwick and I wished to avoid that pressure.

Just after the grand vizier and his party left the waterfront, a message was left for us. The note invited us to a meeting at nine o'clock the next morning. This was no surprise.

Eleven days later, Fenwick and I were riding in the main, accompanying the four rulers we visited earlier on this trip. With the baggage train, our column stretched over a mile in length. Our army left the mountains separating Hier from Vanda five days before. We would spend the night camped outside the closest village to the capital and attempt to enter the city the next day.

Fenwick's and my resolve to return home crumbled when all four of them, led by the grand vizier, announced that they intended to lead their soldiers into battle personally. Fenwick and I discussed the situation thoroughly before agreeing to stay and help them.

"His Majesty suspected they would make it as awkward as possible for us to leave," Fenwick stated in one of our final exchanges about it.

"He did," I agreed. "And since the only one of the four who seems like an experienced soldier is the king of Vanda, the risk to which they are exposing themselves is even greater. It would be a different matter if I felt they were doing this as a lark, with no conception of the danger, but we made sure they were well aware of the substantial risks."

"The only one who displayed any sign of uneasiness was the emir," Fenwick added.

"Now that his troops have arrived, he seems much more at ease," I remarked.

"I think that is because he feared one of his rivals would take advantage of his absence," Fenwick said.

"Was it because they arrived or because the person who troubles him is with the soldiers?" I asked.

"Both, I think," Fenwick said with a smirk.

"If I thought they were merely playing at being soldiers, it would not trouble my conscience to leave," I said. "But I don't feel that is what they are doing."

"I agree. They all know the severity of the danger," Fenwick said, "and the risk to themselves. Yet, there was no hesitation in any of them. It is not arrogant stupidity. They seem to be responding soberly to a grave threat."

"I dread returning to Iradiem," I said, "but I feel it is in Aquiliea's best interest for us to do so. If these inexperienced men are willing to commit themselves to this hazardous undertaking, our departure would damage relations between their countries and Aquileia—whether or not they survive."

"Will our participation enhance their ties to Aquileia?" Fenwick asked.

"I suppose that depends on what happens," I said.

So, with no way to exit either diplomatically or gracefully, Fenwick and I agreed to accompany them. In searching through the clothes Lucy packed in the trunk, I was unsurprised to find she had prepared for this possibility. In addition to a selection of my finer clothing, she included some of my more rough-and-ready shirts and breeches, along with sturdier boots and a quilted vest to wear under my breastplate. There was also a small selection of glass bottles, each clearly labeled as to its use. Fenwick told me that Julienne had packed some of his more durable clothing as well. Fenwick and I took what would be useful and fit in our saddlebags and made arrangements for the trunks to be handed over to the next Traval ship.

The rulers were genuinely pleased when we informed them that we would accompany them to Hier. I did not detect any trace of smugness from them. Indeed, Fenwick and I had, for the most part, avoided their attempts to manipulate our feelings.

The reception we received from the towns we passed was markedly different from when Fenwick and I passed through the first time. Then, we were delivering bad tidings. Now, with an army accompanying us, we came bringing hope of deliverance.

In addition to the rulers and their armies, our number also included twelve priests of the Three Major Gods—three from each of the countries on the southern continent who were participating. The priests would be essential. Before we left camp the following morning, they would recite the incantations that would provide all who heard them with protection against the mage controlling the city and its residents.

If we were successful in reaching the mage and killing him or her, the priests would be the only means by which the people could be freed from the mage's control. None of the priests possessed any experience in confronting the Dark Arts. They knew the proper wording of the invocations to the Three Major Gods, but only because they were written in the weighty tomes they brought along.

The sound of bugles woke us at first light, as it had every day since we departed from Malan. Breakfast was being prepared. Before we attended to that, the groups from each country were assembled. The priests of the Three Major Gods recited an incantation in their own languages. These chants would, we hoped, protect the soldiers from falling under the mage's power until sunset.

When the priests finished, everyone ate. We did not break camp since we planned to return that evening. At the sound of another bugle call, we mounted up and began to assemble in formation. Fenwick and I rode in a small group with the rulers.

"Where do you think we will find the mage?" the grand vizier asked, sidling next to me as we rode.

"One of two places," I replied. "He or she may have taken over the sovereign's palace. I would imagine that is where he sleeps and eats. It is possible that we will find him in a temple of the Three Major Gods, though."

"Why would he be there?" Fenwick asked.

"A mage of the Dark Arts serves the Lord of the Seven Hells. The Three Major Gods cast the Dark Lord down when they observed the evil within him. Because of that, desecrating a temple of the Three Major Gods by having his servant use it as his base of operations would be most pleasing to the Lord of the Seven Hells."

"How do you know this?" the bashaw of Mooresa asked after Fenwick translated, having joined our discussion.

"My wife," I said.

"Princess Lucille is a powerful and learned witch," Fenwick responded.

"A warrior-mage and a witch as the next rulers of Aquileia," the emir commented. "A formidable combination, I think. Who is her primary?"

"Freyja," Fenwick replied, "with her lessers being Eir and Njörun."

"And your wife?" the king of Vanda asked Fenwick.

"My wife has no supernatural ability. She is, however, the daughter of Herbert Traval, and is currently managing a large part of the business," Fenwick answered.

It was interesting observing the reactions of the four rulers. They knew a little about magic but much more about trade. The name of Traval & Company was one with which they were quite familiar. It turned the conversation away from the mystical to the pragmatic immediately.

It was only mid-morning when the walls of Iradiem came into view. Though the wall surrounding the city was thick and tall, when Fenwick and I left the city, I observed that the gates were relatively flimsy. When the original wooden gates fell into disrepair, they must not have replaced them with barriers of the same stoutness as before.

In our baggage train was a ram. With one or two blows from it, I imagined we would force our entrance into the city. Once past the walls, we hoped to find the mage quickly and kill him. The longer it took to find him, the more casualties we would take.

"I am worried that our plan lacks subtlety," I complained to Fenwick.

"Our options are limited," he said with a shrug. "If we had more time to work with, I'm sure we could try something more crafty. We don't. The wards protecting the soldiers give us a little more than ten hours after we reach the gate, but we actually have less time than that. By mid-afternoon, we will need to make a decision on whether to withdraw. If we can't find and kill the mage by then, we need to get everyone far enough away that the mage cannot enthrall them."

"Still, even someone unskilled in warfare would be ready for a frontal assault like this," I said.

"I don't think getting into the city will be our biggest challenge," Fenwick replied calmly. "It's what happens after that worries me. The soldiers need to travel a fair distance through narrow streets to reach the palace. We will lose more than a few along the way. The palace itself will be defended. It's similar to the royal castle in Aquileia—it was the original defense for the first settlement here, built by the old empire. Breaking into it will be more difficult, especially in a timely manner."

When we reached the city walls, the column paused while the ram was brought up. We could see the parapet atop the wall lined with archers. Engineers quickly assembled the protective shell that would offer some overhead protection to the men wielding the ram. Sheets of tin mounted on a frame of poles with wicker sidewalls made a portable shelter that should stop most of the arrows from reaching the soldiers.

It took only minutes to attach the pieces together. Forty soldiers, twenty on each side, grasped the rope handles fastened to the large log that was the ram. Another twenty men supported the protective shell. As they drew within range, the archers began to fire.

The men carrying the ram began to jog toward the wall. They did not stop until they crashed into the gate. I expected the entrance to fly open when it was hit.

It did not. The impact of the ram striking the gate gave off a solid thud, but the gate did not move at all. It was as though the wooden doors were ten times thicker than I knew them to be. The men pulled the ram back a few feet and tried again, with the same lack of result.

"Bring them back!" I shouted after the third attempt.

"What do you think the problem is?" Fenwick asked.

"There are no heavy beams in that gate," I said, "only planks. It must be magically reinforced in some way. We need to try something else."

"What are you thinking?" Fenwick inquired.

"Fire," I said.

Fenwick nodded in agreement, then began telling the different rulers what he wanted. They, in turn, gave orders to their subordinates. In minutes, large pots of oil were hustled forward.

"We will need to put the shell right up to the gate to prevent them from trying to douse the fire," I cautioned. "We should also have archers brought forward to make that dangerous and difficult for those on the parapet."

Fenwick again relayed my instructions, and a group of archers moved forward. The shell moved toward the gate again, but the ram was left behind. Instead, ten men were carrying large clay pots of oil. When the shell was touching the gate, each of the men stepped forward and smashed his pot against it. One of them struck a flint and lit a torch, which he used to light the oil.

Seeing the smoke begin to rise, men above the gate tried to pour buckets of water and sand down to put the fire out. The tin roof interfered enough with these efforts that the fire continued to gain a purchase on the wood. Our archers approached closer and began hitting others atop the wall who tried to put out the fire.

We watched as the gates were engulfed in flame. When it grew too hot for anyone to try to pour water on the blaze from above, we ordered our men to bring the shell back. A fresh group of soldiers hoisted the ram and charged the gates. This time, there was a splintering crash. Our men withdrew the ram from the hole it made, then sent it forward again. This blow burst the gate open.

Three of our men fell to arrows launched from inside. The men carrying the shell allowed the last section of the tin roof to drop to serve as protection for the rest as they ran back to us. A dozen more were wounded, with arrows protruding from their bodies, and their progress was a slower stagger.

Once they were out of the way, the bugle sounded and our horsemen, led by a contingent from Vanda, charged forward. I reached within myself and opened my link to Bellona slightly. Fenwick and I waited only briefly before joining those riding into the city. As soon as we passed through the gate, we encountered another problem. Something had stopped the forward progress.

We overheard someone in front of us call, "Barricades!"

Using my connection with Bellona, I tried to extend my senses. It made perfect sense to me that they would erect obstacles against us on the most direct path. I was trying to "feel" if there was an unencumbered route.

Fenwick must have been doing the same thing. At almost the same instant, we knew that we must head to the left. He caught my eye. When he saw my look of understanding that mirrored his own, he grinned.

"To the left!" he called to the soldiers stacking up behind us as he wheeled Davy in that direction.

He and I were now leading the group who were not pressed forward against the barricade. Arrows started to fly from defenders still on the walls and from soldiers posted in the windows of the buildings along the street. Suddenly, the grand vizier, resplendent in gleaming armor, overtook us, calling to Fenwick as he did.

"He said he wants to give them a better target than the two of us," Fenwick relayed.

A group of cavalry from Scaramouche came charging after their ruler, with occasional sparks flying as their horseshoes struck the cobblestone pavement. As they neared him, they began to raise an eerie, ululating battle cry. It made my hair stand on end. I was glad they were on our side.

Unfortunately, the grand vizier had no idea where he was going. I didn't either, but Bellona gave my mind a nudge as we approached an intersection. Turning to the right seemed to be the correct direction. Fenwick felt it, too, and we turned together, leaving the Scaramangans to rush headlong on their way.

Glancing back over my shoulder, it seemed as though the bulk of our force was following the two of us. Just behind us was the bashaw of Mooresa, his face stretched in a grin. The emir of Garo came close after.

Bellona guided us as we galloped through the city. We would travel through three or four intersections, and then she would let us know to turn. Our course was an irregular zig-zag. I did notice, though, that we were climbing steadily.

Suddenly, a wall of flame appeared, unbroken from one side of the street to the other. I did not need to rein in. Andy stopped of his own accord. Fenwick and Davy did the same next to us. Yet the mental nudge from Bellona urged me to continue.

I gave Fenwick a puzzled look. He held up one finger, telling me to wait. Then he leaned forward and said something to his horse. When he finished, he and Davy took off, heading straight into the blanket of fire. A minute later, he and Davy reappeared.

"It's an apparition," he said with a grin. "No heat."

As Fenwick was sharing this information with those behind us, I said to my horse, "Andy, there is nothing to fear. If Davy can make it through and back, surely you can do the same. After all, Davy isn't half the horse you are."

Andy nodded his head as though he agreed with me. When I pressed my knees only slightly, he surged forward toward the flames. As we reached them, Andy and I both realized Fenwick was correct. There was no heat.

Not all of the horses were as brave or as trusting as Andy and Davy. I could hear most of them refusing to advance. Only a few came through and joined us—less than a hundred.

"Find an officer," I shouted back to Fenwick, "and tell him to find another way to the palace. They will probably need to backtrack in order to find a clear path."

A few minutes later, Fenwick and Davy crossed the flame barrier again. My sense told me to continue forward. We set off again, hopefully drawing nearer to the palace.

17

We encountered three more walls of flame. At each one, fewer of the horsemen accompanying us were able to convince their mounts to pass through. By the time we could see the palace, there were only fourteen men still riding with Fenwick and me.

As Fenwick described, the palace was clearly built for defense. A moat surrounded the high walls. The drawbridge that crossed the moat was raised, preventing access. The area outside the moat was sculpted into magnificent gardens, cleared in all directions.

"Now what?" I asked Fenwick when we stopped to examine the approach.

"I don't think enough of the others will make it through," Fenwick said, shaking his head. "Certainly not in the numbers we would need to force entrance."

"Not to mention the moat and the drawbridge," I said.

"I don't remember a moat from my previous visits to Iradiem," Fenwick said. "We are too far away for me to be sure, but I suspect it is another illusion."

"Then let's go closer," I suggested.

Fenwick told the soldiers with us to wait where they were. He and I rode nearer to the palace. I tried to extend my senses in the direction of the entrance, hoping Bellona could give me some indication of how to proceed. As we approached, some of the defenders atop the walls began to fire bolts at us from skorpios. We stopped outside their range.

As we studied how we might gain access, I began to feel that we should not make the attempt. I looked at Fenwick to see if he was getting the same impression. From the sour expression on his face, he was.

"I don't think we will be able to force our way in," I said.

"Agreed," Fenwick grunted. "What I am wondering, though, is whether that feeling is generated by the Goddess or the mage."

I opened my connection to Bellona more widely to see if that would change my feelings. Shortly after I did this, I became convinced that the moat was indeed an illusion. The sense of wrongness about trying to force our way in persisted without diminishing. I was also reassured that our target was within the walls.

"I think Bellona is trying to warn us not to try the direct route," I said after tamping down my link to its previous level.

"I concur. The question is: why?" Fenwick stated.

For the first time since we rode into the city, I remembered the king's strong wish that I not take unnecessary risks. I felt guilty, realizing I had been too caught up in the excitement. My emotions showed on my face.

"You're troubled," Fenwick remarked.

"Yes. Feeling as though I am not heeding Mark's wishes," I admitted.

"It hasn't been too dangerous—so far," Fenwick commented.

"Still, even an inexpertly fired arrow can kill," I said. "Are we doing the right thing?"

"There are different ways to answer that question," Fenwick said after he thought for a few moments. "The readiness of the rulers to ride put us into the situation, and we could not extract ourselves gracefully. That's one aspect of it. Another is that our ability and experience brought us closer than they have reached, though I do not feel at all like they abandoned us."

"True. I think they would be here if they could have managed it," I said.

"Now, we are within sight of our objective. It's frustrating because we seem to be stymied. I hate leaving a task unfinished. Besides, should we succeed, all four of them, plus the king of Hier—if he survives—will owe Aquileia a huge debt of gratitude. I'm not ready to give up yet."

These thoughts forced me to retreat mentally and regather my wits. I wasn't willing to call it quits, either. Bellona would not have brought us here if there had not been some way into the palace.

"It would be the height of folly to charge within range of the skorpios," I said after a few minutes of silent contemplation.

"Especially with so few of us and not knowing what lies behind that illusion," Fenwick added.

"Even with more men …" I said, then let the thought die.

"More men will not help," Fenwick said.

"We cannot attempt it alone," I said, "but I'm not ready to call it off."

"I do not sense that Bellona is trying to warn us away," Fenwick said.

"Have you ever felt that way? That she does not want you to do something?" I asked. "That is something I have not experienced."

"Yes. Twice—the times I tried to kill you," he said.

"It's nice to know she likes me more," I teased.

"I wouldn't go that far," he snorted. "She just let me feel a sense of wrongness. The first time made me sick to my stomach when I almost killed you."

Thinking about what Fenwick said, I searched within myself, trying to find evidence of any hint that we should not be doing this. Other than the guilty feelings I had earlier, there was nothing. I closed my eyes and prayed to the Goddess—something I had never done while my connection with her was open.

When I finished, I opened my eyes. My sight was immediately drawn to a side street more than a furlong away from where we were. Almost without thinking, I nudged Andy with my knee, and we started in that direction.

"Where are you going?" Fenwick asked.

"I don't really know, but I think I'm going to find something," I answered.

Fenwick and the others followed me as Andy and I walked to the intersection. When we reached it, I knew to turn down the street and then around the corner. I saw a large grate at the curb of the cobblestone street. When I looked at it, I experienced an odd sense of amusement within myself that was not coming from my own feelings. I slid from the saddle and approached it.

"No, Caz," Fenwick groaned. "No-no-no-no-no."

"I hate to say it, but I think this is our way in," I said sheepishly.

"Through the sewer?" Fenwick protested.

"Afraid so."

Leaning over the grate, the smell was nasty but not overpowering. I grasped it and tugged. It came up easily. The hole was easily big enough for us to fit.

"Can we get into the palace that way?" Fenwick told me one of the men asked.

"There's only one way to find out," Fenwick replied. "Does anyone have a torch?"

One of the men had one tied to his saddle. He handed it to Fenwick. Fenwick lit it using his finger—a simple and practical use of magic we both learned on our adventure in Dunland. It impressed the men with us.

"I'll go first," he said. "Hand the torch down to me after I climb in."

There were bricks arranged to protrude from the wall at regular intervals. Fenwick used them as hand-and foot-holds and climbed down. When he was standing at the bottom, the man holding the torch stretched himself on the street to hand it to Fenwick. The rest of us then went down one at a time.

The main channel of the sewer ran through the middle and was roughly four feet in width. On either side, there was a flat raised area about two feet wide. The water level in the main channel stopped four or five inches from the raised area where we were standing. Fenwick started off in the direction of the palace.

We encountered obstacles along the way. There were large branches that must have been swept into the sewer during a heavy storm. From time to time, the group needed to switch to the other side. The jump was far enough that they needed to catch themselves on the far wall, with the result that all of us ended up covered in the muck that coated the sides of the chamber. No one complained, even though it was one of the more prolonged unpleasant experiences I have endured.

We did not encounter another grate overhead for quite a distance. When we reached the first one, Fenwick paused for a moment. Then he shook his head.

"We're not there yet," he said. "The next one we find should be inside the outer walls."

At the next grate, Fenwick stopped. After a moment, he nodded. He waited for all of the group to draw near.

"This is the right place," he said. "We need to climb out as quick and quiet as we can. The guards will probably be looking outside the walls. If we're lucky, they might not spot us—at least, not right away. I'll go first, then the prince. The rest of you follow us."

The men mumbled their agreement. Fenwick dropped the torch in the main channel of the sewer, extinguishing it. He then climbed using the bricks sticking out from the wall. When he reached the grate, he tested it to see how much effort it would take to lift it.

"Caz, I'll need your help. Can you climb up next to me?" he asked.

I started up the wall beside him. When I drew level with Fenwick, things got tricky. We both needed to put a foot on the same brick—his left, my right. I pointed to it, and he understood, shimmying his foot sideways enough for me to get a purchase on the brick. I reached up with my right hand and grasped a bar of the grate.

"On three," he mouthed. "One—Two—Three."

The grate came up easily, but it was heavy and an awkward weight. Our hands were positioned too close to the edge. If we tried to lift it and push it out of the way, it would scrape and make a noise. I nudged him with my shoulder and shook my head vigorously.

We lowered the grate back. I moved my hand closer to the center of it. When Fenwick saw what I did, he nodded agreement and moved his own hand to match mine. He counted again, and we lifted the grate free.

This time, where we held it meant the grate was balanced. We were able to lift and remove it halfway before our arms hit the side of the opening. Fenwick and I lowered it gently, trying to avoid any noise.

He nodded his head upward, then climbed up one more brick. I did the same. We then grasped the grate again and slid it forward slowly. It made a small sound as it scraped the cobblestones, but I doubted that it was heard over a distance.

Fenwick looked at me, raised his eyebrows, and grinned. He clambered out of the sewer. I could see him heading forward and to the left. As soon as he was out of the way, I followed.

As my head came above ground level, I looked around as best I could while not slowing down. We were roughly halfway between the walls and the palace, about fifty yards away from either. Fenwick was heading to an archway, running in a low crouch. I imitated him, keeping my feet low to the ground, trying to make as little noise as possible.

When I joined Fenwick in the arch, I turned to look behind. Nine of our group were above ground now, running to meet us. I watched as the other five climbed out.

The last one was paying more attention to the guards on the walls than his feet. He tripped on the grate, still lying next to the opening. His foot scraped the iron bars on the cobblestones, then he fell, his sword clattering on the pavement.

The noise drew the attention of the men on the walls. They began shouting and quickly turned their skorpios on the last of our group as they ran to join us. Three bolts hit the one who tripped and fell. Others buried themselves in the backs of the two just ahead of him. All three of the men fell, lying motionless.

"We can't do anything for them," Fenwick told the others. "C'mon!"

We left the archway, with the guards behind us raising the alarm. Fenwick seemed to know which way to go, so I followed him. We ran underneath a portico into a courtyard. Fenwick headed to the right when we reached the center of the open space.

No sooner did we turn in the new direction than we saw something to make us slow and stop. In front of huge bronze doors stood a group of fifty men clad in heavy armor. All of them held wicked-looking pikes or halberds in their hands.

"The mage is inside," Fenwick said eagerly.

The sight of the heavily armored soldiers took my breath away. When the king fell at the Battle of Hamil Creek, Fenwick and I may have fought a similar number, but we never had the opportunity to count them. With the king's leg trapped under his fallen horse, we moved instinctively to protect him. This was different.

"Are any of you skilled with pikes? Fenwick asked our men.

All of them indicated they were.

"Good. The prince and I will attack these men," he said. "You need to stay right behind us. When a pike becomes available, pick it up, then guard our flanks."

"Are you afraid?" I asked, with Fenwick translating.

A couple of them hesitated before nodding their heads a tiny amount.

"Good," I said firmly, "for there can be no courage without fear. Just remember, in two weeks, they will be singing songs about your exploits all over the southern continent."

That remark received more vigorous nods and even some grins. I clapped the men on the back who admitted to being scared. Then I turned to Fenwick. He caught my gaze and nodded.

Both of us opened our connections to Bellona completely. I heard the men behind us gasp as the two of us suddenly seemed to increase is size. As I reveled in the strength of the Goddess flowing through me, Fenwick and I approached the defenders waiting for us.

When we were only a few paces away, I looked at the enemy we were facing. There was no expression on the faces of any of them as they lifted their pikes. They may as well have been automatons.

At nearly the same instant, Fenwick and I both darted forward. My sword, given to me by my grandfather upon his death, was designed for just this sort of work—piercing armor. With the strength of the Goddess of war singing in my veins, my blade moved as quick as thought, while otherwise, time seemed to slow.

Enemies fell before me, but there were so many that I could not avoid injury myself. I felt the searing burn of a pike blade piercing my breastplate and scoring my ribs on the left side. Another creased the outside of my right thigh when I turned to kill the man who wounded me. Out of the corner of my eye, another blade was slashing toward my head. Before I could move, someone standing behind me intercepted it and stopped its progress. I danced forward and dispatched the one who tried to deal the blow.

Some of our comrades had retrieved the weapons of our fallen foes. They were now positioned to my left and Fenwick's right. With my left side now protected, I could devote all my attention to the enemies in front of me. I touched the tan-zyan stone in my ring to the diamond in the pommel of my sword. The asomatous energy flowed into me, and I renewed my attack.

An enemy blade sliced my left forearm, slipping through the defense provided by my allies. I ignored the pain and pressed on. One of the fallen men grabbed my right ankle as he lay dying. Distracted while I attempted to twist it from his grasp, another pike stabbed into the calf of that leg. A pike came from behind me, cutting the man's hands from my leg. While this happened, a pike blade struck my helmet, making my ears ring.

I restored my energy again. In that brief moment, I noticed there were only a few of our enemies still standing—perhaps a dozen. Taking advantage of the diminished numbers, I moved to find open space and freedom of movement, away from the fallen bodies and the blood-slick pavement.

Suddenly, there were no more of the enemy standing. I looked around briefly to make sure, then dampened my tie to the Goddess. Fenwick caught my eye.

He stood, his helmet slightly askew, with a feral grin on his face. His sleeves, breeches, and boots were covered with gore. Blood splatters covered his face. I imagined I looked much the same.

Of course, the doors were bolted shut when we reached them. Fenwick, without hesitation, called out to our men. Of the eleven who were able to join us, seven were still standing. One was sitting, holding his side. The other three had fallen.

The seven began attacking the wooden doorpost on the right side with the ax heads mounted on the halberds some of the enemy carried. When they created a split in the wood, others jammed pike blades in the crevices and levered the split wider, cracking the beam bit by bit. While they were attacking the doorpost, I checked my wounds.

Taking off my breastplate and the quilted vest underneath, I reached my shirt. I stripped it off and began tearing the fabric to create bandages. My left forearm and the two wounds in my right leg were bleeding the most, so I wrapped them. The slice on my ribs was shallow and already scabbing over. I tossed the remnant of my shirt to Fenwick for him to do the same, then put my vest and breastplate back on.

I did not sense that there were other soldiers waiting for us on the other side. That is not to say I did not feel a sense of menace. I was certain the mage was waiting for us.

Suddenly, the doorpost gave a loud crack. The heavy bronze door sagged just a bit. Fenwick issued instructions to the men. They dropped their weapons and threw their bodies at the door. With the hinge no longer having a solid purchase in the doorpost, the lower right corner of the massive door gave way—an inch, at first, then two, then three. When the doorpost released its grip on the hinge, they shoved the door back far enough that Fenwick was able to slip inside. I was right on his heels.

At the far end of the room, on a raised dais, seated on a throne of gleaming black stone, sat Julienne Traval. I was stunned. Fenwick was stupefied.

"Why are you here, Fenwick?" she pleaded, sounding as though she were on the verge of tears. "Have you and Caz come to kill me? I thought you loved me. Please—don't. Don't let him kill me. You must stop him."

Fenwick looked at me, grief-stricken. He took the smallest step toward me, then froze. His sword clattered to the floor.

Logic warred with what I was seeing and hearing. I had just enough sanity to use my link with Bellona to extend my senses. With the Goddess assisting me, I suddenly knew the woman was not Julienne.

As quickly as I could move with my damaged right leg, I started toward the throne. The mage kept pleading for Fenwick to save her. I needed to kill her before she broke his mind and heart.

Each step I took was more difficult than the last. I felt as though my feet were mired in thick, viscous mud. Each of my wounds flared with searing new bolts of pain. When I was only halfway from where I began, I despaired of being able to reach her.

I touched my ring to the diamond and drained it of its remaining energy. At the same time, I opened my connection to Bellona completely. I could move no faster than before, but I was still advancing. My wounds were a symphony of burning agony. I let the pain fuel my resolve.

Behind me, I heard the clatter of new soldiers arriving, their armor banging on the bent bronze door as they forced their way in. Fenwick gave a shout. Of warning? Of attack? I dared not turn my focus away from the mage.

The twang of crossbows firing reached my ears just before the bolts hit me. One knocked my helmet off and stunned me. Another buried itself in my right buttock. A third pierced my breastplate just to the center of my left shoulder blade. The last sank into my left hamstring.

On hands and knees, I crawled up the last steps to the throne. When I staggered to my feet in front of her, the mage changed her appearance from Julienne Traval to a demon straight from the Seven Hells. I'd fought too hard to be frightened. With a full backhand strike, I cut off her head. My world went black.

18

I felt as though I was deep under the surface of a lake. Above me, I could see the glimmer of sunlight on the surface. I wanted desperately to swim up, but my progress was slow, as though the water was the consistency of molasses. Swimming was difficult. I felt blazes of pain in different places.

Slowly, ever so slowly, I neared the surface. My lungs felt as though they were about to burst. As I drew closer, I began to hear voices. The sound was consistent with being underwater.

Suddenly, I broke through the surface. My eyes flashed wide open, and I gasped for air. Lucy told me later that all the muscles in my body tensed at that moment and launched me a foot off the mattress.

At first, I did not know where I was. The room was only slightly familiar. Lucy was standing to my right, with the queen next to her. Their presence puzzled me further.

"Oh, praise all the heavenly beings!" Lucy exclaimed, then she launched herself onto me, burying her face in my chest and sobbing.

I felt awful that she was so distressed. When I lifted my left arm to try to comfort her, it was a strain to do so. In addition, the wounds I received still hurt fiercely. Nonetheless, I put my hand on her back and tried to soothe her.

"How do you feel?" Lily asked.

"Weak," I replied after trying to assess my condition. "Confused. In pain. Where are we?"

"You are in your bed, in your quarters in the castle, in Aquileia," Lily answered while Lucy continued to sob into my chest.

That made no sense to me. The last thing I knew, I was in Iradiem, in Hier, on the southern continent. My bafflement must have shown clearly in my expression.

"You have been more dead than alive for nearly three weeks," Lily explained. "What do you last remember?"

"I killed the mage by cutting her head off," I said. "Remembering it, I am puzzled why I did that. It seems unnecessarily vicious. It was extremely difficult to reach her. Every step I took was more difficult. The closer I came, the more my wounds hurt."

"There was clearly a great deal of malevolence in the room. It undoubtedly affected your actions," Lily said. "And perhaps Bellona knew that any blow you struck needed to be one from which the mage could not recover. You will probably never know exactly why you did that."

"Well, that's the last thing I remember until just before I woke," I said.

"What did you feel just before you returned to us?" Lily asked.

I described the feeling I experienced. She asked several questions. The last was the most telling.

"Was your connection to Bellona open when you struck the mage?"

"It was."

"The Goddess saved your life, then," Lily said.

"How?"

"From what happened to you, the difficulty you had in reaching her, and what I have read, I believe the mage had put a powerful spell on her body," Lily explained, "a final form of protection. The spell would capture the soul of any person who attacked her and drag it to the Seven Hells. I think Bellona prevented that, but there was not enough numina in your body for her to keep you in the realm of the living."

"What do you mean?" I asked.

"When you struck the mage, you collapsed," Lily said. "Fenwick thought you were dead. He could not detect a heartbeat at first. Then he noticed your slight exhalation created a spot of fog on his breastplate. From this, he hoped you were not killed. He waited until others arrived at the palace. Among them was a healer, who confirmed that your heart was beating and you were breathing, but very, very slowly. I guessed that Bellona prevented your soul's passage into the Seven Hells but could do no more than that. It left you trapped in your body—more dead than alive. Fenwick brought you home. Lucy and I have been trying for almost two weeks to revive you."

"How did I reach home in less than three weeks?" I asked. "It would have taken riders—"

"The grand vizier's ship apparently shadowed your force as you traveled to Iradiem," Lucy said, lifting her head from my chest. "It sailed into the harbor the next day. Fenwick brought you back on it immediately."

"How is Fenwick?" I asked.

"He has been an emotional wreck," Lucy said. "Other than Mark, Fenwick will be the happiest person in Aquileia to know you have revived. He blames himself for failing you."

"How did he fail me?" I asked.

"He has not explained," Lily said. "We have been gentle with him since he seems so fragile and have not pressed him for details."

'The mage put on the appearance of Julienne," I explained. "Her voice and gestures were identical. She ordered Fenwick to stop me. He froze and dropped his sword. I think he did that so he would not attack me, but we will need to ask him."

"He has not told us that," Lucy said, "but it would explain a great deal about why he has been so troubled. The mage was not Julienne. She is alive and well, here in Aquileia."

"When the mage enthralled Fenwick earlier, she gained access to his mind," Lily said. "She would have used his memories to cast the illusion of herself as Julienne."

"It was an exact likeness in every respect," I said. "Bellona let me know it was an illusion but did not dispel it. If not for that—"

"How horrible!" Lucy exclaimed.

"What happened in Iradiem afterward?" I asked, trying to shift the subject slightly.

"We will let Fenwick explain as much as he knows," Lily said. "His first priority was you, so what he has shared with us has been a jumble. Seeing you might help him sort things out. We have since received letters from the different rulers, including the king and queen of Hier. All of them are exceedingly grateful and have been praying to the Gods for your recovery."

As she said this, my stomach rumbled. It had been three weeks since I last ate. I realized I was as hungry as I ever felt.

"Majors and Minors!" Lucy exclaimed. "Let me get Jenny to work!"

"That seems to be my cue to leave," Lily said. "I will let Fenwick know to come to see you."

She bent down and tenderly brushed my hair to the side. She then kissed my forehead gently. Her eyes bore a maternal look deeper than any I had seen before. It made my heart swell.

Left by myself for the moment, I squirmed my way backward on the bed to a sitting position. My lack of strength surprised and dismayed me. So, too, did the pain from my wounds. Since awakening my affinities, my lesser connection to Eir, the Goddess of Health, has shortened my recovery time. From what I felt now, my wounds did not seem to have healed at all during the three weeks I was unconscious. They felt as fresh and painful as when I received them. When Lucy returned, I was gasping from the exertion of lifting myself up to the head of the bed.

"You're weak as a kitten," she said.

"I am," I admitted, "but I'm also alive. Today, I will be grateful to Bellona and all the heavenly beings for that. I promise to hold off from complaining until tomorrow, at least."

"It's nothing to joke about, darling," Lucy said. "Lily tried and tried to counter whatever the mage did. Nothing worked. She and I have both been poring through her books, searching for something that would help. Last night, I found a reference to an incantation that we had not seen before and thought it might work. It didn't fit exactly, but Lily tried it with different variations more than a dozen times today."

"Well, the last version was effective," I remarked.

"And I made note of it," Lucy said. "Lily will add it to that book. Mark has been as anxious as any of us. He will be relieved to know you are recovering."

"Is he upset with me?" I asked.

"I don't think so, and neither does Lily," Lucy said. "Fenwick explained the circumstances. After Mark calmed down, he surely realized you had no way of exiting the situation without damaging your reputation or Aquileia's. He did threaten to flay Fenwick alive if you did not recover, though."

Jenny came bustling in that moment with a tray. It had short legs and was designed expressly for eating in bed. On the tray were eggs, sausages, some fruit, and a large slice of raspberry pie. There was also a large glass of water, which I seized immediately and began guzzling.

"This is just the starter, Your Highness," Jenny said as I was slaking my thirst. "Princess Lucy told me about your appetite in circumstances like this, so I will begin cooking a second helping as soon as I return to the kitchen."

"Thank you, Jenny," I said. "I do tend to feel a bit peckish at times like these."

Jenny giggled as she curtsied, then dashed off. I began shoveling food into my mouth. It took only minutes for me to devour everything, and I felt as though I'd only just taken the edge off my appetite. I was still ravenously hungry. Lucy rose from the edge of the bed to refill my glass with water. As she walked away, I saw Fenwick peering hesitantly around the door.

"Why are you skulking out there, Aloysius?" I called out. "You've never waited for an invitation to enter any of my residences. Don't tell me you've developed a sense of propriety all of a sudden."

Fenwick came in slowly. His face bore the most ghastly uncertain fake smile I have ever seen. I could tell my attempt at teasing him did not reassure him, if it even registered at all.

"Fenwick, the ladies told me you think you failed me in some way," I said. "From what I remember, you did not. In fact, when the mage ordered you to stop me, you dropped your sword so that you could not attack me if she forced you. That probably took every bit of will you possessed. Be at peace, my friend."

"That's kind of you to say, Your Highness," he responded quietly after blowing out a deep sigh, "but it should have been me who struck the blow. I feel I did not do my duty. My inability to act almost cost your life."

"Fenwick, come closer and sit down," I said, patting a space on the bed.

He approached hesitantly. When he started to sit, he was as far away from me as he could manage. I shook my head and patted the bed next to myself. He crossed a couple of more steps reluctantly and sat gingerly as though he expected the mattress to be holding a concealed bear trap. I tried to meet his gaze, but he kept his eyes averted.

"Look at me, Fenwick, damnit!" I snarled. "That's better," I said more pleasantly when he turned his head toward me.

"That damned woman looked and sounded exactly like Julienne. It stunned me as well. I had barely enough of my wits about me to ask Bellona if what I saw was real. The Goddess let me know it was an illusion, but even so, I was uncertain. If the mage somehow cast the illusion of herself as Lucy, I would have been just as paralyzed as you. There is no blame that anyone could attach to you. If you wish to punish yourself for something you did not do, then your only sin, other than loving your wife as much as I love mine, is that you did not wear your ward when we left the ship. Rebuke yourself for that—not for anything else."

I reached my hand out to him. Fenwick seized it with both of his. He was looking down at the bed for a time. When he raised his head, tears were streaming down his cheeks. I squeezed his one hand.

"I can only imagine how utterly terrible the scene was," I said. "Tell me. Maybe putting it into words will help lessen the horror for you."

"I'll try," Fenwick said with a gravelly voice as he tried to regain control of himself. "Lily explained that she used my memories to create the illusion. I understand that—in a rational way. But to me, she *was* Julienne. The most powerful emotions swept through me. One of them was a sense of betrayal— that Julienne somehow fooled me all this time. Yet, when she ordered me to stop you, my first instinct was to obey. You are correct that it took all the strength I have in my soul to drop my blade. It was all I could do."

Fenwick paused and took a deep breath that was also a sob before continuing.

"Then, the other soldiers arrived. They took my attention away from the mage. I shouted to try to draw their focus. They ignored me. I bent to retrieve my blade from the floor and attacked, but I was not able to prevent them from firing on you. I'm sorry."

"No apologies necessary," I said. "Keep going."

"When you chopped off her head, the illusion vanished. Any relief I felt was washed away by the sight of you collapsing. We've killed men, Caz. When they fall, there is a certain slackness to their limbs that looks like nothing else. You dropped as though dead. I ran to your body and could not detect your pulse. I'm not ashamed to say I collapsed in grief and embraced you. When I recovered my wits a few minutes later and let you go, I saw a small, fogged spot on my breastplate out of the corner of my eye. Taking my helmet off, I tried to clean a spot, then held it in front of your mouth. When it fogged again, I knew you were alive, but only by the thinnest thread. I shouted at the men with us who survived to get help. Waiting for someone to come—those were the longest minutes of my life."

"Tell me about the mage," I asked. "What did she look like, really?"

"She was plain," Fenwick said, "not ugly, but far from pretty. She was fat, like someone who overindulges herself—even worse than Madam Traval."

"Oh, thank all the heavenly beings!" I said with a laugh. "I believe you are recovering your sanity, or at least your sense of humor. What was happening in the rest of the city?"

"It was similar to what we saw in Dunland," Fenwick said. "Most of the people were frozen in place when you killed the mage. They told me there were a handful of men who were moving but were stupefied. Most of the ones who were not stuck in place were not from Hier."

"They came with her from Combrial," I guessed.

"I don't know," Fenwick admitted. "My concern was for you. On the way to the harbor with your body, I did see priests of the Three Major Gods freeing people from the mage's control. Again, it was like what we saw in Dunland."

"I hate to ask, but what happened to the horses?"

"Andy and Davy returned with us."

"The other horses—left behind on the ships."

"I don't know," Fenwick replied. "My concern was on getting you home."

"Did all of the rulers survive?" I asked.

"Yes," Fenwick said with a small chuckle, "and all have the scars to prove they took part in a battle. None of them were seriously wounded, but all of them were very proud of themselves. They are exceedingly grateful to us and deeply concerned about your condition."

"Perhaps that will muffle their complaints when we start seizing their ships," I said.

"Majors and Minors!" Fenwick gasped. "I haven't even checked on the progress of the construction. The first six ships should be just about finished by now."

"I'm surprised the king hasn't brought it up," I said.

"We have been avoiding one another," Fenwick admitted. "I know I did not want to see him, and I imagine he had no wish to see me."

"And here's the wolf," Mark said as he entered my bedroom with Lucy and Lily following him.

Fenwick jumped up from the bed and bowed to the king more deeply than I ever observed before. The king rumpled Fenwick's hair, as I used to do to Jerry, the stableboy. Fenwick jerked away in surprise.

"Your Majesty?" he said in an odd tone, part whine, part puzzlement.

"I *have* been avoiding you, Lord Easton, for fear my emotions might lead me to say something I might regret later," Mark said. "While delivering the good news that Caz was awake, Lily also told me why you might have been unable to act at the moment of crisis. I can only imagine how shocking it must have been for you. I will want to hear the story from both of you soon, but not now. Just know that I bear no bad feeling toward you, Lord Easton."

"Thank you, Your Majesty," Fenwick said.

"As you guessed, the first ships are nearing completion," Mark continued. "Caz, you will need to sort through the letters we have received from those who wish to serve in your force. Lord Easton will help you as you regain your strength. For now, I just wanted to see with my own eyes that you were in the land of the living."

"I understand there have been letters—"

"There have been," Mark confirmed, "all of which sing your praises, Caz, and yours too, Lord Easton. It took them several days to restore normalcy to Iradiem. A force will head south toward Combrial at some point to set things to rights. They have promised to keep us informed. Returning to the subject more closely aligned with our interests—Colonel Yankton should be returning in the next few days. He has been overseeing the construction of a stronghold on Hardscrabble Island."

"Is that the one where we were?" Fenwick asked.

I nodded. Jenny appeared in the doorway with another tray of food. Fenwick and the king saw that as their cue to leave, though Fenwick filched a slice of bacon on his way out.

"Cheeky rogue!" I called after him.

19

For most of the next week, it seemed as though I spent my time eating or sleeping. I hoped to use my connection to Eir to speed the healing of my wounds, but when Lucy brought my sword to me, and I touched the diamond in the pommel, I learned I had used up all the energy I stored there. That meant it was mostly up to me. Draining my body's reserves of asomatous energy always exhausted me (and gave me an appetite).

The first night I can remember dreaming was actually the third since I returned to consciousness. I saw Bellona—it could only have been her. She was tall and broad-shouldered. Her hair was black and straight, flowing behind her as though she faced into a stiff breeze. Her eyes, set above sharp cheekbones, were fierce. She wore a breastplate, arm guards, a leather kilt, greaves, and high boots. She was utterly beautiful and fearsome.

I sensed she was pleased with me. Pleased that I survived and pleased that I triumphed over the dark mage. Yet, I sensed there was something she wanted from me. It was a vague feeling—the merest whisper of a premonition.

The next day, with Fenwick, I went through the letters I received from men volunteering to join the force we were putting together. The captains of the ships were responsible for finding their crews. These notes were from the men we would use to do the fighting. I immediately accepted any men from the Eastern March who applied because I knew them, and they were all experienced soldiers. For the others, I wrote letters to their liege lords asking for their opinions of the men from their holdings.

At the end of the week, I felt strong enough that I wanted to see the ships. Fenwick came with me, along with a half-dozen of the Castle Shield, and we met Mellone and Baldini at the shipyard belonging to Charles Finley. Both ships were already in the water, and I watched as they used a crane on the dock to install the masts on one. Finley saw us and came to chat.

"What do you think, Your Highness?" he asked.

"I'm amazed at how the drawings I saw were transformed into this ship," I said. "It's beautiful."

"She, Your Highness," Finley said.

"Excuse me?"

"She. A ship is a 'she' not an 'it.' You'll need to treat her with the same love, respect, and care you would any woman who is an important part of your life," Finley said. "Have you decided on names for them?"

That was something I had not considered at all. I tried not to let it show that his question caught me off guard. My effort was unsuccessful, as he started to laugh.

"You will need to provide them to us soon. We will be ready to add them in a few days. Your bigger challenge will be getting figureheads carved in time," Finley said.

"Figureheads?" I asked.

"Begging your pardon, Your Highness, but I wrote you about this weeks ago."

"Ah—I apologize, Mr. Finley," I said. "I was out of the country until recently and am just getting caught up on my correspondence."

I had no idea what a figurehead was. I looked at Fenwick pleadingly. Though he was enjoying my discomfort, he did help me.

"Mr. Finley, not only was His Highness out of the country, he also suffered a debilitating wound that has kept him indisposed until quite recently. I must confess that I, too, forgot about figureheads. We will need to engage someone who can create them on short notice *and* make them beautiful. Do you have anyone you would recommend?" Fenwick asked.

"Aye. He'll be hard-pressed to finish in time, but if you speak with him today, he will have a chance. As far as quality, he's the finest artist of all of them," Finley said.

He took us to his rough office and scribbled the name of the man on a small scrap of wood. We thanked him and departed. Fenwick knew the way.

"What is a figurehead?" I asked.

"Have you seen the wooden statues fixed to the front of ships?"

"Oh!" I exclaimed quietly, suddenly understanding.

"The figurehead is usually an iconic representation of the soul of the ship. Sailors are some of the most superstitious people alive," Fenwick said. "They believe a proper figurehead will help protect them from storms and rough seas."

"Will it?"

"Who knows?" Fenwick responded. "Now, before we meet the carver, we need to figure out what we want to name the ships. Do you have any ideas?"

"I've thought of the first four already," I said.

"And?"

"*Princess Lucille*, *Queen Liliana*, *Bellona*, and *Freyja*," I replied.

"I wouldn't dare argue with those choices," Fenwick grinned. "We need two more. Would you have any objection to *Julienne* for one of them?"

"I should have suggested that as well," I replied.

"What about the sixth?" Fenwick asked.

"I have an idea but can't imagine what form it would take," I said.

"And the name?"

"Farsall."

"The final battle of the war," Fenwick remarked. "A well-chosen name for a ship that will prey on the Rhetians. I'm sure the carver can think of something."

We found the shop. It was a small building tucked in next to a chandler's warehouse. A gray-bearded, bald-headed man sat outside—a pipe clenched in his teeth. When we greeted him and confirmed that he was George Chester, he looked at us quizzically for a moment. Suddenly, he jumped to his feet when he saw the men of the Castle Shield behind us.

"Yer Highness!" he exclaimed, bowing slightly and knuckling his forelock. "Majors 'n' Minors! Ah didnae ken wha ye wur! Howfur kin ah hulp ye?"

"You may have heard that we commissioned the construction of six ships," I said. "Four are nearing completion here in Aquileia, with Finley and Hooper each building two. One more is coming from Aurora and another from

Newcastle. I regret to say that commissioning figureheads was a detail I overlooked."

"Howfur dae yi'll need thaim?" Chester asked.

"The ships are close to finished," Fenwick explained. "Finley was stepping the masts today on his two."

"Oigh, that's nae muckle time," he said. "Dae ye hae names fur th' ships?"

I gave him the names. Chester nodded approvingly at the first four. He was not upset with the last two, but I could tell he had questions.

"Wha is Julienne?" he asked.

"Julienne Traval," Fenwick replied.

"That wull be na kinch," Chester said. "Th' ither?"

"Farsall is the place where the last battle with the Rhetians took place a few months back," I said.

"Aye," he nodded. "Ah kin mak' her lik' Bellona, ainlie different."

"Can you get them finished in time?" I asked.

"Ah hawp sae. It wull be dear, ah mist warn ye. Bonny wummin a'—thay need th' best. Nae juist th' materials—ah mist wirk nicht 'n' day tae complete thaim timely," Chester said.

"You must pardon me, Mr. Chester," Fenwick said, "but how can you produce six full-sized figureheads in such a short time, even working night and day?"

Chester turned and opened the door to his shop. Fenwick and I followed him in. Chester gestured toward the back wall. Standing there, larger than life, were the forms of nine women carved from wood. All wore flowing gowns and were complete up to just above their outthrust bosoms. Above that point was an unfinished mass of wood. On the right-hand wall, there were five figures of men, finished to the same extent. On the left-hand side, there were a variety of different sculptures—three horses, a skeleton, and a large bird with its wings outstretched. Clearly, Mr. Chester filled his idle time by preparing for future commissions.

"Ah ainlie need tae dae th'heids 'n' paint 'em," he said with a shrug.

"Would it help if we provided you with some money in advance to cover the cost of the gilt and other materials?" I asked.

"Ah wid nae be 'posed tae th'idea," he said.

"Would six hundred ducats be enough?" I asked.

"Th' hail jab wull nae cost that much. Juist three tae stairt."

"Will you accept a bank draft, or would you—"

"King's own coin if ye dinnae mind," he said quickly.

With that, we concluded our business. As we rode away, I realized I had not been to a bank here in the city since being named the successor. It was something I doubted Albert did for himself.

"Fenwick, how do I get the money to him?"

"Have a member of the Shield take it."

"How do I get the funds from the bank?"

At first, Fenwick looked at me scornfully as if I were an imbecile. His expression changed when he understood what I was really asking. He thought a moment.

"That's a question for Mark, I think," he said. "I'm sure there is some sort of regular procedure, but I have no idea what it is."

When we returned to the castle, I went to the room the king used as his office. I was getting much better at memorizing the twists and turns of the various corridors and did not get lost. At one intersection, I did need to pause for a moment before proceeding but I was still pleased with myself.

Mark bade me enter when I knocked. He was writing something, so I sat and waited for him to finish. When he did, he looked up, and I explained my question to him.

"Quite right," he said. "Well, one advantage you have now is that you no longer need to go to the bank—the banker comes to you. You said your accounts are with Bannister Brothers. My accounts and the ones you inherit from Albert are spread between four different firms, but Bannister is one of them. Just draft a note asking for them to bring three hundred ducats in specie, and someone will deliver it with a note for you to sign. What is the money for?"

"Figureheads for the ships," I said, then needed to explain what they were and why they were not included in the bids provided to us by the shipyards.

"Then that is not a personal expense, Caz," Mark admonished me. "That money should come from the crown, just as the cost of building the ships did. What are we naming them?"

I shared the six names I thought of.

"Good. I approve. You'll have a more difficult time thinking up names for the ones we will build after these," he teased. "It seems to me you used up the most logical choices. Have any other names come to mind?"

"The only one that has is one I will never use—Lord Compote," I said. "Any ship with that name would be bound to run aground regularly."

"I would imagine so," Mark replied with a smile. "By the way, I met with Pierre Luin and have shifted some of our investments to him. If he performs as well as he has for you, we will send more his way."

"I'm pleased to hear it," I said.

"One other thing—the men who traveled with you to the southern continent are due to return from Hier any day now. From the letters we received, most of them survived. Only fifteen of the Shield were killed. Like the others under the mage's control, they were defending against your assault on the city. The king of Hier has cremated their remains, and he is sending the ashes back to us."

"Do you know what happened to the horses?" I asked. "Their fate has been troubling me all along."

"I'm sad to say the horses perished," Mark said with a frown. "And the three ships are unfit to sail without significant repair, as the animals did a great deal of damage. The king of Hier will pay for the ships to be put in order now that normal business is resuming in Iradiem."

The king paused. It seemed he wanted to say something more but did not know how to phrase it. Eventually, he sighed.

"You must know that your condition when you returned upset me greatly," he said. "It also disturbed Fenwick a great deal. Even so, I honestly wanted to throttle him for not bringing you home and avoiding Hier. Lucy told me only a little a few days ago. I would like to hear more from you about why you stayed."

"In the letters Lucy and Julienne delivered to us, you made it clear that you wanted us to depart as quickly as possible," I replied.

I then explained Fenwick's and my dismay when all four of the rulers announced their intention of riding to Iradiem. Our attempts to warn them of the dangers they would face seemed to have no effect. When Fenwick and I expressed our desire to leave, all four of them—both separately and as a group— pleaded with us to stay.

"They played my own hand against me, I'm afraid. I traveled to them as the embodiment of Aquileia, and they all referenced that."

"I see," Mark replied. "And now I must confess that in the dark moments of despair I experienced after your return, I wondered whether you tried at all to heed my wishes. I am sorry now for entertaining those thoughts for even a moment. It is clear you had no choice. In the time since you came to my attention, you have never acted frivolously. I don't know why—"

"Sir," I said, leaning forward and putting my hand on his, "we are still getting to know one another. Do not chastise yourself for a few moments of doubt when the situation seemed bleak."

"Easy for you to say—"

"Like most good advice, easy to say means hard to do," I said.

"Too true," Mark said with a slight smile. "And with you now returned to the land of the living, we could hardly have hoped for a better outcome. All of the rulers have acknowledged a huge debt of gratitude to us."

"Do you think they will remember that debt when we seize some of their ships off the coast of Rhetia?" I quipped.

The king's response was a belly laugh. His amusement sparked my own, and the two of us indulged in a spasm of hilarity. It took several minutes for us to calm down.

"You can go now, Caz," the king said, still chuckling. "Thank you for restoring my good nature. I will have money delivered to the carver."

I headed back to the section of the castle where our residence was. When I entered our quarters, I heard voices raised in excitement upstairs. Curious, I went to see what the cause was.

Lucy and Katie were there in the small sitting room. They stopped talking when they heard my footsteps on the stairs. When I entered, they both looked relieved.

"Katie just had a marvelous thing happen," Lucy explained, somewhat more quietly than they had spoken earlier.

"What was that, Katie?" I asked.

"I can see auras now. I can see yours," she said with wonderment.

"That *is* marvelous," I said. "Do you know what that means?"

"I was just beginning to explain it to her," Lucy said. "Sit down and join us."

I sat down facing them. Lucy turned back to Katie and clasped her hands. Both of them looked excited but in different ways.

"As I was saying, Katie," Lucy said, "You know that Lily and I have magical ability—we told you about that straight off because we knew you heard rumors."

"Yes'm," Katie replied.

"Among many other things, we both can see auras. Lily saw your aura when she visited the market the week before we spoke with you for the first time. It's one of the reasons, in addition to you being quite pretty and highly intelligent, that we wanted you to take a position as my lady-in-waiting. By spending time with me, we hoped that your affinities would manifest and become abilities. That is what just happened."

"So, I'm a witch?" Katie said, her voice both excited and uncertain.

"Not yet," Lucy laughed. "But you can be if you study and learn. You see, there are some people—not many—who are born with affinities—links to the Minor Gods. Most of those folks never know they have them. For a few of them, however, those affinities blossom and become abilities. People with abilities can use magic."

"What wakes them up, then?" Katie asked.

"From what Lily and I have read and learned, spending time with someone who has abilities and whose connections to the Minor Gods are compatible. For instance, Prince Casimir lived with his affinities his whole life but never knew about them until he and I became close. After we spent time together, his affinities bloomed."

"Katie, I am still learning about this myself," I said. "Lucy was taught at an early age by her grandmother, and she knows far more about it than I do."

"Caz did go to the Temple of Bellona to learn more about how to use his dominant link once his ability manifested itself. His lesser ties are to Njörun and Eir. They are also my lessers. My dominant is Freyja, as is yours. That is where the ability to see auras comes from."

"You said the queen can see auras too. Does she have the same—"

"No," Lucy answered. "Lily's dominant is actually not one of the Minor Gods. Her dominant is extremely rare—Ceridwen Sospita."

"Who is that?" Katie asked.

"Ceridwen Sospita is an incredibly powerful spirit," Lucy explained. "Supposedly, she was a real person once—an incredibly powerful white witch who protected an entire duchy from the dark arts. She was killed by the seven most powerful dark mages of the age, who gathered for just that purpose. Though they destroyed her physical form, that act obliterated them at the same time. Her spirit transcended, and her power is available to those with the affinity for it. Someone with that ability can counter the Dark Arts. Back to your question, Lily's lessers are Freyja and Eir."

"If the queen can fight the Dark Arts, why didn't she go to Hier?" Katie asked.

"It was too dangerous," I said. "The king would never allow her to be exposed to that much of a threat. And before you ask, he was not at all happy that Lord Easton and I stayed."

"That was obvious, Your Highness," Katie said, then blushed when she realized how direct she was.

"So, your dominant is Freyja," Lucy said, trying to defuse Katie's embarrassment. "Your lesser connections are with Mielvanir and Sadu."

"What will I be able to do?" Katie asked.

"That will depend on how hard you work in studying what Lily and I can teach you."

20

All of our people who were enthralled in Hier—Mr. Gilbert, the sailors, and the surviving members of the Castle Shield—returned the next day. Mr. Gilbert brought back the trunks I had left on the ship. He was in the lowest spirits and apologized several times.

"Mr. Gilbert, you took excellent care of me while we were away," I said. "You did not fail me. A power you could not fight in any way gained control of you. No shame attaches. In fact, while I have not yet discussed it with the princess, I was thinking that I could add you to our staff."

"Your Highness, I would be honored," he said.

"Good," I replied. "One question though—can you read and write?"

"Of course, Your Highness."

"Excellent. Then my first instruction to you is to stop berating yourself for something that was out of your control."

"Yes, Your Highness," he said, his cheeks flushing with embarrassment.

"You will need to be patient with me, Mr. Gilbert," I said. "I never had a manservant before—I never needed one. Until fairly recently, my life was simple and uncomplicated. In a couple of weeks, I will begin traveling for another assignment the king has given me. I will need you to manage my correspondence. Until I need to depart, together we will go through the letters that arrive. Is that acceptable?"

"Yes, Your Highness."

"Allow me to discuss this with the princess," I asked. "I'm sure she will want to have you shift your lodgings to the quarters attached to our residence. Is that acceptable?"

"Absolutely, Your Highness."

"Excellent."

After he left, I went looking for Lucy. It took me more than a few minutes to find her. Outside the castle proper, tucked under the outer wall near our residence, I found a small outbuilding that appeared to be newly constructed. It was quite similar to the workshop I built for Lucy in Easton. Inside, I found Lucy, Lily, and Katie.

"I don't wish to interrupt," I said upon opening the door, "but I do need Lucy for a moment."

Lucy came out with a broad smile on her face. I shared with her that I wanted to add Mr. Gilbert to help keep me organized. She laughed.

"That happened sooner than I thought," she teased. "I figured you would let yourself get completely buried before you admitted you needed help. Katie and I will determine which room will be his."

"How are things proceeding with Katie?" I asked.

"Majors and Minors! The girl is a sponge! She is very eager to learn and has a keen mind. Lily and I are having so much fun."

"Well, I don't want to keep you," I said.

Lucy kissed me and scurried back into their workshop.

When I returned inside the castle, three different people informed me that the king was looking for me. I made my way to his study. He looked up when I entered.

"There you are," he said.

As we lay in bed that evening, Lucy turned to me and said, "I am starting to understand my Grand-Nan more."

"Your unpleasant grandmother who wished for you to manifest the Dark Arts?"

"Yes. I think one of the reasons she was so cranky is because, until I came along, there was no one in the family with whom she could discuss such things," Lucy said. "When Lily and I began to share what each of us had learned over the years, it was as though a burden was lifted from both of us. Working with my students in Easton was such a pleasure. And now Katie …"

"I could tell you were enjoying yourself when I visited your workshop today."

"All three of us are," Lucy said. "And it made me realize about my Grand-Nan. Even though she was a bitter old woman and disappointed I possessed no affinity for the Dark Arts, I think she enjoyed teaching me. You recall that I told you she latched onto me when she discovered my abilities bloomed. Working with me might have been the only thing that allowed her to maintain a thin grasp of sanity."

"And how is Katie adjusting to life here?"

"I think she still pinches herself multiple times every day to make sure she is not dreaming," Lucy laughed. "One day, she goes to market with her father to help him sell produce, and the next, she is living in the castle. Lily's dressmaker came, and we had her make some clothes for Katie suitable for a lady-in-waiting. That was a fun day. Lily and I have been teaching her better table manners and some of the finer points of etiquette, working with her on her speech and handwriting, and giving her a great deal of reading to do. We have not yet allowed her to look at any of the texts concerning magic. Katie's reading skills need work before she can tackle those."

"And she is not overwhelmed?" I asked with concern.

"Lily and I have both been keeping a close eye on her to make sure that does not happen," Lucy said. "We may need to slow down now that her abilities are flowering. Still, she is so quick and clever. She has a mind like a bear trap—once something is captured, it's locked in forever."

"And what do you intend to do with her?" I asked.

"We mentioned our long-term plan," Lucy said. "We hope to send her traveling next summer. Before that, though, Lily and I intend to introduce her to society and pass her off as my distant cousin when the winter holidays arrive."

"Isn't that putting a great deal of pressure on the girl?"

"It's a reward for the effort she has been exerting in learning so much and so many new things," Lucy explained. "Lily and I reached a point in the first week when we could tell Katie didn't see the purpose in learning manners. Lily said, 'You need to learn so when we host the Solstice celebration this winter, everyone will know that you are a member of a minor noble house, Miss Katherine.' You should have seen her eyes light up, Caz!"

"Are you sure that's wise?"

"Katie is still well-grounded, Caz," Lucy replied. "When the time comes for her to travel on her own, she will be able to appear as Miss Katherine or as Katie, depending on what the circumstances warrant. Which reminds me, Lilly and I want you and Fenwick to teach her to defend herself."

"What?"

"When we send her away, a member of the Castle Shield will accompany her," Lucy explained. "But he will not be in any uniform. Nor will he be as skilled as Fenwick or you. We hope she will never encounter trouble greater than he can handle, but Lily and I would feel better if she possessed some skill of her own."

"That is reasonable," I agreed. "By the way, did you know Fenwick is looking for his replacement?"

"I did," Lucy said. "It will not be easy."

For most of the next two weeks, I rebuilt my strength. It took me longer to recover from my wounds than before. Lucy and I figured out that a contributing factor was that I was completely drained of asomatous energy in my encounter with the mage. It was for that reason, and my near-death state, that my wounds were totally unhealed when I recovered consciousness. In addition to restoring my physical health, it was also necessary to allow time for my supernatural reserves to replenish.

I met with Colonel Yankton. He informed me that the stockade, as he called it, was built. A half-dozen members of the Castle Shield were left manning it.

"It would not do, Your Highness, for some sheepherder to come across it and think we built it for him," Yankton said. "Do not worry about the men. For them, this is light duty—they volunteered."

Mr. Gilbert and I spent time daily reviewing my correspondence. He was as unobtrusive as he promised. My clothes would seem to appear while I was performing my morning ablutions. I knew it was his doing, but I never caught him in the act. Lucy used to tease me occasionally over some of my clothing selections, but with Mr. Gilbert choosing my apparel, she had no opportunity.

"I used to enjoy it when you wore clothes of two different patterns," she complained one day at breakfast. "It is part of your charm. Mr. Gilbert never makes those mistakes."

"I'll ask him to throw in a whopper every so often," I suggested.

"Please don't," Lucy begged. "I think it would make him cry."

"What would make me cry?" Fenwick asked as he entered the dining room and sat down.

"Jenny!" Lucy called out. "One more for breakfast!"

"We were speaking of Mr. Gilbert," I said. "To what do we owe the pleasure of your company?"

"The four ships being built here in Aquileia will be ready to sail the day after tomorrow," Fenwick said. "I think we should go see what Colonel Yankton has prepared for us on Hardscrabble Island and make sure our ships are seaworthy. You also need to begin gathering your soldiers. They should arrive in the city by the first of Haustman. The ships from Newcastle and Aurora should arrive by then as well."

"Fenwick, when the ships set sail for hunting, should I be with them?" I asked. "I'm very much of two minds on the subject."

"If one of those minds is that you fear you would annoy the captains," Fenwick replied, "I would agree with you. After we return from Hardscrabble, set them free. They will only have three or four weeks for 'hunting' as you put it, before they need to return to Aquileia in order to avoid the winter storms. In these early stages, you or I would just be a piece of high-maintenance baggage. Later, after they have found some success on their own, you can invite yourself along. If you did so during Morsug or Porri, when sailing will be as far from a pleasure cruise as you can imagine, they might appreciate your willingness to share the hardship with them."

"You don't think they would welcome my support for the venture?" I asked.

"You are providing them with new ships, built expressly for the purpose of capturing other vessels," Fenwick said. "I think that demonstrates your support. And if you did decide to go, against my advice, I would not be able to join you."

"Why not?"

"The Harvest Fair in Easton," Fenwick replied. "That's where I have been the last ten days—working with Ari to get everything ready."

I looked at Lucy with pleading eyes. I'd missed the last one. She shook her head slightly.

"We can't go, Caz," she said. "It's the same time as the Queen's Cup."

"Majors and Minors! I'd forgotten!" I said.

"Seeing how the queen is now your mother," Lucy said, "we are somewhat obligated."

The last time Lucy and I attended the Queen's Cup, our relationship was still developing. So much had changed since then. Our lives had been a whirlwind, and it did not seem as though it would be slowing any time soon.

"Who of our friends will stay for the cup, and who will be going to Easton?" I asked Lucy.

"If we invite Freddy and Greta, they will come," she said. "Quint and Siobhan will be here. Tom Gibson and Sophie, and Linc and Nellie are going to Easton to visit Fenwick and Julienne and enjoy the Harvest Fair, I think," she said. "I don't know about Ratty and Inger. He might not be able to get away."

"Would it be a burden if I invited those who will be here to dinner the evening before the race?" I asked.

"Invite all of them," Lucy said. "Just don't be disappointed if some send their regrets."

Fenwick and I boarded *Freyja*, the ship Hardy claimed for himself. Before I crossed the gangplank, I wandered to the bow of the ship to see the figurehead. George Chester had done an incredible job. The Goddess Freyja was there, I was pleased to see that she looked more than a little like Lucy, though Freyja's bosom was larger. The figurehead of Lucy was an uncanny likeness, though, again, a bit more blessed in the chest than my lovely wife.

Hardy had one of his men show us to the cabin we would share. It was tiny, as I expected. There were two of the canvas slings called serpentins hanging from the ceiling.

"I hope you wasn't expectin' luxurious accommodations, Yer Highness," Hardy cracked.

"Considering that we half-expected to sleep with the crew, I'd say that's a first-class cabin," I joked back.

"Glad you approve," Hardy grinned, his gold tooth flashing in the sun.

Less than an hour later, we unmoored and raised the mainsail. The other three ships did the same shortly after. The tide was flowing out, and there was a small breeze. Fenwick and I stood at the stern and watched as Hardy gave instructions to his men. I counted eighteen of them.

The water in the harbor was placid. When we reached the mouth, you could see the line of chop. We drove into it.

The wind was stiffer away from the land. Hardy had his men adjust the sails. For a few minutes, *Freyja* had a corkscrewing motion. I reached within myself and accessed my link with Eir, tugging out a tiny tendril to combat my seasickness.

Past the chop, the water settled into regular swells. *Freyja* began to pick up speed and heeled over. I looked behind us to see the other three ships. I couldn't help but grin—it was a magnificent sight.

It seemed to me that we were going quickly—more quickly than any ship I'd been on, even that of Fenwick's opportunist friend, Bebo. Looking over at Hardy standing by the wheel, his face bore a grin similar to mine. Hardy seemed to be muttering something. When he saw me looking, he stopped.

"Jes tellin' 'er she's a real beauty," he explained, patting the wheel. "Never sailed one o' these type afore. I'm liking it. A regular rabbit, she is. We're gonna get along jes fine."

After four days of sailing, we reached the Persimmon Islands. Hardy had his men trim the sails as we approached. He studied a chart carefully, then rolled it up and handed it to me.

"Keep that handy, Yer Highness," he instructed.

He ordered one of his men to the bow with a line. The man tossed it ahead of the ship and let the line play out. As we sailed up to it, he gathered the slack in the line.

"By the deep nine," the man called out.

Another toss, then, "By the mark seven."

"And a half five."

Hardy turned the ship to port slightly.

"By the deep six … by the mark eight …"

"We shouldn't be in no trouble, Yer Highness," Hardy said calmly. "Jes' making sure nothin's changed from the charts."

I looked back, and the other three ships were following us in a line. The man with the line kept casting and calling out the measures. None were less than seven.

We turned to starboard and were heading to Hardscrabble Island. Hardy instructed the men to trim the sails further, and our progress slowed. We approached to within fifty yards of the shore.

"By the mark four. Sandy bottom," the man in the bow called out.

"Drop the sails!" Hardy ordered.

We coasted a bit further, and then Hardy called, "Let go the anchor!"

The anchor chain rattled through the hawse. A moment later, there was a small nudge as the men at the capstan stopped the progress of the chain, and the anchor bit into the bottom. Judging the angle of the anchor chain, two men rotated the capstan a couple of turns to take up some slack.

"Good set!" one of them called back.

I had been too busy paying attention to what we were doing on the ship and had not looked ashore. When I did, I saw the stockade Colonel Yankton built. It was roughly a furlong away from the shore and located on a small rise. Five of the soldiers waved as they approached the sandy shore.

"How long do you intend to stay?" I asked Hardy.

"A couple of hours," Hardy replied. "Tide's still coming in, and I wanna give the boys some practice with the boats. You wanna go ashore, this 'ud be the time, Yer Highness."

Fenwick and I watched as the men swung one of the two small boats out over the side and lowered it to the water. Two climbed down in the boat. Two others handed down oars and then climbed down. When they were settled in their seats on the benches, they gestured for Fenwick and me to join them.

Carefully, we climbed down the ladder with shallow steps built into the hull of the ship. They rowed us to shore with a practiced ease. Remembering Fenwick's and my journey in similar boats and the struggles we had nearly made me laugh.

The soldiers greeted us heartily. They told us they'd been there for three-and-a-half weeks and that any new face was a welcome sight. When we asked to see the stockade, they eagerly gave us a quick tour.

What impressed me were the large quantities of supplies stored. There were barrels of salt pork, bags of grain, and even a supply of dried peas. One of the men showed me the oven they built.

"We'll be making ship's biscuit soon," one of the men said. "Everything a sailor needs."

21

We returned to the ship an hour later. Almost as soon as we were aboard, Hardy signaled to the other three ships. He ordered his men to haul up the anchor. Once that was done, the men quickly set some canvas, and we left Hardscrabble Island. I had a feeling it was not the last I would see of it.

"We made better time getting here than I reckoned, Yer Highness," Hardy said once we cleared the islands and were back in the open ocean, "and we're not far from the Rhetian coast. Sagun is a sizeable port. What say we go have a look?"

"That sounds like a fine idea, Captain Hardy," I said.

"Glad you agree because I already told the others that's what we're doing," he grinned.

"We don't have any soldiers with us," I cautioned.

"Aye," Hardy said, looking me in the eye. "I reckon our men'll be enough. We won't get too greedy. Just thought we'd get a little taste, mebbe."

As afternoon lengthened into evening, all four ships reduced sail. Lanterns were hung so we could tell where the others were. Dinner was served—salt pork stew. As the light faded, from *Princess Lucille* we heard the sound of a fiddle. A flute joined in a minute later from *Bellona.* Several of the men from all four ships began singing.

This had become our regular evening's entertainment since we left Aquileia. Many of the songs were bawdy. A few, though, were hauntingly beautiful, telling of sailors' lives of love and loss.

When the sun rose in the morning, we expanded our sails and headed south by west. Hardy pointed out the port of Sagun as we passed it. He sent one of the men up into the rigging to look for ships. The first one saw nothing. After an hour, he relieved the man and sent another aloft.

"Sail ho!" came a shout not long after the change. "Approaching from dead ahead! Square-rigged!"

Hardy grinned, then ordered one of his men to hoist the "chase" signal to the other ships. He ordered others of the crew to shake the reefs from the sails. This exposed the maximum amount of canvas to the wind. I could see the other ships slightly behind us doing the same. *Freyja* heeled over, picking up speed and bounding through the waves as though the ship itself scented prey.

"Just so there is no confusion, Captain Hardy, please raise our standard," I requested.

Hardy actually knuckled his forelock in acknowledgment, the first real sign of respect he'd shown me. I figured he was excited about what was to come. He barked the orders, and the gold griffin on the gray background that was Aquileia's flag soon fluttered atop the mainmast.

"Looks like two of 'em!" our lookout shouted a few minutes later. "They're tryin' t' go about!"

About an hour after the first sighting, we could see both ships from the deck. They were two carracks lumbering along. Though we were gaining on them, it still took more than two hours to close within shouting distance.

Hardy ordered two of his men forward to man the large skorpio there. They quickly checked the ropes that provided the tension that powered the machine and adjusted them to remove any slack. Satisfied, they loaded a long bolt tipped with a grappling hook into the device. A line, coiled on the deck, was attached to the hook.

"Hauloba ye!" Hardy shouted at the nearest of the two carracks. "Hauloba ye and no die! Sabay?"

"Avast ye and no die!" came an answering shout.

Hardy's response was to laugh. *Princess Lucille* was quickly drawing even with the carrack on the other side from us. Her skorpio was manned as well.

From what I could see, the carrack held roughly the same number of men we did. Several of them were climbing the rigging, carrying crossbows. Some of ours were doing the same.

"If you fine gentlemen would like to partake in the festivities," Hardy said, "get to the fo'c'sle now."

Fenwick and I looked at one another and shrugged at the same time. Unsheathing my blade, I headed forward. As I crossed the deck, I accessed my link to Bellona.

I dared not open it fully. The diamond in the pommel of my sword was still completely drained from Hier. All the asomatous energy I'd generated since recovering consciousness I used to speed the healing of my wounds.

"Fenwick, I can't go all out," I warned.

"I might," he said. "Just for fun."

No sooner did he say that when his appearance increased in size. He appeared to be at least eight feet tall as he manifested the Goddess. It was only an illusion, I knew from my own experience, but it was an impressive sight.

"Avast ye!" came from the other ship. "We hauloba. We hauloba. Sabay?"

"Sabay," Hardy replied.

The captain of the carrack we were approaching gave orders. His men with crossbows climbed down from the rigging partway and handed the weapons to others. They then climbed back up and began hauling in the sails.

Hardy had our men reduce sail, and we drew nearer still. *Princess Lucille* was doing the same on the other side. *Bellona* and *Queen Liliana* were overtaking us, pursuing the other carrack.

"They're Nagahny," Fenwick said. "Captain Hardy, I can translate if that helps."

"Aye. Tell 'em to send six, including the captain, here, and six to the *Lucy*," he asked. "We'll send six and so will Turbot. He'll actually sail 'er back to Aquileia."

Fenwick did the translating. There was a bit of back-and-forth, but eventually, the Nagahny agreed to do as Fenwick ordered. I looked ahead of us. The other carrack had already lowered her sails and surrendered to *Queen Liliana* and *Bellona*.

The Nagahny swung over to our ship, using a line tied to the end of a spar. Our men used the same line to get across to the carrack. The last to come over to *Freyja* was the captain, only slightly better dressed than his crew. He immediately started to harangue Fenwick.

Fenwick allowed the man to vent his spleen for a time, but then responded harshly. The captain stopped protesting. He turned and looked at me with wide eyes, then bobbed his head.

"What did you say?" I asked.

"I explained that we sent the government a letter warning them," Fenwick said. "He knew about it, of course, but was trying to deny that he did. Then he tried to claim that the letter meant nothing because we did not visit in person. I reminded him of the situation in Hier and informed him that you were the one who cut the mage's head off. You saw his reaction."

"Why did he suddenly decide to surrender?" I asked.

"When I manifested Bellona, he remembered from the stories of what happened in Hier that Aquileia has two warrior-mages. He knew resistance would be useless."

"Huh. The whole southern continent knows about us now," I commented.

"They already did, from the rumors about the war and the Battle of Hamill Creek," Fenwick said.

The Nagahny came to Fenwick again, asking something. They held a discussion of some length. At one point, the man was pleading. Fenwick seemed unmoved by his entreaties.

"He wanted to know what will happen to his ship," Fenwick relayed. "I explained we are taking it to Aquileia and will confiscate his cargo but allow him to keep the vessel. He then started to tell me about his aged parents and his sick children, claiming they would suffer horribly if we did not simply let him go. I reminded him that he made the choice to do business with the Rhetians, so the consequences were entirely of his own making. He'll probably come up with a different argument tomorrow."

"What's he carrying?"

"Iron ingots," Fenwick said. "That's one of the reasons he's upset. He knows how close he was to reaching Sagun."

"Is the other ship similarly laden?"

"Yes."

"Pardon me, Yer Highness, I couldna help but overhear," Hardy said. "Iron ingots?"

"Yes."

"Huh. Ain't gold or spices," Hardy said with a shrug, "but that's too much to hope fer. Iron'll sell right quick. How soon do we get the money?"

"Not before you ship out again, I'm afraid," I said. "*Farsall* and *Julienne* will probably be waiting in Aquileia when we return. I don't think we want to wait for the carracks to arrive before we send you out again. Even if the carracks could keep pace with us, it will still take a week or so before the court issues the official ruling and they can sell the iron at auction. Keep in mind, captain, you're working for the crown. I don't think His Majesty has any intention of shortchanging you by even a wheathead."

"True enough," Hardy laughed. "It's jes funny t'think what we did today is on the right side of the law. One more thing. How do I get my men back?"

"Once they reach Aquileia, we'll send them to Hardscrabble Island," I said. "You'll be able to pick them up there. They also have supplies for you in the stockade—salt pork, biscuit, dried peas, and such. I think we'll also try to send regular shipments of carrots and cabbages. They keep for a long time. You might not like either, but they will keep you and your men healthy."

That night, I dreamed of Bellona again. This time, the feeling that she wanted something from me, or wanted me to do something for her, was much stronger. It troubled me enough that I woke and was unable to quickly fall asleep again. I decided to go on deck, thinking fresh air might help clear my head.

In the dim light of the solitary lantern, I saw Fenwick leaning over the rail. He appeared lost in thought. I cleared my throat to alert him to my presence.

"Caz?" he asked softly.

"It's me."

"I should have known," he sighed. "What stirs you out on deck in the middle of the night?"

"I had a dream," I began.

"A disturbing dream, of Bellona in all her glory," Fenwick said quietly. "Wanting something."

"Exactly," I hissed. "You saw her, too."

"Felt stronger than saw," Fenwick said. "She's awe-inducing."

"What does she want, do you think?"

"I don't know," Fenwick replied. "That's what drove me out here—trying to figure it out. Did you feel any hint that something was wrong?"

"The strongest impression I felt was that she wants me—us, probably, if you had the same dream—to do something for her."

"Definitely," Fenwick agreed, "but there's more. I can't quite put my mind on it, which is what is troubling me so much."

"Have you dreamed of her before?" I asked.

"Yes. Once. A couple of days after you woke up," he said.

I shared with Fenwick that I dreamed of her at that time as well. The tone of my dream was different. Fenwick felt less of the Goddess' pleasure than I did, though he did admit to getting the sense she was pleased with him, just not as strongly as I experienced.

"Is it something we are meant to do?" I asked. "Or is it something we left unfinished?"

"That's an excellent question, Caz," Fenwick acknowledged. "It's not anything we left undone. That would feel different. This was more as though—"

"She was asking for a favor," I said, putting the vague feelings I was wrestling with into words.

"I think you're right," Fenwick whispered in an excited tone. "But then, what could it be?"

"Well, it can't hurt to pray for guidance," I suggested.

"Mm," Fenwick agreed.

Leaning over the rail next to Fenwick, I opened my connection with Bellona a tiny amount. *Tell me what you want, Goddess,* I thought silently. *If it is at all in my power, I will do it.*

Fenwick and I went back to our cabin not long after. I fell asleep eventually. The Goddess did not reappear.

We arrived in Aquileia four days later. I was pleased to see that *Julienne* and *Farsall* were waiting for us. I spoke briefly with their captains, Barrett and Ward, who both gushed about the ships and their handling and speed.

Mr. Chester was overseeing the installation of the figureheads on both of them. The representation of Julienne Traval was uncannily accurate, though with a bigger bust, as his portrayal of Lucy was. The figurehead for *Farsall* looked similar to the one for *Bellona*.

Fenwick arranged for the Nagahny to stay at an inn near the harbor where he knew a couple of members of the staff spoke their language. Fenwick left soon after to head to Easton. He was needed for the Harvest Fair.

I returned to the castle. When I found his office, I shared our good news with Mark. He was pleased.

"Wasn't this only supposed to be a trial of seaworthiness?" he asked.

"Yes, but Captain Hardy felt we made such good time that we could spend a day or two on the Rhetian coast."

"And you saw the fortifications Colonel Yankton prepared?"

"I did. They were impressive. Perfect for our needs," I said.

I shared as much with the colonel later and also reminded him to make sure we sent some non-perishable vegetables to keep the men healthy through the winter. He made a note of it, then informed me that the soldiers who would be sailing on the ships were gathered in the Castle Shield's barracks.

In the barracks, I realized I recognized nearly all the men gathered to serve on the ships. I was pleased to see that Major Grunevald had seen fit to provide them all with oilskins. The men would definitely need them for life aboard a ship, particularly in the winter weather to come.

Several were armsmen from the March, and I knew them by name and greeted them warmly. Others, I realized, were from the army who fought the Rhetians. Not wanting them to leave slighted in any way, I made a point of introducing myself.

"Men," I said, after climbing on top of a bench, "I just returned from the first sail in the new ships. Though we were only supposed to give the ships a trial at sea, we decided to swing by the Rhetian coast. We already took two prizes. I imagine there are plenty more left for you. Good luck, and good hunting!"

They greeted this with a small cheer and good humor. I said my farewells and returned to the castle. Upon entering our apartment, I found Mr. Gilbert.

"You need a bath, Your Highness," he informed me before I even drew close to him.

"That bad?" I asked.

"Not horrible, but let's get you cleaned up before you see the princess," he said.

The princess … He meant Lucy, of course. I did not think of her as "the princess," but realizing that others now did, made me happy. Someday, far in the future I hoped, she would be "the queen." She would be the most wonderful queen Aquileia had ever experienced, I thought smugly.

When I finished bathing and dressed, I found Mr. Gilbert again. He was in the small study, sitting behind the desk. When I entered, he stood.

"Your Highness, I am to remind you that in two nights, you will be hosting three couples for dinner: Lord and Lady Rawlinsford, Lord and Lady Tulley, Miss Inger Stevens, and Mr. Ratcliff Hawkins. The following day, you will attend the Queen's Cup with Their Majesties," Gilbert announced.

"Thank you, Mr. Gilbert," I replied calmly, though hearing that Freddy and Greta would be coming to the city for the race made me almost want to dance a jig. "Where would I find the princess, now that I am fit for human company? Is she on the grounds?"

"I believe she is, with Her Majesty and Miss Katherine, in what she now calls her 'workshop.' I'm not entirely fond of the name, I must admit, Your Highness," he said with a small frown. "It seems un—unusual for Her Highness to have a *workshop*."

"Un*usual*, Mr. Gilbert? Was 'unbecoming' the first word you thought of?" I asked, teasing him, "or unseemly?"

"Your Highness, I would not presume—"

"Mr. Gilbert, I take no offense," I assured him. "The princess, as I am sure you are learning, is an un*usual* woman. And Katie is now 'Miss Katherine,' is she?"

"Well, yes, Your Highness," Gilbert said. "The name 'Katie' is suitable for a farm girl or a serving girl, I suppose, but Miss Katherine is no longer on the farm, nor is she a serving girl. She is more of a—how should I say? A protégé? A pupil? A confidant?"

"Mr. Gilbert, I believe you have just described perfectly the role of a lady-in-waiting, at least from what I have observed," I said. "And are others now referring to her as Miss Katherine?"

"Oh, yes, Your Highness," Gilbert said proudly. "Her Majesty and Her Highness both adopted my manner of addressing Miss Katherine immediately."

22

The next two weeks were busy. Taking advantage of people gathering for the Queen's Cup, Mark held a meeting of his council, minus my father and Fenwick, who were busy in Easton with the Harvest Fair. During the meeting, I informed everyone of what happened in Hier and provided an update on our small navy. It helped that news of the arrival of the two carracks came to us during the meeting.

Our dinner party was a success, with Ratty Hawkins' account of how his father reacted to seeing Martin Albrecht's letter being the highlight. After two days of rain, the day of the Queen's Cup dawned bright and fair—a beautiful day that harkened back to summer. Freddy was the big winner among us, which pleased him immensely. Though Freddy placed the bet, he celebrated his win in the character of Lord Compote. I laughed so hard that my sides hurt the next day.

Lucy and I discussed the need to purchase a horse for Katie. Since Carl Stensland displayed such a knack for finding intelligent and intuitive mounts, I cajoled Lucy into allowing us to dine out at his inn. When we arrived at the Foaming Boar, we caused more of a ruckus than I intended. Everyone there recognized the two of us. Perhaps they were tipped off by the members of the Castle Shield who entered before us. Or maybe it was Carl greeting us as Prince Casimir and Princess Lucy.

In either case, the dining room fell silent when we entered. People were staring, though trying to be discreet about it and whispering among themselves. Finally, I had enough. I stood up.

"If everyone will be so kind as to resume normal conversation, I will be absolutely delighted to pay for all your dinners," I announced. "Feel free to come introduce yourselves before our food arrives. We will be pleased to make your acquaintance."

A titter of nervous laughter greeted my request. Still, a couple at a time, people did come over and meet us. Lucy was her charming and graceful self. I was … well, I did my best to be as affable as possible. Lucy is the one with real skill at putting people at their ease.

Dinner was a roast with fall vegetables—delicious and simple. Heeding my request, after our dinners arrived, no one bothered us except Carl. He came and joined us halfway through the meal.

"You do remember what happened the last time the crown prince visited the Foaming Boar, don't you?" he asked. "We were overwhelmed with business for months. I don't know whether to thank you or curse you, Caz."

"Thank me in public," I suggested. "Curse me in private."

We spent some time getting Carl caught up on my latest adventures. He had not heard about Hier. I guess word did not spread, which bothered me not at all. He did hear about the ships because he knew some of the men who volunteered to serve aboard. At last, we reached a lull where I could mention horses.

"I told you how well Andy and Davy performed under frightening circumstances in Hier, Carl. It occurs to me—"

"And to me," Lucy interrupted.

"That you are the finest judge of equine potential we know," I continued. "Lucy now has a young woman who is her lady-in-waiting, who is being instructed in duties that will take her far from the capital. She needs a good mount, but more than a sturdy horse, she requires one who has the intelligence and intuition that Andy, Davy, and Bella possess. Her mount also needs to be trained to your exacting standards—"

"So we can be sure that her horse will keep her from danger as much as possible," Lucy added. "I think a mare would be better for her, but we will yield to your judgment."

"Well," Carl said, stroking his chin, "it just so happens that I was invited to look at a six-year-old mare two days ago—a roan, quite fetching she is. She has been training for steeplechase, but the owners have given up on her."

"Why?" Lucy asked.

"She likes to run *with* the other horses, not ahead of them," Carl laughed. "By herself, she's as fast as they come, but put other horses on the track, and she slows down to be part of the group. She has a wonderful temperament and is smart. I liked her very much but wasn't really in the market."

"Do you think you could still get her?" Lucy asked.

"When I left, I told them I needed to think on it," Carl said, "and I haven't told them 'no' yet. I'll warn you—she'll be expensive. They want eight hundred for her."

"Carl—" I started to say, but Lucy put her hand on my arm to quiet me.

"This young lady is very important to us," she said. "The peace of mind we will have, knowing she has such a fine mount, will justify the high price. Will you get her for us? And train her?"

"I'll be happy to get her for you," he said, "but your visit here tonight might limit the time I will have available to train her. But Jerry knows what to do. If you trust Jerry to teach her—"

"I would trust Jerry about anything to do with horses," I said.

"As would I," Lucy agreed.

"Then we'll be happy to help," Carl said.

"I'll have someone deliver a bank draft in the morning," I said. "Thank you."

"Her name is Serendipity, by the way," Carl added.

"Perfect," Lucy said with a laugh as she clapped her hands.

Though we were slower to finish our meals than the other diners, none of them left. When they saw the serving girl clear our places, we learned why. Led by a man with a clear tenor voice, they started singing the song about me.

Since the last time I heard it, they added two new verses. Both were about Lucy. I applauded after each one. When they finished, I stood.

"Thank you," I said. "It has been a pleasure to share such a fine meal with all of you. May all the Gods, Major and Minor, and all the heavenly beings, bless you and keep you safe until we meet again."

Two days later, my morning started with finding Fenwick sipping a cup of qava when I entered our dining room. Jenny brought me one of my own, and I sat to enjoy it. Fenwick said nothing for a time. I was about to prompt him when he stirred.

"The mysterious and malodorous Dr. Flamel attended the Harvest Fair," he said. "At the urging of everyone in our party, I braved the stench to see him. The cheeky rogue demanded five ducats before he would tell me anything."

"His prices have risen," I commented, "or he had something of unique importance to share."

"I believe it's the latter," Fenwick said. "He said the information applies to both of us—he called me a 'jumped-up orphan' and you 'a jumped-up bastard' by the way."

"That sounds like him," I agreed. "What did he share?"

"He said, 'You will not find the thing that plagues your dreams by searching for it. Misfortune will find you and show you the way.' That was it," Fenwick said with a shrug.

"Hardly seems worth five ducats," I commented. "Anything else?"

Fenwick shook his head.

"He did say the information applies to both of us, so we'll be in it together, at least," I said.

"Such a comfort," Fenwick said with a smirk.

"Well, we leave again tomorrow to join the ships at Hardscrabble Island. Perhaps whatever the misfortune is will find us there?" I suggested.

"That was my thinking, but who knows? Seven Hells! For five ducats, the man could at least speak clearly and not pose riddles."

"How was the Fair?" I inquired.

"Well attended and well received," Fenwick replied. "Ari did a tremendous job in pulling things together. The people were happy that the Fair continued even though you and Lucy were no longer there. I think it did a great deal to reassure folks that they have nothing to fear from my stewardship of the March."

"That's excellent, then. We could hardly hope for better."

"I also learned that our friends on the other side of the eastern mountains came to Oritur to trade not long ago," Fenwick said. "In my absence, someone had the good sense to find Patsy Campbell to translate for them. Cattle and horses for iron implements and weapons—mostly arrows, in great quantity. It apparently took over a week to make the number they desired."

"Is there a problem? Needing such a quantity—"

"Not according to what Patsy told me," Fenwick said. "They usually obtained their arrows from a supplier even further east in the past. Ours were markedly less expensive. Polim, the cousin of their leader Kushedt, was thrilled. His standing in the tribe will improve as a result of the bargain."

The following day, Fenwick and I boarded a small Liburnian vessel, along with the sailors who brought the carracks back to Aquileia. Fair weather deserted us, and the entire journey was made in cold rain and roiling seas. When we reached Hardscrabble Island, we were all exceedingly grateful to dry out and warm up by a hot stove in the barracks of the stockade.

Three days later, *Farsall* approached, and we were ferried aboard Captain Ward's ship. He hoped to find us, as all six ships were now short-handed. Some of the soldiers were being used in place of missing sailors.

That, of course, was good news. Our fleet had captured another eight ships, all now on their way to Aquileia. They had nearly reached the point where they dared not take any more prizes for fear of having no one to sail them. They'd sent *Farsall* to Hardscrabble, hoping that we would have arrived.

We met the rest of the fleet off Sagun. Fenwick and I transferred to *Freyja* and the care of Captain Hardy. He informed us we would be heading to the Rhetian Straits. The ships they had taken since we left were along the western coast of Rhetia, and word had spread. As a result, merchant shipping was staying near the coast, only traveling from one harbor to the next. In addition, the lateness of the season also meant traffic was reduced.

Hardy and the other captains knew any merchant ships heading north or south needed to cross the Rhetian Straits into the open ocean. They would have no ports to which they could escape. We headed south and then west. It took twelve days of sailing against the prevailing winds in mostly bad weather before we spotted the headlands of Drasil, the southern tip of Rhetia. It rained nine of those days.

"We can only stay a week before the weather gets more risky," Hardy explained, "Plus, we are short of men. We can take no more than one ship each before we will need to return to Hardscrabble. We need to get our men back, and then we should really return to Aquileia. The weather will stay unfavorable until the second half of Morsug."

Bellona and *Farsall* caught the first carrack we spotted on our second day near the straits. We decided to send them back to Hardscrabble and then home. Three days after that, *Julienne* and *Queen Liliana* took another ship. They, too, headed for home.

Princess Lucille stayed with us on *Freyja* as we searched for prey. We were heading mostly north toward Rhetia. Another dream of Bellona disturbed my sleep in the middle of the night. It felt almost as though she was pleading with me. I felt tense and anxious when I woke. Going back to sleep right away would be impossible. I dressed quietly and went on deck.

The wind and waves were from the west, and we were on a close reach on the larboard tack. This gave the ship a corkscrew-like motion, and the lantern we hung from the mast was swaying vigorously. Fenwick appeared not long after I took my position at the starboard rail since the ship was canted in that direction.

Looking into the darkness on this rare, clear, moonless night, his arrival did not surprise me. We seemed to be experiencing the same visions. Mine disturbed me enough that I expected it to do the same to him.

"Something is going to happen soon," Fenwick said. "I can feel it."

'The dream?" I asked.

"Yes. It left me restless and uneasy," he said.

"Me too."

Suddenly, the ship heaved up behind us, pitching us both forward and over the rail. An enormous wave crested over the ship and drove both of us underwater. I will admit I thrashed about in a panic for a moment, unable to tell which direction was up. Fortunately, I had a moment of clarity and realized my natural buoyancy would take me to the surface if I relaxed and was patient.

I stopped my frenzied movement and, within a few seconds, bobbed to the surface. When I went under, I inhaled a fair bit of water, and I spent a minute coughing it out. Then I realized I did not hear Fenwick doing the same.

It was so dark I would have no hope of seeing him or his body. Treading water, I extended my arms and tried to sweep around myself. My hand touched his hair. I grabbed it and drew him to me. He was unconscious, face down.

I rolled him over and tried to pull him to my chest. Keeping our heads above the water as much as I could, I clasped him around the chest and tried to squeeze his ribs. I hoped to expel the water and get his lungs working again. It must have been at least a dozen times I squashed him to myself. I was beginning to ponder giving up when he retched and coughed.

While he was doing that, something bumped into my head rather firmly. I let go of Fenwick with my right hand and felt for it. My fingers touched it, and I clutched it desperately, trying to pull it over to us. I needed to get a better purchase and adjust my grip. Whatever it was, it was made of wood, and floating.

"Fenwick, there's something here to grab onto," I said. "Can you manage it?"

"Yes," he croaked.

I guided his hand to the edge of it. When I felt him take hold, I reached up to try to determine what it was. It was only a couple of inches thick but seemed to have a broad surface. I raised myself up and swept my arm over it to try to feel how big it was. My best guess was that it was a hatch cover.

I "walked" around it using my hands and learned I was correct. When I reached Fenwick after traveling all the way around, he was still coughing. I had an idea.

"Fenwick, we're holding onto a hatch cover," I said. "If I give you a boost, do you think you can haul yourself up onto it?"

"I'll try," he moaned.

I dipped underwater and put my hands around his waist. Kicking with both legs in the manner of a frog, I tried to drive us both up. When I stopped, Fenwick managed to get his chest onto the surface.

"Hold a bit, Caz," he said, then began coughing again. "I can do the rest, but I need a minute."

After a short time, I felt him begin to squirm and shimmy. The hatch cover pitched from side to side with his efforts. Then he stopped.

"I'm up," he said. "Let me take hold of the far edge, then you can pull yourself up using my body. Ready? Go ahead."

As I started to pull myself aboard, I could feel it sinking underneath us. Clearly, it was only buoyant enough to hold one of us. I settled back into the water.

"Only one of us gets to ride in style, Fenwick. I guess that's you tonight," I said. "Can you see the ship's lanterns?"

"No," he answered after a minute. "The only light is the stars."

"Well, at least it's a clear night," I said. "Do you think the ship—?"

"I don't think it sank," he said. "At least, I hope it didn't. They probably took some serious damage, though, and I would imagine they are more focused on that than checking to see if we're still in our cabin."

"I suppose that's true," I admitted.

I didn't know what a wave like that, catching the ship almost broadside, would do. The masts might have broken. With the hatch cover gone, they certainly took on a quantity of water. Even if they could spare the attention, the darkness cloaked us, and the vastness of the sea around us made yelling for help a futile gesture.

Thinking back, I should have been terrified. I don't remember ever feeling that way. For some reason, my thoughts turned to what I *could* do, and not how impossible our situation was. Thank all the heavenly beings, the water was not too cold. Enough of the warmth from the summer remained in the surface layer that I was not uncomfortable yet, though further below, it was quite bracing.

Something Fenwick said earlier had triggered a thought, but I could not grasp it for a moment. Then I remembered—he mentioned he could see the stars. That gave me an idea.

"Fenwick, can you keep us pointed north?" I asked.

"Yes," he answered uncertainly, not understanding what I was thinking.

"I'm going to hand you some things. Don't lose them," I said.

I ducked underwater and pulled off my right boot, then slapped it down on the hatch cover. My left boot followed. Then I unbuckled my sword.

"My boots and my sword," I said. "Hang onto them. Now, which way is north?"

"A quarter turn clockwise," he said.

Using my legs, I moved us until Fenwick told me to stop. Then, I started kicking slowly. I figured we had a fair distance to travel, and I didn't want to use up all my energy at once.

"What are you doing, Caz?" he asked.

"Pushing us north, to the shore," I said.

"To Rhetia."

"Well, I would head for Aquileia, but I don't think I'll last that long," I joked. "Unless you have a better idea?"

"Rhetia it is, then," he sighed.

"If we make it, at least I'll have the chance to die with my blade in my hand," I said. "Has to be better than drowning."

23

I pushed us north as long as I could. Just before daybreak, when the gray light of false dawn began to peel away the utter darkness, the wind changed direction and began blowing from the south. I was beginning to feel the cold. The exercise of kicking my legs helped stave it off, but it was seeping deep into my bones.

"Are you planning on doing all the work?" Fenwick asked. "Or would you like me to take over for a bit?"

"That actually sounds like a wonderful idea," I said. "If you feel you're up to it."

"I'll do my best," he said. "Thank you for not letting me drown, by the way."

"Thank Lucy," I suggested. "I only saved you because if I didn't, she might have been quite cross with me for *hours*."

"Remind me when we see her," Fenwick said.

He extended his hand to me and helped pull me halfway onto the hatch cover. As before, our combined weight was dragging it under. Fenwick slid off, and I squirmed on. I noticed he had taken off his boots and sword as well. Before I flopped myself on top of them to prevent them from going astray, I tried to look around.

Neither of the ships was visible. I thought I saw a faint smudge on the northern horizon, but it was not yet light enough out to even mention it. It was probably only wishful thinking on my part.

The cold I felt did not dissipate, but it no longer grew worse. I had the thought to try to access my connection to Eir to see if that might dispel the chill. I opened that connection slightly and plucked a thin tendril from the mote. With my mind, I tried to flow that tendril into the parts of my body where I was most chilled.

It worked, but it took more than just a whisp of her power to chase away the cold. I used as much as I dared without draining myself. When I finished, I was not warm, but I no longer felt so soddenly chilled.

Not long after the day broke, I noticed Fenwick was just hanging on and not pushing. I appreciate that he gave me a respite, but it was clear he was not up to the task. After all, he had drowned a few hours before.

"My turn," I announced, offering him a hand.

He took it gratefully, and we changed positions. Getting back onto the hatch cover winded him noticeably. He lay there panting for a moment. Suddenly, he gasped.

"Caz! I can see the Drasil Heights! Off to the right," he said with quiet excitement.

Carefully, he raised himself to his hands and knees. I presumed it was to see better. He lowered himself just as cautiously to avoid tipping the hatch cover.

"We are less than half a league from shore," he said. "The coast is relatively flat here, similar to what we encountered when Bebo landed us on the eastern shore. I could see a small hill not too far away, with what looked like one of their ugly temples."

"That means a town is nearby," I said. "Is that a good thing or a bad thing?"

"It's a bad thing if it leads to trouble," Fenwick said, "but might be a good thing if we can obtain food, shelter, and a means of escape."

It was the middle of the afternoon by the time we reached the pebbled shore. By then, I was exhausted and starting to shake with cold. Fenwick and I stumbled around and gathered wood. When we felt we had enough, after arranging it carefully above the high tide line, Fenwick lit a twig using his finger. From that, he carefully allowed the fire to grow. In five minutes, we had a roaring blaze.

The wood was seasoned and relatively dry, so our fire gave off little smoke. Fenwick and I stood near it, warming ourselves and drying our clothes. We put our boots as close to the blaze as we dared to dry them out as well.

In less than an hour, I felt almost human again, though extremely tired. I clambered up the scarp and stuck my head up to see what I could. About fifty feet away was the stubble of harvested grain. A small barn was the closest building. I imagined the farmer's hut was on the other side of it. Looking out to sea, I saw no sign of either of our ships.

"I think we stay here and keep warm until the middle of the night," I said. "Evening is approaching. After midnight, when people sleep most soundly, we can go exploring."

"Food would be welcome," Fenwick said. "Will we return here?"

"Only if we don't find someplace better," I replied. "But we should gather enough wood to keep the fire going through the night."

We gathered more wood, taking care to stay below the scarp. Before the light faded, I crawled up to the top of the slope just past where we were sitting and surveyed our surroundings again. This time, I was looking beyond our immediate vicinity, hoping to find some indication of where the nearest town might be.

As I looked, my eyes kept stopping on the unattractive temple on the knoll not far away. It wasn't that interesting, but something made me want to look at it. It was difficult to tear my gaze away from it. I had a thought.

"Fenwick, climb up and have a look to see if you get an idea where the town is," I asked.

"No idea," he said when he returned a few minutes later.

"As you looked around, was there anything in particular that caught your eye? Something that seemed to arrest your gaze?"

"The temple," he said after he took a minute to reflect. "I would be scanning from shore to shore, but every time I passed the temple, my survey would be interrupted. Why?"

"I felt the same thing," I said. "When we go out later, I want to see that temple, if only because it's on the highest ground nearby, and we might learn where the town is. But I have a strange feeling there is something more there."

"What sort of something?"

"I have no idea," I admitted. "When we get there and find nothing, I suppose we can have a quiet laugh."

I went back to the slope. Peering over it at their temple, I accessed my connection with Bellona. The blood in my veins seemed to thrill at the sight. Closing my link, I slid back down.

"We're meant to go there," I said. "No question about it. It's related to our dreams. I looked at it with Bellona."

Fenwick understood what I meant. He nodded, and a thoughtful look came over his face. Smiling, he shook his head.

"The rogue wave that swept us away was no random accident," he said with amused wonderment. "Majors and Minors! And Bellona, most of all! I'm not accustomed to being a pawn in a game greater than I can understand. This is a strange feeling."

"I have felt that way for some time," I admitted.

"Have we no free will?" Fenwick asked after minutes of silent contemplation.

"Of course we do," I replied. "But all the experiences of our lives shape us into who we are, and that influences the decisions we make. We are free to make the wrong choices. It does not mean that the overall outcome will change. Instead, the path to it alters and perhaps becomes more difficult."

"When I first tried to kill you," Fenwick said after thinking about what I said, "I chose to, of my own free will, even though I had misgivings. Are you saying that if I decided instead to—I don't know—approach you and warn you that your stepmother wanted you dead, that it would still lead us to be where we are, here and now?"

"I think so," I said. "Fenwick, from what Lucy shared with me, I should have died that night. That was not allowed to happen."

"You have felt this way since?"

"In part," I said. "My understanding is limited. It is like peeling away the layers of an onion. At the time, I thought it was Lucy's love that saved me. I know this to be true, but I have since come to think that was only part of the answer."

"And this onion," Fenwick said, "are you getting to the heart of it?"

"Majors and Minors, no!" I laughed. "About all I can say is—that when we find ourselves in circumstances like this, it is comforting to think that we are where we are meant to be—that there is a reason behind it. I may not ever understand the reason, though. I accept that."

"This is not the conversation I thought I would have, stranded on a beach in Rhetia," Fenwick said, shaking his head and laughing softly. "I suppose that actually makes perfect sense, though."

"You're probably right," I chuckled.

We stayed by our fire, enjoying the warmth, until well into the night. When Fenwick stood to put on his boots, I did the same. We buckled our swords around our waists and climbed up the scarp, heading in the direction of the temple.

The night was just as black as before. The moon, waxing crescent, disappeared hours before, shortly after sundown. From being near the fire, our eyes were unaccustomed to the dark, and we stumbled at first, walking over the uneven surface of the farmer's fields.

When we reached a slight incline, I knew we were heading in the proper direction. After a few more minutes of walking, we sensed rather than saw the bulk of the temple building. We found the entrance. The door was unlocked, and we entered.

I made the end of my finger glow. With that dim light, Fenwick found a torch in a sconce by the door. He lit it, and we stepped inside. It was not as large as the temple we were forced to attend on our previous visit to Rhetia.

We proceeded toward the altar. As we drew closer, my eyes were drawn upward. On the wall behind the altar was a spear. I knew with certainty this was why we were here.

It was slender and about half again longer than the short lances to which I was accustomed. It had a leaf-bladed tip. Though tarnished, I suspected that the tip was made of steel. As I approached it, I saw a small plaque fixed on the wall underneath it.

"The so-called 'Lance of Bellona'—one of the false gods worshiped by the infidels of Aquileia—brought here by Erasmus Litchey, the soldier who took it from their temple, dedicated in this dwelling of the one true God as a testament to His power," Fenwick read.

"Give me a leg up so I can get it down," I asked.

Fenwick set the torch on the floor and cupped his hands. I put my left foot there and raised myself up. As soon as my fingers closed around the shaft, supernatural strength filled my body. I was no longer cold, tired, or hungry. I felt invincible and also filled with a sense of the deepest satisfaction.

'Touch it, Fenwick," I whispered once my feet were on the ground.

"Oh, my!" he gasped after a moment. "Oh, my!"

I touched my inner connection to Bellona, intending to withdraw only a thin amount in order to learn in which direction we should head. Power from the spear surged into me until I knew I was "full." I also knew where to go.

"Fenwick, open your connection and touch it again," I suggested.

"Whoa," he replied with amazement when he did.

Fenwick picked up the torch, sputtering on the floor. We headed to the entrance. He snuffed it out before we opened the door. Despite the darkness, I could see everything as though the moon were full.

"Fenwick, keep a hand on it," I said. "I think it will help."

He put his hand on the shaft next to mine. We fell into step immediately, making it easy for us both to hold it. The direction we were heading was away from where we started. On the other side of the rise where the temple was built, we dimly could see the town. We headed for it.

At least one person was awake and beginning his day—the baker. The smell of bread reached me and reminded me how hungry I was, even with Bellona's influence. Fenwick must have felt the same.

"Give me a minute," he whispered, then darted inside the building.

I heard muffled voices. Fenwick's threatening, the other pleading. A few minutes later, Fenwick returned. He pressed a loaf of bread into my hand. It was not warm.

"Yesterday's?" I asked.

"It is," he replied. "And we should count ourselves fortunate. With the way I trussed the baker up, the first batch today will be burnt to a crisp. Where are we heading?"

"I hear water," I said, "so I hope there's something we can sail away from here. Even though our recent experience with stealing small boats in the middle of the night has not been good, I have a feeling our luck has turned."

We resumed walking. I gnawed off mouthfuls of bread as we went. For day-old bread, it was not too stale. I'd certainly eaten far worse in my lifetime.

In less than two furlongs, we saw the small harbor. There were a couple of fishing boats tied to the docks, but I kept looking. Toward the mouth of the harbor, I saw what I hoped for.

"Toward the mouth," I whispered. "Do you see the Liburnian?"

"I see it," Fenwick replied.

"That's the ship for us," I said. "If we took one of the fishing boats, the Liburnian could catch us. In the Liburnian, none of these others have a chance."

Still holding the lance, the two of us made our way to the small ship. Before we stepped onto the dock, we both stopped. Something was urging us to be cautious.

"Two aboard," Fenwick hissed. "I'll deal with them."

The gray light of false dawn was on the horizon, enabling me to watch as Fenwick approached the ship slowly. He stepped onto the gunwale of the ship gingerly, trying to avoid making the hull rock and alert the inhabitants. In this, he failed.

Under his weight, the ship moved more than expected. It also screeched as the hull rubbed against the piling. Fenwick leaped forward. He dispatched one of the two, but the other was now awake.

"Help!" Fenwick told me later the man shouted. It was in Rhetian, so I did not understand. "Murderers! Thieves! Help!"

The man scurried forward, away from Fenwick, and jumped from the bow. When he surfaced, he was swimming to the shore, still yelling. I put the lance down and trotted to where he was slogging out of the water, withdrawing my blade as I moved.

The man was looking over his shoulder, worried that Fenwick would follow him. He never saw me. I cut his throat in mid-holler. His shout died, turning into an obscene gurgle.

I sheathed my blade and picked up the lance. Fenwick was already untying the ship. I jumped aboard and laid the spear down, then searched for the oars.

Fenwick cast the lines off. I handed him an oar and the two of us used them to pole ourselves away from the dock.

Lights began to appear in response to the man's hollering. The water was now deep enough that we could no longer push against the bottom. Fenwick put his oar in the lock and began pushing it to turn the bow of the ship to the sea. I locked my oar in. Once we were pointed more or less in the proper direction, we both began to pull. The oars were too long and heavy for one man to handle both.

The Liburnian was much heavier than the rowboat we stole the last time we escaped from Rhetia. I felt as though I was making no progress at all despite using every bit of strength and weight I possessed. Fenwick had me take a break. He got busy with the sail, untying the lines that kept it furled against the boom.

Lit torches were coming to the water's edge. We were clearly visible, only a few yards away from the end of the dock. If anyone had a crossbow, we would soon be in trouble.

Just as I started to worry, Fenwick began to hoist the sail. After he raised it, he tied the line off and darted to the stern to adjust the boom. He returned to his oar, and we resumed rowing.

One of the men coming to the waterfront stopped halfway, then turned and ran back. A couple of minutes later, he reappeared, a crossbow in his hands. I was about to curse when suddenly, the job of pulling the oars became easier. Cocking my head, I could see the sail filling with a small breeze.

The man ran to the end of the dock and cocked the crossbow using his foot. As he brought it up to fire, Fenwick and I both ducked. I heard the whistle of the bolt fly past Fenwick. The man on the dock cocked the weapon again. Behind him, I saw two others carrying similar weapons. They were not joining the first on the dock but running further along to catch up with us.

The first one fired again and missed Fenwick a second time. He saw the two men running along the waterfront and left the dock to join them. Fenwick saw them as well.

"Bring the oars in," he said as he crouched down and moved to the tiller. It was all I could do to bring the oars aboard without getting a bolt in my ear. I would stow them properly when we were out of range. Fenwick cursed.

"Hit?" I asked.

"No. Almost," he replied. "Felt the breeze through my hair."

"Better there than through your ear," I cracked.

We were picking up speed. As we neared the harbor mouth, the breeze grew stronger. Fenwick steered us so that we were now at least a hundred yards away. Any shot that hit us now would be a matter of blind luck. We still kept our heads down.

The chop waiting for us when we reached the boundary between the small river and the sea was teeth-rattling and kidney-jarring. The waves slammed into us with no discernible pattern or rhythm. Often, we had not yet settled from one impact when another hit. The only good thing about it was that the men with crossbows gave up, realizing they were just wasting bolts.

24

Once we were clear of the chop and well past the headland, Fenwick turned us so we were running before the west wind. I took it upon myself to explore our new ship. The first thing I found was the man Fenwick killed.

I dragged him up from the cabin and over to the side of the ship. Since the Rhetians followed a religion I believed to be a fraud, I said no prayers as I slid the body over the side. Then, I returned to the cramped cabin below the deck to see what there was inside.

There were narrow bunks for twelve people along the bulkheads. Only two of them were recently occupied, and they smelled foul. The other bunks held sleeping pallets rolled together and tied with twine. There was a small galley—filthy. Bits of food and spills made the deck tacky underfoot. The cupboards in the galley held no food. There was a small barrel of water with a ladle. Permeating the air was the coppery smell of the blood from Fenwick's victim.

Returning up to the deck, I saw that Fenwick found a locker holding weapons. He gestured to it. Inside were four crossbows, two axes, and six short swords.

"Crossbows would have been nice to have," he commented. "What's below?"

"A job of cleaning," I answered, pulling the rest of my uneaten loaf of bread from inside my shirt where I'd stashed it. "And I'm not in the mood."

"That bad?"

"If need be, I believe I can make it as far as Hardscrabble Island without venturing below, except for the occasional gulp of the little water I found," I said.

"What if we run into weather?" he asked. "Those are mares' tails in the sky to the west. If they turn into mackerel scales tonight, we'll be in for a bit of a blow."

"If we find some oilskins, I'll just have you lash me to the mast, Fenwick," I moaned. "I'm in no mood to tidy up after pigs at the moment. It's been two days without sleep, and whatever the surge I felt from the lance has worn off, and I'm done for now."

"Fair enough," he agreed.

I did venture below once more and came back with four of the sleeping pallets. Unrolling two of them, I stretched out on one and used the other as a blanket. With the rocking of the ship, I was asleep in no time at all.

Fenwick woke me sometime in the night. He needed a break, and I took over the tiller. I will admit I dozed off, sleeping sitting up with the tiller bar under my arm. Daybreak woke me. Fortunately, Fenwick was still sleeping.

Looking to the sky, the high wispy clouds Fenwick called "mares' tails" were gone. In their place was a lower level of scallop-shaped clouds I guessed these were the "mackerel scales" he mentioned. Given that his nautical knowledge was more than mine, I took for granted that a storm was on the way from the west.

"Oi! Lord Easton! Stir your stumps!" I shouted.

Fenwick rolled over and extended his head from underneath the sleeping pallet he was using to cover himself. He fixed me with one baleful eye. Thinking better of complaining, he sat up and looked around. We passed the Drasil Heights sometime in the darkness. They were still visible behind us. He also noticed the change in the sky.

"We held a vote while you were asleep, Lord Easton, and decided that you should clean the cabin to the best of your ability before the weather shifts," I announced.

"Who is this *we* of which you speak?" he grumbled.

"Everyone aboard," I said cheerfully. "You abstained. Therefore, the decision was unanimous. You shall clean while I steer."

"That hardly seems fair."

"I could just command you to do it, as your prince," I said, "but I would rather not pull rank. Please, Fenwick?"

"Fine. The 'please' wins, seeing how you did bring me back from drowning," he said.

"Aw—I was saving that," I complained.

Unbelievably, Fenwick found a broom, a mop, and a bucket. He set about cleaning the cabin. It didn't take long—a couple of hours at most. I ended up taking over halfway through—after he cleaned up the blood.

When we finished, it was clean and tidy enough that one of us could stay below when the storm hit. I took the lance below to protect it from the weather Fenwick predicted. Under the bunks were lockers. I went through them when I finished cleaning and found more weapons. The prize was some oilskins. I showed them to Fenwick with pride.

"Well done, Caz," Fenwick acknowledged. "Now, if you could only find us some food and some more water."

"One thing at a time, Aloysius," I responded. "One thing at a time."

We sorted through the oilskins to find pieces that fit us. As I was finishing the job of cleaning the cabin, it did not escape my notice that the wind and waves were gaining strength. At present, they were coming from nearly dead astern. We needed to begin heading north, though, and that would make things trickier. Before I mentioned it to Fenwick, he turned us to a broad reach and asked me to trim the sail.

"I'd like to get as far north as possible," he said. "With any luck, we will avoid the worst of what's coming."

The storm reached us just before sundown. We may have enjoyed a bit of luck. Perhaps the storm was worse to the south—I don't know. It was plenty bad where we were. After a few hours, we turned west by north, close-hauled under only enough sail to keep us pointed into the weather. The waves broke over the port bow, and our ship resembled a porpoise diving up and down.

Fenwick and I rode it out, clad in our oilskins. We lashed ourselves to the ship, not wishing to repeat our swim to shore from three days earlier. Not long after the day broke, we judged the worst was past and turned north by east again on a broad reach. This imparted a corkscrew motion to the ship, and I was glad Eir was able to keep my seasickness at bay.

By mid-afternoon, the sky lightened, and the rain stopped. The wind was still brisk, and the swells were still sizeable. We'd had the presence of mind to fill buckets with rain during the storm. The water was drinkable, but enough spray reached it that it had a hint of brackishness.

Fenwick went below to sleep first. When he returned to the tiller, I dropped into a bunk and fell unconscious quickly. I think I remember laying my head down, but I can't be sure of that.

'Your High-and-Mightiness," Fenwick's words woke me, "you need to come see this."

Groggy, I stood. The movement of the ship was less choppy than before—the rise and fall (with accompanying twists) were more regular. I stopped and drank some water before joining him.

Less than a mile away, through the light fog that surrounded our vessel, I saw two Liburnians approaching on both sides of one of our caravels. The caravel was crippled. Both the main and mizzen masts were broken off to half their length. I hoisted our sail all the way and trimmed it to give us as much speed as possible.

As we drew closer, we could hear the sounds of shouts and curses. The caravel was the *Freyja*—the one from which Fenwick and I were tossed. I wondered where *Princess Lucille* was. Even though the fog around us was lifting, we could not see her.

We were closing the distance quickly. I hoped our men did not see our arrival and lose hope, thinking more Rhetians were coming to attack. Fenwick kept us pointed straight at the Liburnian on the port side of *Freyja*.

"Get the crossbows and grappling hooks out," Fenwick instructed. "Only provide about twenty feet of slack and have the lines secured to the mast. Just as we reach them, drop the sail and grapple on to their ship. That will kill our momentum and snug us in tight. Then you and I can go save the day."

I cocked all four crossbows. Two, I laid on the deck at Fenwick's feet. I placed the other two below the gunwale where I planned to be when I used the grappling hooks. The men on the nearest Liburnian thought we were allies. They continued to focus their attention on *Freyja*.

I retrieved the hooks and bent lines to them. The other end of the line was secured to the foot of the mast. Fenwick took us right to the Liburnian. I dropped the sail, and he put our side hard into the side of the other ship with a screech and a thump. I did not toss the hooks. Instead, I planted them carefully, then made sure my feet would not be entangled when the lines went taut.

The lines yanked our ship to a halt. If I were not braced for it, I would have lost my footing. As soon as I recovered my balance, I opened my connection to Bellona all the way. I felt the strength and power throughout my body as I picked up the two crossbows, firing both into the chest of attackers who turned when their ship was jarred by ours. I scampered over onto the attackers' ship.

The pirates were just figuring out that we were not their allies. Having four of your number drop with bolts in their upper chests was their first real clue. Fenwick and I, appearing larger than life, boarding their ship with blades drawn was another.

The pirates put up not much more of a fight than the sheep on Hardscrabble Island. Fenwick and I had surprise, speed, and skill on our side, not to mention the strength of the Goddess Bellona singing in our veins. One of the soldiers on *Freyja* recognized us.

"Cap'n Hardy, the prince and Lord Easton just showed up!" he shouted as he left this side and ran to the other.

Fenwick, displaying that same illusion of immense size as I was, vaulted over the gunwale alongside me and onto *Freyja*'s deck. Captain Hardy and his remaining men were crouching below the gunwale on the other side, with the ones from our side scurrying to join them. I saw that four of our men were down, two on each side of the ship, crossbow bolts protruding from their chests. The planks of the deck were covered with spilled blood.

Captain Hardy whipped his head around. He was clearly surprised to see us. Fenwick and I did not delay. We crossed to the gunwale where he was.

"Draw their fire," Fenwick ordered, "and we'll board their ship."

Hardy nodded to his men. The eight armed with crossbows stood and loosed their bolts, ducking back down quickly. We heard the thunk of a couple of bolts hitting the side of the ship and the whiz of others that sailed overhead.

Fenwick and I then leaped over the gunwale and down into the attacking Liburnian. These men were more prepared than the first group. One of the men facing me was able to slice the top of my left forearm when I was engaged with someone else. He paid for it with his life. First, I cut off his offending hand, then, lifting my blade, I sliced his throat with the tip.

After that, there was little artistry in this fight. It was close-quarters work—a brawl with bladed weapons—between the two of us and eleven of them. Within a minute, it was over. The attackers were dead. I looked over at Fenwick, and he grinned back at me. He was covered with blood. I imagined I looked just as feral. We both started laughing as we both closed our connections with Bellona and returned to the appearance of normal size.

"Where in the Seven Hells did you come from?" Hardy asked, leaning over the side of the caravel.

"A long story, captain, with a happy ending, it seems," Fenwick said.

"Well, thank all the heavenly beings you showed up when you did," Hardy said. "I don't think we would have been able to hold them off."

"We got that impression," I said.

"You got another ship?" Hardy asked.

"Among other things," Fenwick said. "What we did not manage to grab on our way was any food."

"I think we can feed you," Hardy said. "But we have a bit of unpleasant work to do before we light the galley fire."

"What happened to *Princess Lucille*?" I asked.

"The wave that hit us and washed you two overboard missed her," Hardy explained. "She's undamaged. We saw the storm was coming. Turbot and I agreed there wasn't any sense in him sticking around, so he sailed on. Neither of us figured the Rhetians would be on the prowl after the storm. They sailed up on us, easy as you please, right out of the fog. They were probably looking for someone storm-damaged. That was us. Only the wave did it, not the storm."

"What do you want to do with their ships?" I asked.

"Take them to Aquileia, of course," Hardy replied. "They're worth money."

"Do you have enough men to crew them?" Fenwick inquired.

"Barely. May I ask you to sail the ship you captured back?" Hardy requested.

"Food," I reminded him.

"I can give you a small barrel of salt pork, some dried peas, a few carrots, and some biscuit," Hardy agreed. "Easily enough to see you to Hardscrabble, or even Aquileia, if you wish to press on.

"I think we'll press on," Fenwick said.

Hardy gave orders to one of his men to retrieve the items he promised. The man returned a minute later with the small barrel, then went back and brought a tin of ship biscuit and a small sack with the vegetables. I took the tin and the sack.

Before we left, Fenwick and I told Hardy what happened to us, beginning with being washed overboard. We told him about the Lance of Bellona. His eyes widened.

"What will you do with it?" he asked.

"We haven't thought about it or discussed it," I answered. "We may keep it in the castle or return it to the Temple of Bellona. The Goddess will give us an indication regarding what she wants. That much I think we can count on."

Hardy assured us he would be able to return to Aquileia. He urged us to depart immediately. Having three Liburnians tied to his ship, with his masts only half-length, was three more than he wanted. His men were already trying to clear the deck and couldn't toss the bodies of his fallen men over the side until at least one of the sides was clear.

I took the tin and sack of vegetables, climbed down off the ship, across the first Liburnian, and onto the one Fenwick and I stole. Fenwick followed me. After stowing the food in the galley, I unfastened the grappling hooks and shoved us away. I then quickly raised our sail while Fenwick manned the tiller. Within minutes, we had already opened up a gap between us and *Freyja*.

"You realize we burnished the legends more today," Fenwick smiled. "By the time those men make it back to port, you will have killed a hundred pirates today, single-handedly."

"You don't think you'll be part of the story?"

"Story? Seven Hells, Caz—I'm talking about the new verses of the song," Fenwick teased.

"Oh, that," I replied, pretending disinterest. "What do you think we should do about the lance?"

"I think you gave the best answer," Fenwick said. "The Goddess will let us know. She may let you keep it at the castle. If she would prefer we take it to her temple, I imagine we'll have another unusual dream or two."

We sailed back to Aquileia, not stopping at Hardscrabble. Rain clouds seemed to follow us the entire way. The seas did not act up, and the wind stayed steady from the west, so we needed only six more days.

Upon arrival, we needed to find the harbormaster. We had to inform him that the Liburnian needed to be assayed by the prize court. We unloaded the lance and searched for his office—a weatherbeaten shack. He recognized me immediately, which I learned was a good thing.

"Ya tied up in the wrong spot," he said. "Over there is where we keep the prizes 'til the court rules. The furrin ships, they let 'em go after we unloaded the cargo. The Rhetians we sold at auction."

Where he was pointing was a fair distance away. Fenwick and I would need to row the Liburnian over there—a good quarter-mile through the drizzle that was falling. I was tired, hungry for a decent meal that did not include salt pork, and soaking wet despite our oilskins.

"Ordinarily, I'd be askin' ya to do that yerselves," he said. "But it don't feel proper me askin' Prince Caz t' row the boat 'round t' the right moorin'. Lemme git some men t' do that fer ya."

"Much obliged," I said.

"Do you have any money?" I asked Fenwick.

He looked at me and laughed. "No."

"Neither do I," I said. "I guess we're walking back."

"Wait," Fenwick said. "The Traval office is just over there. I can get some money from Julienne or her father so we can pay for a hackney."

"But then, how do we carry this?" I said, bobbling the lance that was resting on my shoulder slightly. "Never mind. You pay for the ride, and I'll carry this up top with the driver."

"If you're sure," Fenwick said doubtfully.

"I'm sure."

25

The guards manning the gatehouse were horrified when I rode up on the top of a hackney. My appearance took them aback first—wearing dingy oilskins and soaked, with my wet hair dripping. Once they recognized me, they tried to take the lance away from me, but I refused to turn it over. I trudged across the bridge with it on my shoulder.

Navigating the corridors inside the castle was tricky. Due to the length of the lance, I needed to plan a couple of maneuvers at corners. Eventually, I reached our apartment. I opened the door and shoved the lance inside. I then propped it against the wall in the entry hall and began stripping off my wet clothes.

Mr. Gilbert found me first and immediately took control of the situation. He quickly scurried upstairs and returned with a dressing gown before I completely disrobed. He then set about gathering my wet things.

"I imagine you would like a bath, Your Highness?" he suggested. "I will also lay a fire in your bedroom. In the meantime, there is already one burning in the parlor if you would like to warm up."

'Thank you, Mr. Gilbert. That sounds quite nice," I said.

Not long after, I was enjoying a soak in hot water. I was so relaxed I did not know Lucy had returned until she slid into the water facing me, entwining her legs and mine. I opened my eyes slowly, and a grin crept onto my face.

"You look like a scruffy brigand," she said with a smile, referencing my unshaven face.

"You'd best be careful then, missy," I said. "We freebooters have been known to take liberties with saucy wenches like you!"

I sloshed toward her and wrapped my arms around her. She gave a playful shriek as I started to rub my whiskers on her face and neck, growling like an animal. I let her push me away after a bit so I could kiss her.

"What is that in the hall downstairs?" she asked. "I felt it before I saw it."

"That, my dear, is the Lance of Bellona, if the plaque in the Rhetian temple is to be believed," I replied. "And the reason Bellona has been disturbing Fenwick's and my sleep since our return from Hier."

"Majors and Minors!" Lucy gasped. "You and Fenwick didn't mention a thing about retrieving a sacred artifact."

"Well, we didn't know until it happened," I said.

I then proceeded to tell the whole tale, starting with the dreams Fenwick and I shared. Lucy climbed out of the tub and returned with a razor. She bid me continue while she shaved the beard from my face.

I told her of the wave, and our long swim ashore, being drawn to the temple, finding the spear, and stealing the ship. By the time I finished, the water cooled. I wanted nothing more than to be dry and warm.

Lucy helped me dry off. We dressed and headed downstairs. As we went to the parlor, she stood and looked at the lance in the hall. After a moment, she went to it and touched it with her fingers.

"Definitely a sacred artifact," she said as she slid onto my lap on the sofa in front of the fire. "It even has an aura. The thing just radiates numina—divine energy."

"When I put my hand on it, it restored my reserves of asomatous energy," I said. "Fenwick's, too. I was even able to fill the diamond in the pommel of my sword to capacity. The power in the lance did not seem to diminish in any way."

"Tomorrow, Lily and I will need to go through our books," Lucy said. "I remember reading about relics like this, but thought they were all lost, or figments of myth. The Lance of Bellona is one I never heard of."

"Which one did you know about?" I asked.

"Andvar's hammer," Lucy said. "And Freyja had a spear as well, I think. I would imagine all the Minor Gods would have had some talisman if they actually existed and are not just legends with no substance. What will you do with it?"

"Unless Bellona tells us otherwise," I said, "I plan to keep it here. I imagine it would be something quite useful to have in war."

"You just finished a war," Lucy said, "and another isn't likely to break out for several generations."

"Then Bellona will let us know that she would like us to return it to her Temple," I said. "She hasn't been too shy about communicating, though she hasn't been very specific."

The next day Lucy disappeared after breakfast. I went to find the king to give him my report. He was in an expansive mood.

"Come in, come in," he urged when I knocked on the door of his study. "Sit down, Caz. I have excellent news to share."

The excellent news was the preliminary report on grain production from the Eastern March. On average, the amount of grain and produce that would ship from Port Charles would be eighteen percent higher than the previous year. That was indeed good news. Commodity prices in Aquileia would remain stable or decrease slightly. Farmers in the Eastern March would profit even more than the previous year.

"What is the reason for the increase?" I asked.

"Duncan said the growing season was no better than previous years," Mark said, "and the land under cultivation did not increase more than seven or eight percent. He attributes it to nothing more than being more aware of the opportunity. Now, you and Lord Easton just returned with another prize, I understand?"

"Fenwick and I had an unexpected adventure," I said, then went through the whole tale.

"And Lily and Lucy are researching what the thing might be?" Mark asked.

"I believe so," I replied. "Lucy darted away right after we ate this morning."

"You said a Rhetian soldier brought it back," Mark mused. "It must have happened in the last war, nearly two hundred years ago. The Rhetians briefly controlled the area where the Temple of Bellona is."

I must have looked surprised because Mark said, "Just because I'm uncomfortable with the supernatural doesn't mean I don't know where the Temples of the Minor Gods are. In examining the events of the last few years,

I've become convinced more than I ever thought possible that the Gods play an active role in our lives. I've always had faith, Caz, but that faith is now solid belief. I don't have to be comfortable with it in order to understand how it has benefited the kingdom—just grateful."

"Fenwick and I had a conversation eerily similar to this when we were stranded on the beach in Rhetia," I said.

"It flatters me that I am in agreement with perhaps the two cleverest men of your generation," Mark smiled.

"Men, perhaps," I agreed, "but I'm afraid Lucy is far more wise than I am."

"As Lily is compared to me," Mark said.

"The Lance of Bellona is mentioned several times in both my and Lily's books," Lucy told me over dinner that evening. "In the hands of someone like you or Fenwick, who has awakened his bond with the Goddess, it is supposed to provide unlimited strength and endurance to both rider and mount."

"It is definitely of a length too great for a foot-soldier," I said. "Interesting that the influence would extend to the horse as well."

"All the books said the same thing," Lucy said. "They also mention it was stolen from her Temple by the Rhetians."

"As it was."

"It is also not the only relic associated with Bellona," Lucy continued. "There is also a sword. The books say it was last seen in her Temple on the Southern Continent, in Nagah. According to what we read, it also provides the user and his mount with unlimited strength. It will cut through anything—even solid rock. Miss Katherine copied a picture of it that we found."

Lucy slid a piece of paper over to me. The drawing was quite neatly done. The design of the sword was simple. Instead of the swept hilt my blade possessed, it had only a cross guard. From the drawing, the proportion of the pommel was different as well—longer. Of course, from just a drawing, it was impossible to tell the size of it, but I sensed it was longer than my rapier. Since Lucy said it also benefited the user's horse, it was a cavalry blade.

"Miss Katherine has a talent for drawing," I commented.

"She does," Lucy agreed, "and her handwriting has become quite elegant in just the short time she has been here. It has been so much fun to teach her. She is so quick to grasp everything."

"And she is enjoying herself?" I asked.

"I am trying to find some young ladies her age for her to meet," Lucy explained. "It has been difficult. Katie needs a friend who has varied interests and is curious about the world. Someone who is only interested in gossiping over needlepoint—"

"You need to find her a young Lucy, or Greta, or Julienne," I said.

"Or a younger version of any of our friends," Lucy added. "Siobhan, Inger, even Nellie—maybe not Nellie. Nellie would be perfectly happy to spend a day entirely in gossip."

I laughed because it was true. "Is she lonely?" I asked.

"It's difficult to say," Lucy said. "Whenever she does have free time, we can always find her in the library, and she seems perfectly happy, immersed in whatever she is reading. I suppose she is no more lonely than I was."

"You were lonely? I never got that impression," I said.

"Oh, I had my cousins and siblings," Lucy said, "and they are good company, but I could never talk to them about what I was learning from Grand Nan. Their interests were much more practical."

"I doubt you'll find anyone Katie can talk to about what she's learning from you and Lily," I remarked.

"Perhaps," Lucy said. "Carl purchased Serendipity while you were away. I haven't told Katie yet. Would you like to go see her tomorrow? Jerry won't have school tomorrow, so I think it would be a good day to visit."

"That sounds fun," I agreed. "Katie will be thrilled."

The following morning dawned clear. I let the Castle Shield know about our visit to the Foaming Boar. At ten, we set off. Katie was riding a horse provided by the Shield.

During the ride, she was full of questions, trying to learn where we were going. Lucy would not tell her anything—only that it was a surprise. Katie was extremely puzzled when we reached the inn and rode to the back.

Hearing us ride into the small stable yard, Jerry slid down from his room in the loft above the stable. Seeing Lucy, his eyes lit up. He immediately came over to offer her a hand as she dismounted Bella. While he was doing so, he saw Katie for the first time. He stood agog.

"Please help Miss Katherine down, Jerry," Lucy requested.

Jerry did not react for a moment. Then Lucy's words penetrated his brain. He quickly moved and offered Katie a hand, staring at her with wide eyes. A year earlier, Lucy and I noticed that Jerry was suddenly aware of the difference between boys and girls. He manifested that in puppyish worship of Lucy. Katie was much closer to Jerry's age, though I would guess at least five years older. It was an insurmountable gap at that point in their young lives, but it was clear Katie made a different impression on Jerry than Lucy did.

"We are here to meet Serendipity," Lucy said. "She will belong to Miss Katherine."

"What?" Katie screeched.

"Caz and I bought you a horse," Lucy explained. "Her name is Serendipity."

"Miss Sera," Jerry corrected.

"No," Lucy said. "Her name is Miss Katherine."

"I'm sorry, Lady L—Your Highness," Jerry stammered, his eyes still fixed on Katie. "Serendipity much prefers to be called Miss Sera. Much as your horse prefers Bella instead of Isabella."

"You bought me a horse?" Katie exclaimed, over the top of Lucy and Jerry's exchange.

"Yes, Miss Katherine," I said. "If I'm not mistaken, she's the strawberry roan over there.

"And her name is Miss Sera?" Katie asked, addressing Jerry over her shoulder as she ran to the stall.

'Y-yes, m-miss," Jerry stammered, frozen in place, his eyes glued to Katie.

When Katie reached the stall, the horse peered at her for a moment, then took a sniff. Katie stepped forward hesitantly. When she did, Miss Sera stretched her head out and laid it alongside Katie's. Katie's arms immediately went up to hug the horse around the neck.

"Are you training Miss Sera?" I asked Jerry.

"I am, Mr. Caz," he said proudly once his brain registered the words. Thinking about horses freed his mind from befuddlement, and he was able to speak again.

"Miss Sera is just as smart as Andy, and Bella, and Davy," he gushed, "though not as clever as Thunder."

"Of course not," I said. Thunder was Jerry's own horse.

"She's brilliant at jumping, and quick, though not as fast—"

"As Thunder," I said.

"Jerry, you don't need to tell me. Tell Miss Katherine," I suggested. "Though you don't need to compare Miss Sera to Thunder. Miss Katherine will learn all that soon enough, I'm sure."

"Oh! Right," he said, then strode off to join Katie and Miss Sera.

I walked over to Lucy and put my arm around her. Lucy was smiling at the view. It was definitely love at first sight—between Katie and the horse.

"Can I ride her?" Katie asked Lucy.

"That's up to Jerry," Lucy replied. "He is in charge of Miss Sera's training."

"Please, Jerry?" Katie pleaded.

Lucy needed to turn away to keep from laughing. With that tone of voice and the look on Katie's face, Jerry would be able to refuse her absolutely nothing. He stood frozen, momentarily incapable of speech.

"Why don't the two of you go on a ride, Jerry?" I suggested. "You can take Thunder, and Miss Katherine and Miss Sera can begin to get to know one another."

"Oh, let's, please?" Katie begged.

"Um, certainly, uh, Miss Kath—"

"Call me Katie, Jerry," she said as she finally released the animal's neck. "Do you have tack for her? I'll saddle her."

"Uh, Miss, uh, Katie, that's really my job," Jerry tried to explain.

"Jerry, until a couple of months ago, I was just a farm girl on our family's place just outside the North Gate," Katie said. "Lucy and Lily are making me into a lady, but I haven't forgotten how to do things."

"Well, it will be much quicker, if you don't mind," Jerry admitted.

"Jerry, when you finish, would you please bring Miss Katherine back to the castle? Then you can bring Miss Sera back here," Lucy suggested.

"Yes, Your Highness," Jerry responded.

"Miss Katherine, Jerry helped train Andy, Bella, and Lord Easton's horse, Davy," Lucy explained. "Though he is young, he is extremely gifted and has a way with animals. He was taught by Mr. Stensland, who owns this inn. Mr. Stensland trained horses for the Rangers, and trained Andy, Bella, and Davy to that level of performance. That is the standard to which Jerry is training Miss Sera. Anything to do with Miss Sera, you should listen and pay attention to what Jerry says."

Hearing that, Jerry's posture changed, and he snapped out of his daze. He did know horses. The praise Lucy gave him helped put his feet back on solid ground.

"Katie, the saddle I think will fit you best is this one," Jerry said, walking into the stable and pointing to it. "Blankets are here."

I offered Lucy my hand, and she swung onto Bella. Putting my foot in the stirrup, I slid onto Andy. I nodded to the men of the Shield, and we departed.

26

The months of Gorman and Ylir dragged by. Our fleet was stuck in port due to the weather. That meant I became more familiar with the kingdom's account books than I ever hoped.

Based on our success thus far, Mark ordered six more ships to be constructed. The new ships would be named *King Mark*, *Prince Albert*, *Ceridwen Sospita*, *Sparrowhawk*, *Griffin*, and *Njörun*. They would be ready by the beginning of Harpa, toward the end of spring.

The king was slightly embarrassed that we chose to name a ship after him but was highly pleased that we honored Albert in this way. As far as I knew, there were only four people in the kingdom who understood why I would wish to name a ship *Sparrowhawk*. Lucy and Lily laughed when I told them about it. For these ships, I made sure to notify George Chester in plenty of time.

Though Fenwick and I were expecting Bellona to appear in our dreams again, to let us know to return the lance to her Temple, she did not appear. I did move it from our apartment. We hung it in the Throne Room in a prominent location.

The one bit of excitement was the upcoming holiday season. Lily allowed us to invite friends to the official observance of the Winter Solstice here in the castle. Fenwick and Julienne, along with my father and Ari, would be entertaining the notables of the Eastern March at the manor. Lucy and I asked Freddy and Greta, Quint and Siobhan, Linc and Nellie, Ratty and Inger, and Tom Gibson and Sophie.

I also invited the young Lords Houlsin and Chafter, who took over the soldiers from their counties when their fathers proved to be incompetent blowhards in the recent war. To be sure, I did not know them well, but I saw them both rise to the occasion in exceptionally difficult circumstances. I hoped they would come and, with Lucy and Lily's permission, invited them to stay in the castle. Everyone we invited responded positively.

"Good," Lily said, "young blood. That is exactly what the party needs. I have never enjoyed it because Mark has always insisted on conducting it the same way his father did—stuffy and boring. It is the solstice! The time when days begin to lengthen, and the world renews. It is a time for celebration—for music and dancing—not for serious and dull conversations. We shall have a festive night of it!"

Lucy and I were also invited to Linc Ellsworth's party, the Earl of Dorch's gala, and a brunch the morning after the solstice at Freddy and Greta's. I wrangled invitations to those events for Houlsin and Chafter as well. It promised to be nearly a week of fun and frivolity.

I resumed my training after not having visited my salle since before my adoption. While I could no longer attend the salle, I had the Castle Shield and their trainers at my disposal. When I sparred with the men, I never accessed my connection to Bellona—something that would have made things unfair. Even so, there were few who could come close to matching me in fencing. In fisticuffs and wrestling, I did not enjoy the same advantage, and a few of the men had the great pleasure of thumping me a time or two.

There were also mounted sessions outside the city walls. Andy enjoyed the exercise. Lucy and Lily often came to observe and get their own riding practice in, with their own trainers. Katie and Jerry made a couple of appearances as well.

Jerry was over being awestruck by Katie. It seemed they developed a different relationship—more akin to siblings. The only thing they really had in common was horses, but that was enough.

Lucy and Mr. Gilbert contacted the tailor to commission clothing for me to wear to the upcoming parties. I was not allowed to know what they ordered. The night of the event is when I would finally see. As I have mentioned before, the Earl of Dorch's gala was an event where women, in particular, went to great lengths to appear as beautiful as possible. The celebration here at the castle called for understated elegance, and Linc and Nellie's party was just plain fun, and we would see a wide variety of dress.

One thing that pleased me greatly was a project I started after speaking with Lily. I explained to her that I felt awful for not getting Lucy a present for our anniversary, so I wanted to compensate with an extra-special gift at solstice. Lily made an excellent suggestion.

On the rear wall of the Castle Shield's barracks, facing south, I had a room constructed with glass walls and a glass ceiling. There was a stove inside to fend off the cold of winter. It was not quite as big as Lucy's workshop but could be expanded easily due to how it was made. Inside were long tables with raised edges four inches in height.

We filled the top of each table with, according to Katie, the best quality topsoil. With Katie's guidance, we selected the herbs and plants that Lucy used in her workshop and that would thrive in this environment. I could hardly wait to show it to Lucy, but I reined in my enthusiasm and made sure she did not catch wind of what we were doing.

Lords Houlsin and Chafter arrived the day before Linc Ellsworth's party. The good impression they made upon us during the war continued on this visit. I learned both of them attended the same boarding school I did. Though my experiences there were mostly not pleasant, it did give us some common ground.

Neither of them brought a young lady with them. As they were both young, decent-looking, and titled, I imagined the women at the first two parties would be eager to make their acquaintance. Lucy promised to warn them away from anyone with whom they would not want to be involved. They were good company, and I thought they might be solid additions to the council I intended to form. For now, I merely asked if they would write me once every other month and let me know how things were going in their holdings. Both of them seemed honored that I would ask.

Linc and Nellie Ellsworth's party was every bit as much fun as I remembered. Lucy and I danced and mingled, catching up with friends and acquaintances. No one seemed to treat me differently than in previous years, which was one of my worries.

Houlsin and Chafter enjoyed themselves immensely. They were in great demand as dancing partners from a variety of young ladies. Wisely, they spread themselves around and did not allow anyone to monopolize their attention.

For the Earl of Dorch's gala, Lucy wore a dress with a glittering silver bodice and a full blue skirt—matching the traditional colors of the holiday. She wore the tiara Queen Liliana gave her at my adoption and looked every bit like a princess. My outfit matched with colors reversed. My jacket and waistcoat were blue, and my breeches—though not a glittery silver, were a light gray that looked silver.

I wish I could say I enjoyed the evening, but that was not the case. In my previous scribblings, I've mentioned how conscious I have always been of my illegitimate birth. Certain members of the older aristocratic families always made it clear that they did not approve of my presence at a function like this. When someone would try to introduce me to one of them, at best, I might get a reluctant handshake. Sometimes, the person would simply turn his back on me as though I did not exist.

Some of these people were present. They stayed as far from me as possible, but I could tell from their expressions that I was the topic of their conversations. I could also tell that they had nothing nice to say.

"Don't let them bother you, dear," Lucy whispered in my ear. "None of them are as important as they wish they were. In fact, if you consider their holdings, none of them have any real importance at all."

"I know," I sighed. "It just triggers unpleasant memories."

"Dear, living well is the best revenge," Lucy said. "Would you trade your life for any of theirs?"

I only needed to think about it for a moment. With the broadest grin, I pulled Lucy to me and kissed her passionately. She was absolutely right, and I told her so when we broke apart to catch our breath.

The bright spot that evening was reuniting with Count Dunland. He was overjoyed to see us and embraced us both. The last I saw him, he and his holding were a mess, having been plagued by a practitioner of the Dark Arts. He was hale and healthy now and reported that his territory had also recovered.

The following day was the solstice, and it dawned with snow falling heavily. The actual moment of the event, according to the astronomers, would take place that evening, in the middle of our celebration in the castle. After Lucy and I ate breakfast, I asked her to dress for the weather and come for a walk with me.

Katie, Lily, and I did everything we could to keep Lucy's gift a surprise, all the while knowing that Lucy's gift of clairvoyance might spoil things anyway. Nevertheless, I felt I needed to try. Lucy did not seem to know what I intended. Whether she was being kind and pretending ignorance or really did not know, I would need to guess.

We left the castle and crossed the bridge. When I steered her in the direction of the barracks, she appeared to be genuinely puzzled. Turning the corner of the last building, I showed her the growing room we built.

"What is this?" she asked, not recognizing it.

"It's yours," I said and placed the key in her hand.

"But—what is it for?"

"Open the door and find out," I suggested.

Lucy took off her mitten and unlocked the door. She stepped inside and stopped. The door was narrow, so I could not see her reaction. I did not have long to wait.

Lucy whirled around and jumped into my arms, wrapping herself around me. Her cheeks were covered with tears already. She kissed me passionately and repeatedly.

"Oh!" she gasped suddenly, releasing me. "Come in and shut the door. We can't let the cold in."

The glass-enclosed room was warm and humid. Moisture clouded the panes except where condensation became too much and drops slid down. Sprouts were beginning to appear all over where Katie, Lily, and I had planted seeds. Katie made little signs indicating what was growing where.

"Oh, Caz!" Lucy sighed happily. "This is *perfect!*"

"You didn't know?" I asked.

"I knew we would build this eventually," she admitted, "but not so soon. Oh, thank you!"

She embraced me again, though not quite as vigorously. When she let me go, she quickly began moving down the tables, reading what we planted. Her excitement reminded me of a child in a sweet shop. When she reached the end of the tables, she turned to me and grinned.

"Come with me," she said happily, pulling me by the hand.

She tugged me outside, pausing to lock the door. Grasping my hand again, she nearly ran back to the castle. Still pulling me along, we reached our apartment.

Delaying only long enough to drop her cloak, hat, and mittens, leaving them on the floor of the entry hall, she began pulling me upstairs. When we reached our bedroom, she shoved me inside and locked the door behind her. Turning to me, the excitement on her face was evident.

"Are you ready for your present?" she asked.

"I think so."

Lucy turned her back to me and backed up. She took my hands and placed them on her belly. All of a sudden, I knew what my present was. Joy filled me and took my breath away.

"Are you—?" I gasped.

"Yes, my love. We are going to have a baby boy," she said, turning to face me.

"How long—how far—?"

"Three months," she said. "We can make an announcement tonight if you wish."

As I absorbed this news, I did not realize at first that Lucy was undressing me. When I did begin to understand, she began shoving me toward our bed. By the time we reached it, my shirt and waistcoat were unbuttoned, and she was reaching for my breeches. I finally caught on to her intent and began trying to remove her clothes. We didn't quite remove them all.

"As far as an announcement tonight," I said much later, "should we ask Mark and Lily?"

"They already know," Lucy said. "If you don't wish to tell everyone, Mark certainly will."

"Am I the last to know—again?" I whined.

"I'm pretty sure Fenwick doesn't know—yet," Lucy said. "But Julienne is giving him the same present."

"They're having a baby, too?"

"A girl."

"He will be so scared," I commented.

"What about you?" Lucy asked, rolling over and looking down at me from an inch away.

"I'm too excited and happy to be scared. That will probably come later," I said.

"You should be excited," Lucy said, kissing my nose. "Your son's primary affinity is with Bellona. You will need to teach him well."

"Really? How can you tell?" I asked.

"His aura," Lucy replied. "Lily and Katie both spotted it right away. His lessers are Njörun and Freyja."

"Majors and Minors!" I whispered in wonderment.

"Fenwick's daughter also has affinities," Lucy said. "Her primary is also Bellona, and her lessers are Freyja and Mielvanir."

"They will be compatible?" I asked. "They will get along?"

"Oh yes," Lucy laughed. "Don't start planning their wedding, dear, but I'm sure they will be friends."

"When will the baby arrive?" I asked.

"There is a chance he will be a solstice baby," Lucy said.

In our superstitious Aquileian culture, babies born on the day of either solstice were considered blessed by the Gods. I don't know whether it really mattered, but given my experience, I would not dismiss the idea. Of course, our son would have every advantage, growing up as a prince, with loving parents. A dark thought crossed my mind then.

"We have to make sure he's normal," I blurted.

"Normal? In what way? He won't be normal. He has affinities," Lucy said.

"I don't want him to grow up in isolation," I said. "Consider what happened with Wim and Albert. Growing up in the royal family warped them both. Albert recovered from it, but Wim—"

"He will grow up with friends," Lucy assured me. "He will not be isolated."

"And you know this?" I asked.

"You know I cannot share specifics," Lucy smiled. "Let me just say they will not be the only children born next year."

"Well, of course not," I agreed. "Oh! You mean—will some of our friends—?"

"Some," Lucy teased. "Like Fenwick."

"I'm happy for Fenwick and Julienne," I said, "but I'm happier for us. Thank you for my fabulous solstice gift."

"It is our gift to each other," Lucy said, then kissed me.

That evening's solstice celebration was quite different from the two we attended before. Before you even entered the room, you could hear music. The dancing would not begin until after dinner, but even so it provided an atmosphere that had been lacking in previous years.

There were more people, the numbers swelled by the addition of others of our generation. The friends we invited, even though we saw them at two previous parties, were excited to be here (in the *castle*!). They added an energy to the room that infected everyone.

Katie was there—excuse me, Miss Katherine was there—looking poised and sophisticated. Lucy introduced Miss Katherine as her lady-in-waiting without any further explanation. Most assumed she was a daughter of some minor noble house. It did not take long for Houlsin and Chafter to find her, and I could see that she was reveling in their attention.

Earl Montgomery, Quint's father, wanted to know about what transpired in Hier. As I began telling him the story, I found myself speaking to a larger and larger group. While everyone present knew about what happened in our war with the Rhetians, knowledge of what took place in Hier was not widespread. I tried to relate what happened as succinctly as possible, as I wished for everyone to mingle and converse among themselves.

When we were summoned to dine, Lucy and I were seated with Mark and Lily at the head of the room. All the women took their seats while the men remained standing. Mark then lifted his glass.

"Let us thank all the Gods, Major and Minor, and all the divine beings, for the many blessings which they have shared with us," he said. "It has been a tumultuous year—a year of war and victory, a year of change, and a time of renewal. May all the Gods and heavenly beings fill our hearts with hope, and our spirits with resolve, as we enter into the new year."

Muttered assents of "hear, hear" followed as everyone lifted a glass and drank. Mark did not sit down, which puzzled our guests. Instead, he looked at me.

"To His Majesty's words, I would like to add my own thanks," I said. "Princess Lucille just told me earlier today that she is with child. May all the Gods and heavenly beings, and all of you, provide her with your care and protection."

The room erupted with applause. All the women stood, except for Lucy. In the midst of the noise, I heard Freddy shout, "Huzzah!" in his Lord Compote voice. It took all my self-control not to burst into laughter.

Fortunately, Lily sat down, followed by Mark, and the ruckus died down to a loud buzz of excited conversation as everyone followed suit. I noticed Lucy gave Freddy a look of mild reproof—she heard Lord Compote as well. Freddy shrugged as if to say, "What would you expect?"

27

After dinner, the dancing began. It got off to a slow start, as nearly everyone wanted to give Lucy and me their best wishes and congratulations. By the third tune, we were able to join everyone on the floor.

Mark pulled me aside when Lucy and I decided to rest for one number. His face was flushed. He looked happier than I had ever seen him.

"Lily was insistent that we do things differently this year," he said to me quietly, "and I only agreed grudgingly. How wrong I was! This is what a celebration of the solstice should be!"

Shortly after ten o'clock, the band stopped playing. The royal astronomer, whose garb was normally indistinguishable from any other court official, appeared in a blue gown and conical blue hat, both decorated with crescent moons and stars in silver. Though lacking the long, unkempt beard and straggly hair (and horrid smell), he looked in every other respect just like the mysterious Dr. Flamel.

He watched the clock carefully, and at the precise moment of the solstice, he rang a small gong. Cheers rang out in the room. Couples kissed. Lucy and I were no exception. I dipped her down and planted the most passionate kiss on her lips I could muster. Then I gave and received kisses from Lily, all our female friends, and, finally, a chaste kiss on the cheek from Miss Katherine.

The music resumed, and dancing began anew. From the corner of my eye, I noticed the seneschal appear and head straight for the king. Mark and Lily stepped away from the dancing and separated from the others. The king caught my eye, and the slight movement of his head indicated he wanted to speak with me.

"Mark needs me for something," I whispered to Lucy.

We left and crossed to Mark and Lily. I could tell they were troubled by what the seneschal shared with them, but they were trying not to show it. Lucy saw it, too, and squeezed my hand.

"An emissary from Mooresa just arrived," Mark said. "His Aquileian is not good, so we have sent for a translator. Let us carry on for now, but when our guests leave, we need to hear what he has to say."

"Do we know what brings him here at such a dangerous time to sail?" I asked.

"He was difficult to understand, Your Highness," the seneschal said. "I don't know any of the particulars other than this is a matter of the most dire urgency."

"We will have the band stop playing at eleven," Lily said. "That will be a signal for our guests to depart, though many of the older generation are already doing so. Return to the festivities, and act as though nothing is amiss. There is no sense in casting a pall on such a fine evening."

As we returned to the dancing, I could tell that Lucy knew what was coming. She was not happy about it, but there was none of the fear I remembered that she displayed when Fenwick arrived at the manor, not quite a year before. I took her hand and brought it to my lips.

When we rejoined the group, Lucy's expression was returned to one of animated happiness. I did my best to match it. We continued to dance with everyone until the band stopped.

Then, there was the process of goodbyes and well-wishing. Mark and Lily were doing the same. Finally, the last guests left the hall. Mark caught my eye, and Lucy and I followed him out.

He led us to the room where the council met. Inside was a man I remembered slightly from Fenwick's and my last visit to Mooresa. Sitting with him was another man who looked like a sailor—the translator, I reckoned.

"What has brought you across the Surrounded Sea at such a dangerous time of year?" Mark asked through the translator.

"Disaster. After you freed Hier and departed," he said, addressing me, "we spent months in Hier, helping them to return to their normal lives. Three weeks ago, the bashaw and the other leaders took our forces south to Combrial, where the trouble in Hier originated. In the first week, we lost all of our leaders and half of our soldiers."

"Killed?" Mark asked.

"Worse. Enslaved," the man said. "We began to retreat. Our priests have learned how to prevent more of us from enslavement. Those of us still able to resist knew we needed help. It was decided that I would come to beg for your aid. We need the assistance of the warrior-mages. Without them, we believe the entire southern continent will be under the thumb of the Dark One. We have heard that much of Nagah is already under the control of the Dark One as well."

"Do you need soldiers as well?" Mark asked.

"Yes. And priests of the Three Major Gods to cast the spells of protection for them."

"I thought the protection only lasted from sunup to sundown," I commented.

"Our priests have learned another spell, but it must be renewed every day," he explained. "And, of course, that is the time when the enemy tries to attack. Our men are brave and fighting as hard as they can, but their resolve weakens day by day. That is why I am here. You are our last hope—the last hope for millions to avoid enslavement."

Mark asked the seneschal to take the emissary and the translator to another room. When they left, the king sat down heavily. The rest of us took seats as well.

"I am extremely loath to allow you to go, Caz," Mark sighed, "even more so as a result of what happened in your last encounter. But I fear what will happen if I do not."

"I cannot say I am eager to return," I responded. "It is a dangerous time to sail. The dark mage in Combrial is likely to be more powerful and skilled than the one we faced in Hier, and she nearly killed me."

"But—" Mark interjected.

"But the Gods have seen fit to bless me with unique abilities," I said, "perhaps for just this purpose—I don't know."

"Do you want Fenwick to join you?" Mark asked.

"Of course," I said.

"I will send a rider immediately," Mark said.

"I can get to him more quickly," Lucy interrupted.

Mark looked at her with a puzzled expression. Lucy's familiar, Chauncey, the owl, knew the way to the manor. What's more, Fenwick would recognize Chauncey's appearance as a summons. Lily tilted her head, and the king understood what she meant. He nodded.

"Please do," he said.

"I sent him on his way before the guests departed," Lucy said.

"Let's find the Mooresan and tell him we will respond," Mark said, heaving himself from his chair. "Then to bed. There is nothing more we can do tonight. Tomorrow, Caz, you will need to ask Traval, Hawkins, and Albrecht for as many ships as it will take to transport the Castle Shield."

Three days later, Fenwick arrived at the castle. Chauncey made the trip to Easton in less than a full day. When Fenwick saw the owl swoop down at his head as he stood by the stable that afternoon, he knew he was needed in the capital. He packed and left immediately, riding through that night and the next day, using only two days for what was normally a three-day journey.

I already met with Herbert Traval, Ben Hawkins, and Martin Albrecht, and informed them of our need for carracks. Between the three of them, there were enough ships, but the holds needed to be reconfigured to transport the horses. We were taking all two thousand men of the Shield, which required fifty ships.

In addition, I summoned Captain Hardy. I ordered the caravels to accompany us. Though I doubted we would come under attack from pirates at this time of year, I was taking no chances. Plus, the caravels, due to their speed, would be useful to deliver messages back to Aquileia if necessary.

Lily met with the priests at the largest Temple of the Three Major Gods. She demanded they find the spell which would provide our men a full day of protection and ordered them to provide us with nine volunteers to join us. Getting the volunteers was the easy part. They still had not found the correct spell by the time Fenwick arrived. We sent the Mooresan emissary and his translator to the Temple in the hopes that he could share whatever wording he remembered.

Lucy met with the healers attached to the Shield and made sure they had the medicines, bandages, and other tools they would need. They had all come to know Lucy during the war with Rhetia and were grateful for her assistance and instruction. In addition, Lucy and Katie packed a crate with additional items. Some of them were for Fenwick and me. Half of the space was devoted to bottles of the restorative elixir she brought when we traveled to Eatonford and, later, Dunland.

I'd just returned from the harbor, my shoulders covered with the snow that was falling. The seneschal met me when I crossed the bridge and informed me of Fenwick's recent arrival. When I entered my apartment, I called out his name as I took off my cloak.

"In here," Lucy called from the parlor.

Fenwick was standing by the fire, a steaming cup of qava in his hands. Lucy was on the sofa but stood when I entered and came to give me a kiss. I shook hands with Fenwick and sat down. Lucy slid onto my lap.

"Thank you for coming so quickly," I said. "Has Lucy told you what is happening? Congratulations, by the way. I'm sorry that such happy news is marred by our need to pull you away from home and hearth."

"Lucy just finished telling me about the Mooresan," Fenwick said. "And I understand you have received similar good news. Julienne and I both wish you every blessing."

"As we do for you," I replied.

"When do we depart?" Fenwick asked.

"Tomorrow morning on the tide," I said, "if all goes well. I just returned from the harbor, and they are nearly finished making the carracks ready."

"And when is the turn of the tide?" he asked.

"Just before midday," I said.

"Good. I can catch up on my sleep a little," he said. "What is our destination?"

"Iradiem. It's the closest to where we should find what is left of the allied forces if they have not been overwhelmed yet," I said.

"I suppose we will learn the rest when we arrive," Fenwick said with a wry smile. "Now, I understand you are having a boy? Have you come up with a name yet?"

"Compote," I joked.

"Not on your life, Caz," Lucy threatened as she laughed.

"What about Theo?" Fenwick suggested.

That made us laugh even harder.

"All I know for certain," I said, "is that he won't be named either of those. Neither will he be a Casimir nor an Aloysius."

"We've discussed various combinations of Duncan, Mark, Albert, and Noel," Lucy said, "and like none of them. Besides, if we include one, the others might feel slighted. Mark and Lily did not name their children for family members, so we are free to set our own path. We have plenty of time to decide."

"What about you and Julienne?" I asked.

"Diana," Fenwick stated. "Julienne chose it, and I like it very much."

"You do know the child will have affinities?" I asked.

"Julienne told me that Lucy shared that information with her. In a way, it makes the challenge of fatherhood seem even greater," Fenwick said. "Difficult enough to raise a child properly, but one with supernatural connections? An even greater responsibility."

"Do you have your ward?" Lucy asked.

"I have rarely taken it off since you gave it to me, Your Highness," Fenwick said with a small bow. "Are you bringing the lance?"

"Yes," I answered. "I think we will need every possible advantage on this mission."

Fenwick stayed for dinner. Lucy had forewarned Jenny that he would, so there was plenty. He departed after we finished, and Lucy and I retired to bed early. Lucy tucked herself in tight, with her head on my chest. I could smell her hair—my favorite scent in the world.

"When I see you next," she said, "there will be no disguising the fact that I'm pregnant."

To be continued in the next FitzDuncan adventure …

ABOUT THE AUTHOR

John Spearman (Jake to his friends and colleagues) has been a Fortune 500 sales and marketing executive, a Latin teacher and coach at a prestigious New England boarding school, and is now an author. He lives in coastal Maine with his wife and their dogs. He began writing because his wife challenged him. He was lucky enough to find an audience and has not looked back (except to fix the mistakes he made in the early days!).

This book is the eighth of the FitzDuncan series. Spearman has four other book series, all in the category of military science fiction. The first was the Jonah Halberd series of four books. The Sandy Pike series is set in a different universe from the Halberd books. The next series is of three novels featuring a female hero named Perseverance Andrews which is related to his first four books, the Jonah Halberd series. The Andrews books take place in the same universe as the Halberd series, though over three hundred years earlier.

Spearman's latest series is published by AethonBooks. Set in the new universe, it features a main character named Cliff Rawlins. Mr. Rawlins' story has a rocky beginning.

If you enjoyed reading this book, please consider leaving a positive review on amazon.com or goodreads.com. It will help other readers like you find books they might enjoy. To learn more about the author's different works, please visit www.johnjspearmanauthor.com